THE NICE PILL

By: Peter Scott

Copyright 2021 Peter Scott

To: Chris my wife, and to those who are kind and considerate.

With thanks
To
Will Ingrams
and
Alison Williamson

Table of Contents.

'Jihadists turning nice?'

'That's what they said.'

'OK.' The Major flattened his hands on the table and leaned forward. 'So why?'

'The radio and phones were tuned to music.'

The Major grinned. 'It's best to avoid music like that.' They laughed together.

'Maybe it was too good for them?' suggested Jim.

'You mean they were affected by it?'

'It might have been more than they could cope with.'

The Major thought over what he had been told. 'So, the hostages said their guard had turned nice?'

'They said he seemed upset as well.'

'Were the corpses fresh?'

'The blood was still tacky. They died at about the same time I would guess.'

The Major walked over to the window. Hazily shimmering in the rising heat, the escarpment rose just above the compound wall and, against the foreground of military hardware the scene appeared contrived, like a bad film set.

'OK, so music can be mood changing. Maybe it touched on their sensitivity?'

'I thought sensitivity was knocked out of them?'

'It is, and usually by group brutality. Kindness would be a betrayal.'

'So, if one goes soft, he lets down the group.'

'And if he does something really soft, like releasing hostages, they'll contrive a death for him which will make a bullet seem fun.'

'Would a tune do that sir? I mean make him soft enough to release hostages?'

'Possibly,' The Major shrugged. 'If he was alone, it might press what was left of his sensitive button.'

'One tune wouldn't have pressed it for long?'

'Maybe it was long enough for the jihadists you found.' He thought for moment. 'But it probably wouldn't have worked if they'd been grouped together.'

'You mean they would have each been too scared to admit to each other that they had soft spots?'

'Exactly. Weren't you the same? I was.'

Jim thought back to his fights with the Leigh Gang at Silver Woods sandpits. It was nasty kick and gouge stuff, even with a lad he once liked at school. But nothing would have been worse than losing face with his mates. They had created a mutual bond to out-hard each other, so there could be no going back. Fortunately, the police became involved before the growing arsenal of knives and airguns resulted in serious injury.

He agreed. 'But we weren't as bad as that lot.'

'No?' The Major was doubtful. 'Try convincing weekend A&E staff.'

'Not public beheadings and burnings.'

'Plenty like watching it and worse.' The Major unbuttoned a tunic pocket and took out his mobile phone. 'All the nastiness you could ever wish for in a tiny box. Even the dear old UBC pushes it after 8pm.'

'But that's pretend.'

'Not all of it, and viewers like to believe it's real.'

'No one actually gets killed.'

'But if hate and savagery is enjoyed from safety of armchairs, are viewers much better than the perpetrators?'

The Major was correct. Jim remembered being pressed into a crowd of sniggering schoolmates and being made to watch a hideous sequence on a mobile phone. In an instant he had been contaminated in a way that even the army couldn't erase, and like a poisonous splinter it still leached depravity and cruelty into moments he might otherwise enjoy. Yet his so-called mates pretended it was a big laugh.

'The Roman games would get top box office billing office now.' added the Major.

'And we're involved in the real thing,' claimed Jim.

'Yes, but it's usually short and noisy; occasionally brutish admittedly, but it's difficult to hate someone you don't know, and it's not deliberately tailored to be savoured like modern day entertainment.'

'Except this lot torture people to death.'

The Major shrugged.

'True, but they will claim morality by avenging a deity who is greater than all of us. Sadists or not, a place in the hereafter is a powerful motive for doing what they do.'

Jim pondered this. 'I wish I could believe in a God that much. But if that's what they believe, what chance do we have of beating them?'

'I can't answer that question, Sergeant.' The Major grinned. 'Correction…I won't answer that question. But it's the end of your tour and de-mob for you soon, isn't it?'

'Next week sir.'

'I thought so. Not long for me either.' The Major stepped forward. 'It will be a radical adjustment for both of us. War is dangerous but usually straightforward. Life decisions as a free agent can be complex and stressful. We'll both need luck.'

They exchanged salutes.

'By the way HQ have approved my recommendation for you to receive an award for extreme bravery.'

Jim reddened.

'Thank you, sir, I was lucky.'

'No, your men were lucky because you were there.'

He walked to the NCOs' Mess.

OK, so he half expected to be put forward for an award and it was great to know it had been approved, so he decided on a celebratory spell at the bar before bed and the morning patrol.

The Major was right. He didn't want the hassle and worry of adjusting to life outside the army. Given the choice he would sign on, but he hadn't been given the choice. He'd be on reserve of course, and there might soon be a new recruitment drive given the way things were hotting up everywhere. For him though, it was nearly Job Centre time. He'd decided on training as a paramedic if he could get it, but beyond that, his options seemed limited. He recalled the discussion he had with a career's advisor before leaving school, and the army came out as the most likely prospect. There was no chance of higher education with his predicted GCSE grades, and none of the local opportunities held any appeal. Besides which, his mates would drag him down whatever he did, and he knew he would be better off without them. He even mentioned this to the careers advisor who saw the sense of his reasoning

1. The Sound of Music

Aebid pressed his forehead hard against the muzzle of his trusty Kalashnikov and wept.

Only yesterday he had reduced that traitorous village headsman to his component parts in front of his family and he didn't feel bad about it then, so why did he feel so bad about it now?

Embracing the gun in a prayer position, he slid down over its lumpy bits and banged his head repeatedly on the ground in torment.

'That tune! Oh, that tune!' No wonder they had been forbidden to listen to music. Why hadn't he decapitated those western infidels before rummaging through their rucksacks? That's exactly what he was supposed to do, but he took the radio and was stupid enough to turn it on.

'Oh, that tune!'

He clawed the ground. The tune had gone, leaving only a desperate need to hear it again. But he couldn't hear it again and had released the hostages.

Bonding with comrades in competitive cruelty should have protected him against such an intense outpouring of remorse, and now he would die as a traitor. With luck he would be shot, but his compatriots would almost certainly arrange a more sophisticated and prolonged method for his disposal.

He shuddered, and raised himself high enough to look across the arid landscape stretching below the escarpment. Somewhere beyond the heat haze lay his village. He could have returned on many occasions, but chose not to. It would have meant arguments with his father, and he had little in common with other relatives. That brief liaison with the butcher's daughter had gone nowhere, leaving nothing to entice him back. It was just a place where he would simply get older; no more than that. A place full of nobodies who were content to be nobodies. He wanted a reason for living; something to satisfy his youthful energy; something much bigger than himself to fight for, and until a few moments ago he believed he had found it.

'Oh, that tune!' He dropped his head hard down onto the butt of the gun as the armpity embraces of his mother, and shouted lauding of compatriots became vacuous recollections. Desperately hoping that he might hear the tune again, he fiddled with the programme dial, then cursed and threw the offending radio over the edge of the escarpment; following it down until it skidded intact into a patch of scrub. He wanted to see it fly into a thousand pieces in atonement for the damage it had done, yet still tried to re-capture that moment as he leaned forward and pulled the trigger.

Further along, and just out of earshot, his commander bounced off a rocky outcrop and thudded onto the base of the escarpment.

'Suicide?' suggested the lance corporal.

Sergeant Jim Kettle was doubtful. 'They don't usually do suicide - it's bad for their afterlife.' He retrieved the Kalashnikov and glanced at the head wound. 'This could have been caused by the fall.'

'You reckon Sarge?' The young lance corporal was unconvinced. 'A hole like that?'

'Yes, well…whatever.' They climbed back into the patrol vehicle. 'Better check around.'

A short distance further on they stopped before the butt of another Kalashnikov jutting onto the track. He unlatched the magazine, and walking a few meters to the body of the commander picked up a mobile phone.'

'Careful Sarge, it could be a trap.'

'Thanks for the warning Corp, but it's a 'Soncya' phone; standard issue for ISIL round here.'

A tinny rattle of music came from a disconnected earpiece.

'Got a big hole in his head as well hasn't he Sarge?'

He nodded, and carefully unplugging the phone left the earpieces in situ.

Rounding the escarpment, they approached the buttress which nosed onto the track leading back to base.

'Two more there Sarge!' The lance corporal pointed ahead, and they stopped close to the bodies. One was draped over a smooth boulder still tacky with blood. A few meters away two legs protruded upwards from a cluster of smaller boulders.

They recovered the Kalashnikovs and two more phones.

'Big holes in their heads as well Sarge?' The lance corporal was becoming irritating.

'Yes, big holes,' confirmed Jim quietly. The phones were also tuned to a music station.

The hostages waved them down a mile or so along the track. Thirsty and dishevelled, they had made it from the escarpment.

The young woman spoke flatly between gulps of water.

'They were going to kill us, but then one of them cut us loose while the others were away.'

'Something was really bugging him,' cut in one of the men.

'Yeah, he sorta turned nice,' said the other. 'He just said *Go*! but his face was all twitchy like he was holding back tears.'

'Turned nice?' chipped in the lance corporal. 'I didn't think they did nice.'

'Well nice-ish,' qualified one.

They drove back through the village past a small yard where a goat was being openly slaughtered with a knife. The squealing animal sounded over the engine noise and Jim hated the whole village.

One of the hostages started to shake.

'Gee that's done it for me!' He squeezed his eyes hard shut and shook violently. The young woman hugged him while speaking over his shoulder. 'He came to us. Seems there were three of them, then something happened.'

They arrived at base.

Jim handed in the phones and Kalashnikovs, and shared farewells with the Americans. Soon they would be winging back home and he wouldn't be far behind. Maybe a couple of patrols more and IED's exempted, he'd be in the UK waiting to be demobbed.

'Suicide you think?' The Major was doubtful. 'It sounds more like a squabble.'

'The hostages said their guard turned nice - well nicer.'

and arranged an interview at the local army recruitment office.

Staying with his sister and her screechy son wasn't an attractive prospect either, but Dawn had made the offer, and since she had split with hubby, he could make himself useful in her tiny semi until a job came along.

First checking his watch, he ordered another pint. Just two more patrols with that irritating lance corporal, then it was on the plane and back home…well, the UK.

The discovery of huge gravitational waves headed the news on the bar radio. Two black holes getting it together had created quite a disturbance way up in space; just as astronomers had predicted years ago. Who knows? It might even start off the answer to life, the Universe, and everything.

He thought further.

So why couldn't everyone get excited about something like that, instead of contriving hate, and throwing bombs about. It was so much bigger than all this stupid: 'My god's better than yours, so I'd better kill you in case yours takes over my patch,' sort of stuff. He was at the sharp end of this of course, and had to bump off as many of the enemy as he could. But the killing business had got so systemised that by the time he'd got himself geared up, and checked all he needed to check, he might as well be shooting at skittles.

Someone switched the radio over to football, and the far end of the bar erupted into 'Yesses' Groans and raised fists. Man' United had scored against Arsenal to keep their place in the first division. He lukewarmly supported Arsenal because the manager did less shouting, and didn't wave his arms about so much, but that was about the extent of his enthusiasm. The result would of course be exploited by the lance corporal on the morning patrol.

He fancied another beer, but a voice welled up to him from the days of childhood… *'And now it's time for bed.' said Zebedee.*

He obeyed the voice and walked across to his quarters.

'Thrashed again eh, Sarge?' The lance corporal grinned provocatively.

Jim concentrated on the track ahead. 'There's always a next time.'

'It'll be a long time coming though, won't it Sarge?'

'It'll be worth waiting for.' He scanned each side of the track. He really didn't need a morning of football banter.

'Might help if you changed Penn,' persisted the lance corporal.' What do you think Sarge?'

Jim groaned inwardly. The lance corporal always spoke in questions, and who was Penn anyway?' He was already out of his depth, and with five hours to go the subject had to change.

'How about the manager then? You could cha…….

2. Confusion.

A blonde angel gazed down to him through a circle of diffused lights.

'Welcome.' Her smile waxed and waned as she drifted in and out of his vision while conferring with someone nearby. 'You've joined us at last.'

The bliss faded as he dozily reasoned he probably wasn't in heaven. He could have reached a half-way house of course, and might have to answer some probing questions. But that possibility was also quashed by some nearby grunts and energetic jerking as he was circled round and moved away from the lights. Clearly, he was being pushed somewhere on a trolley and was woozily trying work why the trolley seemed to be pressing up on him.

'Should the trolley do that?' he wondered, but the blonde angel was smiling at him again.'

'We'll take you up now, my lovely.'

Overhead, the strip lights continued alongside a galvanized ventilation duct until they stopped and reversed into the confines of a lift, which rose a few meters and clunked to a stop.

'Third left isn't it?' asked a male voice. The lift doors opened and they followed another corridor ventilation duct.

'Yes, it's all ready.' The blonde angel gripped the side rail of the trolley, and swivelled it through some swing doors, past some beds and into a vacant cubicle.

'About three inches more,' she instructed, and then hissed an expletive close to his ear as the trolley jerked and bumped over something.

'Sorry about that.' She leaned over to apologize. 'But that was my foot and it bloody hurt.'

She curtained him off.

'Somebody will see you soon my lovely…well, as soon as they can. We're all going doolally here, but you're just out of theatre which makes you a priority.'

He settled back. Most of the wooziness had gone and he was starting to hurt. That was a good sign of course. He checked what he could of his working parts by flexing, prodding, and testing everything down to his toes. He was never able to move his big toe independently, and the occasional jab of carpel arthritis in the joint between his thumb and forefinger had been there since unarmed self-defence training. Nothing seemed to be seriously amiss, although his upper back and neck prickled uncomfortably. Tentatively rubbing behind a shoulder, he felt the tips of some splinters just above the surface of the skin. It was satisfying to pull them out, although some were quite long and caused bleeding. He'd been bandaged in places, but there was no plaster and no numbness. Neither had he been fitted up with drips, so hopefully most of his internal bits and pieces were intact. The trolley was still pressing upwards though, and this was puzzling, because he normally felt that gravity was pulling him downwards. He raised an arm and felt it being pulled downwards which was normal. But once on the trolley it felt as if it was being pressed upwards just sufficiently to stay where it was. So why did he feel he was being pressed upwards, when he usually felt he was being pulled downwards? And why was he thinking like this anyway?'

A prolonged screech came from just outside the ward.

'Help me! Help me nurse! It's getting worse!' Loud clucking noises followed.

A second voice chimed in: 'Go away go away! Can't bear it, can't bear it!' For a while both voices primed the air with apprehension, generating audible signs of interrupted sleep and irritation in the ward.

Someone said, 'I wouldn't have my mother like that.'

'You've no choice,' replied somebody close-by. 'My mother was like that.'

'I'm sorry.'

'So were we. She wanted to go before getting that bad, and we wanted her to go before getting that bad, but there's no choice.'

More shrieked demands punctuated the conversation.

'They don't sound happy.'

'Probably don't know what they are.'

'I want the chop before I'm like that.'

'It would be a DIY job unless someone did time for you.'

Some assenting murmurs confirmed a wider audience in the ward, then the curtain parted and the consultant entered.

'How do you feel?'

'As if I've been punched all over, but everything seems to work fairly well.'

'Good, keep moving and exercising gently. You should be walking soon, but we need to have you under observation for a few more days.'

'Did anyone else survive?'

'Sadly not. I understand that the crew in the rear of the vehicle took the full force of the blast.'

Jim thought back to the lance corporal. He was on the winning side of the football banter, but an improvised land mine seemed a cheaty way of settling it.

'Lucky me then?'

The consultant agreed. 'You were very lucky, but we need to check for anything below skin level.'

'I've removed some splinters already.'

'Try to leave them for the nurse. Some will take time to emerge and the sites need to be treated for possible infection. Is there anything you'd like to ask me?'

A prolonged screech cut across Jim's reply, and the consultant winced as he opened the curtains to leave. 'If only I could move you on, Mavis.' He spoke with concern.

'You'd be doing her a favour,' said Jim.

Visibly puzzled, the consultant half turned before closing the curtain, and once outside, his silhouette hesitated uncertainly before moving on.

'Maybe there's something he's forgotten to tell me,' thought Jim.

Another trolley drew alongside and made light contact with the wall. The blonde angel parted his privacy curtain and poked her head through.

'You've got a neighbour my lovely. I'll be with you in a second.' She withdrew and spoke to an assistant.

'I'll attend to this one. Those up front will be too busy with Mavis.' She slid the curtain further aside and came in.

'You've to stay where you are for a couple of nights, which is why you're catheterized at the front.' She reached under the trolley and brandishing a bed pan pointed to a red button. 'Press this if you need the pan, alright?'

'Alright, thanks.'

She showed him how to use the radio.

'Has the ward sister seen you yet?'

'No.'

'Right, I'll get her to move her fat arse.'

'She won't lose much weight that way.'

The blond angel seemed taken aback. 'No, I suppose not.' She closed the curtain and hesitated outside as if, like the consultant, she was discomforted by something left unsaid.

'She knows more than I do and isn't telling me,' decided Jim. 'It could be serious I suppose.' He succumbed to a sinking feeling. 'Probably waiting for the tests to confirm what it is.'

A prolonged groan nearby, told him all was not well with his new neighbour either, and another spate of outbursts from Mavis and her roommate triggered more listlessness and moans throughout the ward. The curtained enclosure blocked him from visual contact, and removed any obligation to interact with fellow patients while trying to come to terms with such an abrupt change in his lifestyle. With the radio off, he put on the headphones to simulate the sound of the sea, which was something he used to do by placing teacups over his ears as a child. The headphones weren't very effective, but they were better than the ward sounds. Eliminating all else, he imagined the sea as a vast grey matrix moving smoothly towards him, and against that mental backcloth he laid back on his pillow to think about death.

Death had never been far away of course. He had witnessed it in its varied and messy forms on numerous occasions, but now it was close up and personal. It would be a big let-down if he died and nothing happened afterwards. On the other hand, it could be a big worry if something did happen.

Deciding his future after the army was difficult enough. After death it would be mind-boggling. Heaven would be OK of course, but he couldn't relate to it in job, or even pleasure terms. Would everyone have to start from scratch, or would those who had lived extra virtuous lives have a head start? Perhaps top-up training was given for those who had only just made the grade. Work of some kind had to be part of whatever form Heaven took. Even nooky on tap would surely lose its appeal in the absence of some form of heavenly vocation.

He considered this further.

Maybe a different heaven came with each different belief. After all, there were plenty to choose from, and how could he tell which one was the best? He'd never had the chance to chase round and compare them all. He went to the local church like everyone else in his village, and no one, not even the Vicar, had told him he might be in the wrong place.

He thought back to those early church services. They were always well attended, and Hell was in vogue then. The Vicar may have had a covetous eye on Godfrey Jones, but it didn't stop him risking popularity by making Hell so hot that the local youths put aside crudity and catapults for just long enough to earn a few heavenly top up points at the Sunday Service.

So, it was Heaven or Hell or an endless nothing, and he'd certainly blotted his record with Islam.

His spirits sunk lower as he thought about Hell.

Hell made sense.

If there was a heaven for being good there had to be a hell for being bad, and it was probably on a sliding scale from 'burnt to a cinder' to a nasty scorching. He'd done some good in the army. Saving the crew from that burning 'Mastiff,' should have given him some plusses, so on balance the 'nasty scorching' category would seem about right if it was to be Hell. But then what? Even a mild scorching couldn't go on forever surely? There had to be some way out of Hell, although the Vicar had never mentioned it.

Then there was the endless nothing, and that was hardest of all.

The surface of the matrix ruffled and his spirit bottomed.

He tried to imagine an endless nothing. No feeling, no hearing, no seeing, no smelling, and no awareness - just nothing. The world; space, friends, and life in all its manifestations would continue without him, and he would be gone; finished, kaput, and that would be that.

He really didn't want to accept an endless nothing, and grappling for straws that might convey some hope, he recalled the moment when his sister stepped back from pushing a small wooden cross into a freshly dug mound by the garden hedge. They had hugged each other in a trio of grief and Mum said: 'We'll all miss Biggles, but he'll give life to the hedge.'

It was consoling to know that Biggles would be nurturing the hedge, and after years of diffusion might even leave an infinitesimal something of himself in a future cat. Sadly of course Biggles would never know, so it would still be an endless nothing for him.

But what makes us so special anyway? Why should we expect Heaven or Hell when all other life forms have to be content with recycling?

A teeny chink of enlightenment cut through the gloom. Heaven wouldn't make sense to other creatures because being good or evil isn't the way they think. Only humans knowingly choose to be good or evil, and in a world so vulnerable to human behaviour, surely there must be a final judgement, or where's the come-uppance for doing horrible things if the kind and selfish also perish into an endless nothing?'

He felt slightly better, but only slightly. There were just too many imponderables. Anyway, what made him so sure that other creatures can't tell good from evil, and what for instance, should happen to his sister's son? It was hard to imagine a nastier shouty, punchy, and scratchy child. Perhaps judgment was suspended for those under sixteen, but what criteria could possibly be applied in the years following his premature death or murder. Where should he go?

With each unanswered question the journey into an endless nothing seemed ever more likely, and a nagging foreboding summoned up a monster from the deep which began to circle inside the matrix.

The scene before him had now become surreal, and visualising all the components compacted together, he turned it into a picture, then simulated his own flatness and entered it.

Depth had vanished, yet the monster created an illusion of distance, because its fin appeared to get bigger and smaller as it circled round the matrix. He slowly turned a hand. It was flat from every angle. Then he took a risk and grabbed the monster. Without depth it didn't look so lethal, but oddly, he could feel its girth, and his hands felt solid even though they appeared flat.

If he was aware of only two dimensions, was this how he would experience a three-dimensional world? He allowed time for this to sink in while a tiny glimmer of something other than an endless nothing tried to squeeze its way through.

So, if, at that point, he was given the ability to see the third dimension, everything would gain depth, and the mystery of living in a flat world would vanish in a flash of perspective. It would be a revelation.

He struggled to keep his thinking together, when the thought struck him that it would be an equally big revelation if he was given the ability to comprehend the fourth dimension.

Could that explain last minute shouts of 'Stroll on! So, it's that bloody simple!' sometimes called out with the onset of death?

He felt constrained inside the picture, but it channelled his thinking right back to his Uncle Bill's funeral service. He really liked his Uncle Bill, and when the Vicar had read: 'My father's house has many mansions.' the words comforted him with their mystery and hope. At the time he was heavily into 'Doctor Who,' and here was the Bible of all books, offering a trendy 'Tardis' like solution to heavenly overcrowding, and even a nod towards a fourth dimension. But that was before the magic had been sucked from the passage by someone changing 'mansions' to 'rooms.'

He removed himself from the picture and made the matrix swallow the monster. His head swam, but in a confused way he'd decided that death might be something more than just an endless nothing.

A figure approached, and the matrix collapsed as the curtains were swept apart by the ward sister.

'Jim Kettle? I'm Beryl your ward sister.' She picked up the patient's notes at the end of the bed.' So, are you comfortable?'

'Yes thanks.'

Simultaneously his pulse was taken and a thermometer placed in his mouth.

'Have you opened your bowels yet?'

'Not yet.'

She checked her watch. 'There's still time, although we need get you scanned today.'

'Why?'

'You need an X-ray to check below skin level.' Her voice went buzzy. 'From whoever had to be scraped from your back, I suppose.'

'I was lucky. His rifle would have been hard to scrape off.'

She frowned with puzzlement. 'Well, yes I suppose so.' Still looking puzzled she waddled round to the other side of the bed and drew the curtain right back.

'Do you know what's wrong with me?' he asked.

'We won't know until you've had all the tests.'

'I've waggled everything from my toes to my ears with no problems.'

'That's a good sign; keep waggling. But some bits don't waggle, and we must check everything.' She looked up from the patient's notes. 'And keep drinking the water.' She gave him his glass. 'It'll help you to poo.'

Her expression changed to exasperation as Mavis chimed up again with her mantra. 'Go away! Go away! Can't bear it!'

More moans circulated the ward.

'Please God, put her out of her misery!' exclaimed Sister Beryl.

'Agreed, and you can do away with me if I get like that.'

Looking up in surprise she used the pen from the notes to point to herself.

'What did I say?'

He repeated: 'Put her out of her misery.'

She seemed shocked. 'You heard me say that?'

'I agree with you.'

'But...' she was worried. 'Did you really hear me say that?'

'It was clear enough to me.'

She chastised herself while writing the notes. 'Well, it was unprofessional. I shouldn't have said it.'

He placed a finger over his lips. 'Let's keep it a secret then, and I'll drink plenty of water.'

They shared smiles and she thanked him, yet remained puzzled.

Dawn arrived after lunch.

She had gained weight since the evening Jim had spent with her and ex-husband Darren. They had been to the new bowling alley, and had later shared a spicy chicken take-away in Dawn's semi-detached. Darren had previously announced that he, 'didn't do politics or religion,' and demonstrated further strength of character by refusing the green salad on the grounds that he, 'wasn't a rabbit.' Luckily the TV was tuned to 'Match of the Day', and Darren was snoring well before Jim was on the A12 and driving back to base.

It was on the same evening that Dawn had announced her pregnancy. Jim made a few congratulatory sounds, but could think of nothing to explain her attraction to Darren. Perhaps she just wanted to have a baby, and he had delivered the goods. Neither did she express much concern about his occasional shenanigans which led to their divorce. Darren had vanished quite amicably by the time Shaun was able to crawl, and was rarely mentioned in later conversations.

Now, son Shaun was beside her with his head and shoulders just above the level of the bed. A seventy percent amalgam of Darren and thirty percent of Dawn, Shaun was prodding the screen of his 'Z' Deck'. Every so often he would glance upward to check his surroundings, then down to a reassuring world of bleeps, guns, and gangsters. Jim was clearly outside his zone of interest, and Jim was content to leave it like that.

Dawn gave him a look of concern and tried leaning over, but Shaun stayed where he was.

'So, what have they found Jim?'

'Mainly bone splinters, and a few bits of cloth.'

'Have they removed everything?'

'Just about, apart from a brass button they found on the scan.'

'Is that serious?'

'Not really; they should have it out soon'

'Does anything else need to be done?'

'Just physiotherapy which should begin tomorrow. But I can't help feeling there's something they're not telling me.'

She acquired the diagnostic expression used during their childhood patient and doctor games, but he spoke first.

'Do I seem different somehow?'

'Not so far. But Jim, it's a bit too early to ask me that. I haven't seen you since I split with Darren. What do you mean by different?'

'A bit remote…distant. I feel I'm on the outside of everything.'

'Well sometimes I feel like that, but you've just been blown up - it's hardly surprising, is it?'

Shaun tilted sideways and pulled a face as she reached over to pat Jim on the arm. 'Give it time brother.'

He liked his sister. There had never been much childhood jealousy between them, and even during his feral period they had got on well together.

'OK, I'll give it time.' It was pointless trying to convey how he felt, especially when he wasn't sure about it himself.

'Have you made any plans?'

'I'll take what I can get. It could be security, or maybe paramedic training.'

'Well, stay with us at least until you get something.' She sounded hopeful.

Shaun had been tugging at her arm because he wanted a wee, and continued to look pointedly at her as Jim gave directions to the loo. They went off together, and immediately on return Shaun grabbed his Z Deck and noisily voiced objections at being made to stay any longer. As she was pulled away, Dawn managed to exchange goodbyes with Jim, and repeated the offer for him to share her semi.

Living with Dawn made sense. Apart from finding lodgings, he didn't have anywhere else to go, and they could share the rental, but Shaun would be a continuous splinter in the head. He wasn't too keen on modern children, and since they had become 'kids' he liked them even less. Still, like them or not, Shaun came with the package.

He snoozed until dinner and darkness came. Outside, the thunderstorms competed with each other, and a sort of clubby feel prevailed as sparkling rivulets of water flowed erratically down the ward windows in time with the lightning. He donned the headphones and listened to the weather forecast. Flooding was predicted in the South West and valleys in the North. It was almost a repeat of the forecasts given the year before, and the year before that. Once again, the government was blamed for inadequate funding of flood defences. Once again, the immediate concern was for those whose homes and farms were in valleys vulnerable to flooding, and once again the climatologists warned of more weather extremes unless atmospheric pollution levels were drastically reduced.

Global warming wasn't on his personal agenda until he met a drunken entomologist in the British Club during a detachment in the Sudan. Employed by the Sudanese Government to control white fly on cotton crops, the entomologist advised on the frequency of aerial spraying, and gave Jim a morose lecture about damage being done to the natural environment because of it. A patrol northward into the encroaching desert took him through vacated villages; bleached cattle skeletons and dead trees, all of which confirmed the entomologist's forebodings. But global warming and the environment soon dropped from his list of concerns during postings to other areas of conflict.

Anyway, what was all this guff about climate change and protecting the natural world when politicians were forever rabbiting on about growth and making more stuff? How were they squaring all that with climate protection? And again, why was he thinking like this? If he hadn't long to live, it was a bit late to be getting seriously worked up about all the stupid things going on in a stupid world.

Outside the air had become explosive, and it reflected his mood. Hail rattled on the windows, and the continuous flashes and bangs had now transformed the feel of the ward to a refuge inside a war zone. He turned up the volume. The weather forecast had moved onto an interview with someone who had damaged his libido through a daily diet of porn, so he quickly tuned onto another programme featuring a shouty presenter playing AI simulated bonky-bonky music, and seeking views on the merits, or otherwise of obscene slogans on T- shirts. Reaching flash point he clouted the radio button to off, and launched a tirade of expletives at the ceiling.

But why was he ranting at the radio?

In his loutish days of catapults and punch ups he would have enjoyed an 'up yours' strut through the neighbourhood looking hard in an obscene T- shirt. Neither had porn done much to damage to his libido. So where did he get the right to be so precious?

This was turmoil.

There were too many contradictory feelings swilling round. He'd lost his centrality. All the emotions, knowledge, and experiences, which had been interlinked and bonded into a single 'Jim' were becoming unstuck. He thought he knew who he was, but now he wasn't so sure. Something was seriously amiss, and it could be something he hadn't been told about.

Seen through the windows on the opposite side of the ward, a reflected stream of blue lights tracked across the wet upper frontages of nearby office blocks, and sirens clashed discordantly with the thunder. More trolleys were wheeled in, and the nurses whispered urgently to each other as they hurried between patients. Anxiety and tension rippled through the ward, occasionally enhanced by a harpies' chorus from Mavis and her friend.

Sister Beryl made a beeline towards him, but was grabbed by the elbow to assist with a snagged curtain being drawn round a new arrival.

'Been a big pile up on the ring road,' someone announced.

'Some birdbrain pushing his luck,' speculated another voice.

'You're probably right. Last time it was a druggy. I feel sorry for this lot having to cope with us as well.'

The conversation criss-crossed over Jim, but a more fundamental need had forced its way downwards. He debated whether to hang on until the emergency was over before pressing the button, but Sister Beryl was already bustling towards him.

'You should need this by now.'

'I didn't want to bother you while the emergency was going on.'

He missed the smile as she reached for the bed pan.

'You're no bother.'

She drew the curtains and sprayed the cubicle with air freshener.

'Someone will collect it when you've done.'

'Do I ring the bell?'

'No need to, you've rung my bell already.'

Did she really say that, or was this also part of going nutty? It was more a sensation than something spoken and conveyed a hint of wistfulness.

The bedpan pressed upwards. This was crackers! The whole miserable world had crowded into his head, and now he had to cope with a flirtation on a bedpan. How did that happen? Or did it really happen?

The thunderstorm moved over, and the ward reverted to a clubby feel as silver rivulets again chased down the windows in a departing burst of rain. He checked for the time and stared at the pale circle on his wrist. His watch had been a constant in his life ever since joining the army. Now even that had gone.

Preceded by another large burst of air-freshener, he was efficiently dealt with by a nursing assistant, and longing to achieve a sense of proportion, tuned into some classical music until his headphones were removed and the blond angel was again looking down on him.

'Time for you to go in the lift again my lovely.'

'Button removal time, is it?'

She nodded. 'It shouldn't take long.'

'What else is wrong with me?'

She consulted the notes.

'It doesn't say anything here. What makes you think there's something else?'

'I just feel I'm not being told everything'

She swung him into the lift and pressed the down button. 'Well, you'll get it straight from me and no messing.' Her Norfolk burr was enhanced in the lively ambience of the corridor. '…But if you think you're in the dark my lovely, you should try the shoes I'm wearing.'

'So, we've got that in common then?'

'You mean straight talking?'

'Yes, and being kept in the dark.'

She frowned. 'Well, I suppose so.'

Performed under local anaesthetic, the operation was brief, and he was given the brass button; it was distorted.

The blonde angel wheeled him back to the ward. 'Will you keep it?

'I'm not sure.' He viewed it uncertainly, and thought back to army parades and uniform inspections. 'It needs a polish.'

'Were you friends?'

'He was a good soldier.' Jim spoke as he felt. Perhaps he should have pretended some affection for the lance corporal but it would have been insincere.

'Was he married?'

'I think so.' He rolled his thumb over the button and decided against keeping it. After all it was hardly a gift, but if the lance corporal had a wife, it seemed wrong to just get rid of it.

Sister Beryl joined them on the ward. 'Job done?'

He showed her the button. Yes, job done, but 'I'm not sure what to do about this.'

She examined it.' 'If I was his wife I wouldn't want it, but we can't be sure. Once we've got this rush over, I'll ask the Chaplain what he thinks.'

She produced his watch from her top pocket, and smiled at his expression as she placed it on the side locker.

'This came up from radiology, and boy! How I wish you would look at me like that.'

Her wish was fleeting and buzzy, but very warming.

Sleep came, but it came as a succession of creepy moods and a misty déjà-vu liaison leaving him crestfallen at what might have been. So, it was pleasant to wake up to some light banter.

The Club Bouncer was speaking.

'Anyway, why should I be nice? The cruds I have to deal with would walk all over me.'

'But if it made them nice as well, you could all be nice together.'

'Yeah, a sort of Saturday night love in.' wheezed a third voice.

'And I'd be out of a job.' said the Bouncer.

'You wouldn't be in here though, would you?'

Some laughter followed as the subject moved on.

'Do you remember the council rigging up speakers playing Mozart to keep the clubbers nice?'

'Yeah, the street cleaners got chipboard and bits of wire mixed up with the usual chicken and pizza boxes.'

A hesitant voice chirped up from the bed opposite.

'But think about it...I mean, well, if everyone became nicer, you know? Wouldn't it be a better world?'

'You mean the whole world like Russia, China, Africa, the Arabs and all that lot?'

'It would have to be the whole world because, well, think about it, we don't want any more Hitler's in power, do we?'

'We've had plenty since he got sorted. Anyway, what's to stop them?'

'I'm just saying if everyone was nicer, it would be harder for the nasty ones to get into power, if you know what I mean?' It came across as a plea for understanding.

'So how would you do that?'

'It wouldn't be easy.' The Chirper paused for thought. 'Every country would have to agree.'

'I thought we had a United Nations for that?'

'But it isn't working, is it? And this is something different.' The Chirper knew he was on uncertain ground. 'I'm just saying it might help with all the trouble in the world. Something's got to be done.'

'Being nice won't do it.' declared the Bouncer. 'Anyway, what world? Why should I worry about the world and that lot out there? The wife and kids are what matters. It's the survival of the fittest here as well.'

'Seems like you lost out again,' wheezed the Wheezer.

The Bouncer persisted over more laughter.

'Yeah, well alright, but my dad soon got me into fighting. He wasn't going to have me bullied at school.'

'So, you got your bullying in first, you mean?'

'Maybe, but I got respect. It was a rough school. Being nice wouldn't help there.'

Jim thought back to his feral days. The Bouncer was right. It was just the same in his school. The toughs usually received more respect than pleasant pupils and the swots.

'But what about the kids that were brought up to be kind and…well nice, you know? They're the ones who usually get bullied.' The Chirper whinnied slightly.

'So what?' The bouncer was uncompromising. 'They need to get hardened up. Countries are big gangs fighting for what they want…what else are they? So, I make my kids tough, so they can fight for what they want - anything wrong with that? If someone wants to make their kids soft more fool them. If I was their kid I wouldn't thank them for it.'

A few grunts of assent followed.

'Yes,' persisted the Chirper. 'But it doesn't have to be a nasty world does it? I mean, being nice doesn't mean being soft?' He faded off uncertainly. 'Does it?'

'It's the same in my book.' asserted the Bouncer.

Jim joined the debate.

'So, what's this all about?'

'Someone's come up with a nice pill.'

'I thought we were trying to get rid of nice pills?'

'Seems this one is different; it just makes you nice or nicer. It doesn't do anything else.'

'What sort of nice? Nice to people? Nice to animals?'

'Didn't say, just generally nice, I suppose.'

Jim thought about, 'generally nice.' He knew what being nice meant but wished there was another word which had more bite. Again, the Bouncer was right. It was a tame, almost effete word with no energetic macho alternatives. It was almost an insult to be called nice. Maybe it would have more bite if action words were added to it by saying something like, 'Dangerously nice', or even: 'Punchy nice,' but they still missed the mark.

The Bouncer spoke again.

'They'd have big trouble getting me to take a nice pill. Anyone trying to make me nice would soon have a fight on their hands.'

'Can't see these pills catching on somehow.' concluded the Wheezer.

Jim felt some sympathy for the Chirper, but the meal trolley came round and the debate faded out.

Taking his watch from the locker, he calculated that less than twenty-four hours had passed since his arrival, and although his injuries seemed trivial compared to the accident victims, it was about time he was told exactly what was wrong. Perhaps he wouldn't be in such turmoil if he knew.

He donned the headphones and returned to the radio.

Another shouty presenter was already seeking opinions about the nice pill.

'Well listeners, if you think you've heard everything, listen to this. It's claimed that a pill might soon be available which will make everyone nice. Yes, a pill to make everyone nice. 'Think about that!' Didn't you know you were nice already? Well, if you're not sure, you may soon be able to take a pill.'

With me is Professor Grillwood; Head of Humanities at Grimston. 'So, there you have it Professor. Your views please.'

'Well, I can only give you my opinion, but I doubt if colleagues elsewhere would disagree. A range of drugs and treatments are of course used to control and alleviate a variety of emotional and behavioural problems, but I am very uneasy about any artificial agent being widely used to modify our natural characteristics. We have enough mind-changing drugs already, adding yet another can only do more harm.'

The presenter came in. 'I understand that the same ingredients are common fare across many Andean Regions of Latin America, and they are thought to enhance well-being.'

The professor was unconvinced. 'And coca leaves were used by Andean Indians to cope with extreme altitude and cold. Then they were of course refined and misused.'

'I suppose there's a danger they could cause extreme niceness if refined,' speculated the presenter. 'But I'm informed that it doesn't work like that.'

'Perhaps not, but evolution over thousands of years has finely tuned us to survive in a competitive and sometimes hostile environment. Being artificially nice could reduce our perception of danger in a variety of ways.'

'Surely it won't weaken our resistance to disease or anything like that will it?'

'Frankly I don't know. But it would almost certainly make us more vulnerable in some situations.'

'You mean by being in the wrong frame of mind to perceive danger?'

'Yes, of course.'

'But we've already fought off most of our natural enemies. Fellow human beings are surely the main threat we need to consider?'

'That maybe so, but I simply cannot subscribe to the position that human beings as a species are incapable of modifying their behaviour without recourse to artificial methods.'

The presenter moved on.

'Well thank you professor, and that's a definite thumbs down for the nice pill. Now let's call in Bishop Pocklington. So, you've heard the professor. Do you agree Bishop?'

'I do, although from a different perspective of course. As the Professor says, we are fashioned into who we are by a myriad of life experiences from the moment of birth, and even before birth if we include our parents' characteristics… and isn't that such a wonder?' He paused and smiled while savouring the question. 'People are a complex array of loves, desires, dislikes, and regrettably hates sometimes. Conflict, disease, and starvation have always blighted human life, and sadly it is very true of the world we live in today. Those of us who are fortunate enough to enjoy happy circumstances should do everything we can to alleviate the dreadful conditions that so many are forced to endure, and much is already being done. Just consider the bravery of medical professionals working in the heart of war zones, and those who volunteer to control infectious diseases in countries with inadequate facilities. I should also mention those in our own benefice who have given sanctuary in their homes to refugees escaping the horrors of war. They don't need nice pills to enhance their humanity. There are so many occasions where our love for each other overcomes seemingly impossible hurdles. Goodness! The selflessness of motherhood is surely proof of that, and I cannot possibly endorse the wholesale distribution of a substance to make us artificially… well… nicer. Neither can I accept that God would ever approve of such a way to sustain good will towards our fellows. Let us celebrate our common humanity by doing what we can for our fellow men, but not by taking strange pills.'

'Thank you Bishop. So, let's hear from Brian who runs 'Spikewell Youth Boxers!'

'Yes, OK…Well, some of our kids get a lot of stick for bad behaviour. We get problems where we live, and started boxing clubs to get them off the streets. Loads of them round here are deprived because families don't have enough money, and their schools can't always cope. The ones I see aren't bad kids, it's just that they get into bad company and there are too many toughies around getting them into crime and drugs. They don't want help from a stupid pill.'

'Wouldn't it encourage them to make better friendships?'

'Sounds like it would make them into cissies. Cissies don't cut it here.'

'Well, what about the toughies?'

'Try that if you want. Not sure where the pill would end up though.'

The shouty presenter moved on.

'Well so far, it's still thumbs down for the nice pill. But what's wrong with everyone being nice? Surely it would make a better world, and surely someone out there must think it's a good idea. So, would you take one? Let's hear from you!'

The next listener was introduced after the football summary.

'Come in Edith, I believe you have a different point to make!'

Edith was hesitant.

'Yes, well, what about all the horrible things we are doing to animals and forests and the oceans. I mean something's got to be done hasn't it? Why does everything always have to be about people?'

'Thank you, Edith,' concluded the presenter, 'and that's a thoughtful note to end on.'

The news headlines followed, and the same presenter moved to another issue.

'Lip filler ops are getting popular, and you may have heard that top model Cincilla Juba is suing a private clinic a cool million dollars for a botched lip filler operation. Seems she hasn't been on the catwalk since visiting the clinic. So, are you planning a lip filler op, or like Cincilla, have you had a similar experience you can tell us about?'

More bonky- bonky music followed.

Jim's anger boiled up again. Seems that he and the lance corporal had been blown up so that shouty presenters could have the freedom to make that sort of jollop newsworthy?'

He silenced the radio and simmered at the bishop's contribution.

Did he really believe that people would ever cease warring with each other, and that 'humanity' would ever create a golden age of peace? Come to that, was parental love entirely selfless?

Even Dawn, bless her, had been so besotted with newborn Shaun that her eyes never left him whoever she was talking to. Far from being unselfish, this was a mother and baby love bubble leaving others to coo sycophantically from the outside as her little bundle of joy shrieked: 'Me! Me! Me!' Perhaps Shaun's progress towards a mini Darren had removed some of the shine from motherhood, but it was taking a long time.

Yes, it was always about people and how people felt. Rarely if ever, was it about the decimation of so many other living things and the wholesale pollution of air, land, and sea. His anger increased. And yes, he had been part of it, and yes, he'd killed. Yet his antipathy for the bishop almost topped that of the jihadists who blew his patrol up.

But again, why was he thinking like this? He never used to.

Hopefully sleep would come, but there wasn't much chance of that while Mavis and her friend were in serious chat mode, and once again it was loo time.

He pressed the button and rising from the nurses' station, the blond angel came towards him, then hesitated and turned into an alcove and reappeared with a wheel chair.

'You may need this, my lovely.'

'I'd like to try without it.'

He slid tentatively from the side of the bed, and the floor pressed upwards to take his weight. Walking felt strange, but no more than that, and if he concentrated hard enough, the pushing up sensation went away.

He managed in the loo, and returned to the bed without assistance.

The blonde angel seemed satisfied.

'It's a thorough check-over with the physio next.'

'Is everything else alright?'

'I can't tell you what I don't know now can I now? You've just been blown up my precious. We must check everything, and this place can kiss me goodbye if those litigation shits get me in trouble again.'

'Pity they can't be dragged into Saturday night A&E', he suggested.

'I wish….' she began,' then stopped. 'What did I say?'

He repeated her litigation rant and she lapsed into a shocked Norfolk drawl.

'Doon't taal me I raally said that!'

'I bet most of you feel like that.'

'I might have thought it, but I didn't say it, and I didn't swear…did I?'

'Yes.'

'Well. I'm sorry, I shouldn't swear in the ward.' She looked at him reproachfully. 'And it seems I have to be careful I how I think as well.'

Sleep came as a nightmare inside a gigantic funnel-shaped arena filled to capacity with a jeering crowd rising towards the cloud base.

Determined not to lose face, Jim confronted the opponent chosen by his feral chums. Pushing his chin forward until his neck tendons stuck out like straining hawsers, his opponent curled his lips back in an expression of pure hate and mouthed an obscenity while the referee circled around them conducting the crowd to fever pitch. There were no break bells, and the floor of the ring was gritty, offering little traction as they tried pulling, tripping, and punching each other down. Any semblance to boxing had gone well before mutual exhaustion took over, but Jim got in a lucky punch, and with a groan of recognition, slumped over himself lying prostrate on the floor. The referee pulled him to his feet and held his arm aloft as the victor, but by then, the crowd and his mates had gone, leaving the arena littered with cups, cans, and fast-food wrappers.

Saturated in sweat, and half conscious, he managed to grab and gulp down the glassful of water from the bedside cabinet, then flopped back into total sleep until the rattle of a breakfast trolley and some clarion calls from Mavis and her friend brought him back into an awakening ward.

Sister Beryl gave him a few moments to recover, then placed a thermometer in his mouth.

'Looks like you've had a rough sleep?' She checked the thermometer and seemed satisfied that nothing was seriously amiss.

'I had a bad dream.'

'That's hardly surprising after your experience. But let's have you in that shower, you'll feel better for it.' She checked his steadiness as he shuffled out of bed, then walked part way with him to the shower cubicles.

'How much longer will I need to be here?' he asked.

'You'll need physiotherapy and observation for a while. The consultant may give you some idea this afternoon.' A hint of informality entered her voice. 'But remember, you were only blown up two days ago, so don't be so impatient.'

He returned from the shower and settled into fresh bed sheets just as the consultant arrived with a lady holding a laptop computer.

'Mr Kettle, let me introduce Doctor White who is the Senior Psychiatrist at the Benton Institute.'

Doctor White smiled as she drew up the visitor's chair and opened her laptop.

'And I gather that you survived a land mine explosion without too much damage?'

Jim nodded. 'I was lucky.'

'You certainly were,' confirmed the consultant, 'How do you feel now?'

'The aches and pains are going.'

'Good,' the consultant read the patient's notes. 'We're keeping you under observation for a few days more, and will fit in a brain scan if Dr White feels it necessary.'

Dr White conveyed informality with authority.

'Does the possibility of a brain scan surprise you?'

'No, it makes sense. I've changed since the explosion.'

'In what way have you changed?'

'I feel I'm on the outside of everything.'

'You mean detached?'

'Yes, and I get angry at things that didn't bother me before.'

'Give me some examples.'

He attempted to explain the whys and wherefores of his ranting and imaginings, but found it difficult to put over.

'I'm not putting it over very well, but you've probably heard enough.'

She disagreed.

'No, I haven't heard enough. Please go on and include everything, whether you think it's relevant or not.'

Suitably chastised, he continued right to the end of his fight in the Stadium.

'So, you defeated yourself?'

'He looked like me, but I'm not sure who I defeated.'

'Does it still feel as if you are two separate people?'

'Not so much now. It's as if he was always there and the fight somehow stirred him into me.'

'Would you say that your new personality is an improvement?'

'I'll have to pass on that, but I mostly share his feelings.' He smiled. 'Although, with him being me, and me being him, I would say that wouldn't I?'

She frowned and tapped into her laptop.

'Has anything else struck you as unusual during your stay here?'

'I think something's being kept back from me. I'm not complaining, and the nurses are fine, but they seem to go peculiar at times as if there's something they don't want to tell me. If I'm going to die, I want to know.'

'I can assure you that no one here thinks you are going to die.' She eyed him carefully. 'But you have created quite a stir among the staff.'

'How?'

She added the hint of a smile. 'Do you sometimes have an inkling that you might be…' She winced as her question was swamped by an outburst from Mavis and her friend, and broke off to exclaim: 'If only you could get peace ladies!'

'They should have been given the chance for peace before now.' remarked Jim.

For an instant Dr White was nonplussed.

'What did I say?'

'You said, 'If only you could get peace ladies!' I agree with that.'

'She was intrigued. 'I certainly didn't say it, but I did think it, and somehow you picked it up.'

'It sounded as if you said it. That's how it came over.'

She allowed herself some excitement.

'You certainly timed it nicely, because I was about to ask if you had an inkling that you might be able to pick up thoughts.'

'I've heard about mind reading. It's unusual, isn't it?

'It's extremely unusual.'

'Well, if I can pick up thoughts, they usually come with a buzz.'

'Did my outcry come with a buzz?

'Yes.'

She tapped into her laptop while regarding him with interest.

'Well, on the surface, it seems that you have the ability to receive suppressed emotions, but that can only be confirmed by testing.'

'Didn't someone called Eric Teller put on mindreading shows?'

'Yes, but he was never formally tested.'

'Well, it's good to know I'm not dying, but I'd be avoided everywhere if I became known as a mind reader.'

Dr White was adamant. 'It need not be known. The tests results remain strictly confidential, unless of course, you wish to exploit your ability in some way.'

'The buzzes I get would be too unreliable for a mind reading show.'

She jotted more into her laptop.

'Perhaps, but you certainly need a brain scan to check for any injury caused by the blast, and I also recommend further tests to determine whether you have telepathic powers. She added tentatively. 'It would contribute greatly to our understanding of the human psyche.'

'Please say you'll take the tests.' came with a buzz, and he sensed her relief when he agreed to her unspoken request.

3. Far Away

A retired mobster looked down to a trashed wilderness from the top terrace of a palatial villa high above his tiny fiefdom. The remaining greenery straggled over patches of bare earth cluttered with excavation sites, and far into the distance, wispy plumes of dust trailed over the bordering territory into the lush canopies of an undamaged rain forest. This was all his handiwork, and now he didn't feel very good about it.

Below on the middle terrace, his henchmen lazed around on deck-chairs cradling M15's and scanning the narrow road which snaked up to the guardhouse. Behind them, the forest slanted upwards towards a steep granite escarpment rising like a giant step into a bluish haze overlaying the lower foothills of the Andes.

Ostensibly a dictatorship, the small nation of Miser Tellus was effectively ruled over by Respectico Phaulius, and as long as everyone did exactly as they were told, the money kept flowing into various dodgy bank accounts across the world. This of course benefitted Dictator Marshal Otiosum who was just as nasty, but morbid obesity and a hankering for cocaine had eroded both his ability and desire to govern. Anyway, the money kept rolling in, so why should he bother?

But now Respectico Phaulius was seriously contemplating his real worth.

He just wasn't happy.

An ominous void had only recently replaced the satisfaction that power had given him, and the tiny figures labouring for emeralds in excavation pits weren't happy either. The older ones could remember fresh fruit; fishing in bountiful lakes, and family bonding over meals. Times were hard then, but this was soulless. Beer, bread, imported veg and sweetie pops from Respectico's 'Emerald' stores had become the norm, and video games gifted out at Christmas hadn't done much for family or community harmony. Respectico instinctively knew how to disrupt the cohesion of a simple community by introducing commercial practices and the promise of individual wealth. The whole process took about three years from the time he bought residence, and now he could exploit a submissive workforce with unchallenged authority.

But he wasn't happy.

A sudden spell of dizziness had prompted a check-up in Miami, where he was advised to lose weight and take tablets. Suddenly he was vulnerable. He might even die one day, and should that happen, how would he be remembered? What could be chiselled on his headstone, and who would lay flowers on his grave? Would any of the Panama rent girls shed tears when his luxury yacht ferried them home for the last time? Monogamy had never been his thing, and money gave him choice, so why go for trouble? He'd bought the girls like everything else, and could think of no one who had done anything for him out of affection. But who was he going to leave all this money and power to? His relatives had disowned him years ago, and a brief altercation with the Mafia during a bad early career move had ensured there would be no offspring.

And who among those labouring down there in the pits, would harbour fond memories of him? He'd provided a rescue team, and five percent wholesale value as a bonus for extra unearthed stones. What more could they expect? He'd even made his helicopter available for emergency hospital treatment, but not once had he received a hint of gratitude.

A chill mountain wind dropped over the veranda and down to the excavation sites, stirring up more dust which brought on a fit of sneezing. He turned to go back inside the villa, and as he was about to open the door, the sound system started up and embraced him with a tune that burst into all those gloomy hollows he had long chosen to ignore. More like a flash of enlightenment than a tune, it pushed aside all the guile and ruthlessness he had employed over the years, and filled him with an aspiration that no amount of power or wealth could ever satisfy. Not once had he experienced anything close to it. It had been a sudden jolt of awareness that he was a senior member of the sad global club for pointless living, and now he desperately wanted to do something about it.

But what?

Maybe he could re-employ the locals in a massive replanting scheme, but after that would they go back to a co-operative lifestyle? Some had already grabbed the chance to make extra money; especially the young, who had eagerly absorbed the raw commercial morality streaming into their tablets and smartphones. New enterprises were growing apace; not all of them savoury, and a developing gang culture had displayed itself in some nasty confrontations between rival booze producers. None of this had been of the slightest concern to Respectico. Lawlessness and extortion were part of his DNA, but growing community disorder in the ramshackle settlements were affecting emerald extraction and therefore profits, so he increasingly had to employ his henchmen to keep the peace.

It soon it became clear that he, and he alone, had left Miser Tellus with no option other than to take on the ways of the modern world, but his was a modern world with even less checks and balances.

He stubbed his cigar on the balcony rail and swore.

It was as if he had led healthy and happy children into an X-rated video store with full rein to indulge, and to hell with the consequences.

But what to do? He had to find a solution.

While he deliberated, his henchmen were glancing upwards, screw-faced at the cacophony of the speakers blaring out music from different radio stations. But he desperately needed to hear the tune again, and kept the sound system going until the air chilled and a bright moon had cast its steely pallor over his vast estate. It was no good. He couldn't keep everyone awake until dawn. A triple whisky and bed were called for, and as he walked over to the patio door for a second time, a radio presenter jokingly announced the production of a nice pill in Fortunatus Viridis, his neighbouring state.

A bejewelled hand beckoned him inside.

'You are thoughtful, my Respectico?'

He grunted and nodded, 'Did you just hear about nice pill?'

'You don't need nice pill my Respectico?' She feigned surprise.

'Maybe I try one,' he muttered, 'and you get me information please.'

The crackle of distant shooting failed to penetrate the triple glazing during the night, and several jogs from the bejewelled hand were needed to drag out some waking grunts from a dozing Respectico the following morning.

Later, on the middle terrace, a henchman handed him some binoculars.

'Big bust up last night using guns.' He indicated a rubbish strewn patch close to the nearest settlement. 'Some dead ones there.' His finger moved over to an excavation site. 'More there.'

Respectico scanned the patch and counted about five corpses.

'Better get down and see what's happened.'

A few months had passed since he had last gone 'below' and the area had deteriorated. Many of the cultivated patches fronting each dwelling were now covered with scrubby red earth as the spoil from the excavation pits had extended into the domestic sites, and everywhere was littered with all kinds of debris. The corpses were lying together in a rough semi-circle, and some were already draped in blue plastic sheeting brought over from the excavation site.

'Looks like an automatic did this.' The senior henchman closed up to a corpse in the foetal position. 'Probably one of these.' He tapped his M15.

A workman dragged across two more plastic sheets, and while draping them over the remaining corpses, acknowledged them with an indifferent shrug, and shouted at two boys as he turned to go back.

The boys waited until he had gone, then ran over and played tag round the plastic sheeting while pretending to shoot each other. Some doors opened, and their mothers screamed at them to get inside.

'Like home, eh?' grunted Respectico.

'Yeah, takes me back Boss.'

They had both been reared in the favelas and could have been viewing the aftermath of a serious gangland altercation.

Seemingly from nowhere, a boy with a toy gun quickly unrolled a plastic sheet from one of the corpses to snap a 'selfie'. A distraught mother ran out screaming at him to get inside, then changing direction, halted before Respectico, and burst into tears.

'They all young… they evil!' She shakily pointed back to her son who was grinning into his phone. 'He, my son…yes, he my son!' she screwed her eyes up and dropped to her knees. 'He evil… Oh God, how they get like that? My son…yes my son he is evil!' She clawed Respectico's shoes and looked upwards. 'You do something please! You kill him, you kill me! Please you do something!'

He palmed her to rise and cupped her face in his hands. Tears had cut through the grime on her cheeks - she had been beautiful once.

'I'll think of something lady.' he grunted, and tried to look reassuring.

The boy glanced indifferently at them from his doorway, and then back to grinning at his phone and the images he was sharing with the other lad.

Respectico climbed back into the Humvee.
Something had to be done.

'It is here my Respectico.' The jewelled hand laid
his tablet on the desktop and pointed to the news
item.

*'Adelita Justica, State Governor of Fortunatus
Viridis is planning to go ahead with a new facility to
produce Sapiens Carduus Soup in addition to Sapiens
Carduus Tablets, or 'nice pills' as they are popularly
known.*

*'Sapiens Carduus' or (Wise Thistle) is a common
thistle in the lower Andean regions and has been an
essential ingredient in many popular dishes
throughout Fortunatus Viridis for centuries. It is
thought to enhance moral awareness, and recent
studies into the behavioural effects of Sapiens
Carduus have concluded that it may account for the
long-term stability of those regions where it is
consumed. It is also a good source of vitamins 'C' and
'D' and is known to be non-addictive. While said to be
an acquired taste, it is planned that 'Sapiens Carduus'
will be an essential ingredient in a variety of food
products from Fortunatus Viridis, and that Sapiens
Carduus Soup will soon be widely available.*

*A number of respected voices have raised concern
that any artificial means to modify human traits is
ethically unsound, and could result in social
problems.'*

Respectico gazed uncertainly at the phone in his
office. His only meeting with Adelita Justica was to
agree on financing a dam to stabilize water supply
between Miser Tellus and its bordering territories. He

had been expecting a hard time given the damage he was doing to the Miser Tellus ecology, but Adelita had conducted the meeting with so much authority and good humour, that he even felt a passing twinge of guilt about his activities.

He picked up the phone and hesitated. Adelita had charisma, but he had been steeped in the harshness of a corrupt life and would sound coarse and ignorant. That mattered to him, but the cupped face of the distraught mother mattered even more. Urgent action was needed.

He dialled, and was efficiently transferred to Adelita who was visiting a community garden. She answered on her mobile phone.

'Respectico, it's been ages since we last met. So, how are you?' There was no hint of wariness or pretence.

'Not too bad.' He cringed at the drabness in his voice. 'Can we meet?'

'Of course we can. Goodness, we've been neighbours for long enough. We should have got together well before now. What do you want to discuss?'

'I want to change things here, and could do with your help.'

'I hope I can help. Please give me some idea how.'

He shrugged his shoulders at the phone. Might as well shed pretence, and come clean.

'I've messed up here Adelita, and now it's big trouble. I've got to do something before it gets real nasty. The Marshall won't be any good.'

She sensed his anxiety. 'It sounds urgent. Do you still have your helicopter?'

'Yep.'

'Well, why not fly over straightaway and join me for a snack and coffee?'

He thanked her as a subaltern might thank his next in command, then phoned the army Captain to advise extra patrols in case of further trouble, before sprucing himself up and taking the roof lift to his helicopter.'

The Governor's Residence was a white, stuccoed Spanish mansion which had been modernised and equipped with solar roof panels and ground source heat pumps. Flower decked balconies graced the frontage of the building, and the bottom floor included a reception area; a large open plan living space, and a meeting room.

Respectico looked into the distance while having coffee on the patio with Adelita.

Ahead, the green expanse of lawn sloped down to a river which cut diagonally across their line of sight through a patch of flowers, and into the raggedy border of a rain forest.

His helicopter had settled onto the lawn, partially obscuring the view, and a flock of blue birds had perched on the rotor blades in an attempt to camouflage such a tasteless intrusion into their territory.

Contrasting it with the vast area of scarred vegetation seen beyond his own balcony, he shook his head in self-reproach.

'Miser Tellus could have been like this.'

'Don't be too hard on yourself, Respectico. Marshal Otiosum would have sold out to a palm oil company if you hadn't taken over.' She directed his attention to the forest. 'All this could have been sold five times over, and the pressure is still mounting.'

'Big money speaks.'

'It's speaking loud enough to persuade our politicians. I will fight it of course, but palm oil, or cattle ranching will take over unless our thistles come to the rescue.'

'And you make special thistle pills?'

'We always have.'

'And we get nice if we eat them?'

'Yes, if you must put it that way.'

She frowned.

'I wish the media hadn't used 'Nice pills' to describe them. 'Considerate pills' or 'Thoughtful pills' would have been better, but we'll have to live with 'Nice pills' I suppose. The soup we are producing will be marketed simply as a healthy food, and we are making no other claims.' She spoke with determination. 'The pressure is relentless, Respectico, but I don't intend to lose our beautiful Fortunatus Viridis to corporate greed.'

Respectico closed up to her over the table. He had been doing some strategic thinking while flying over.

'And you don't have to lose your beautiful Fortunatus Viridis lady.' He pointed to himself and grinned horribly. 'You just have to trust a corrupt emerald dealing hoodlum?'

'Ugh, revolting!' She shied away while managing a smile, 'But how?'

He walked over to the patio doors, and gestured towards the view.

'You keep all this. I've trashed Miser Terrace, so grow your thistles there.' He turned to face her.

'Look, I've blundered big time. Maybe I got an excuse. I fought nasty, that's all I knew. Most favela kids fight nasty. That's how they make it, and I made it by being nastier than most. Yeah, and I've got big money. So much that I don't know how much, and big money gets power, and people calling you 'Boss'. So, it's: 'Bravo for the favela kid who made it'. He pointed to himself. 'Bravo for the kid who brought the favelas into Miser Terrace…OK?

He kept pointing to himself.

'And now they're shooting each other. Bang! Bang! Just like home.'

'It's that bad?'

'Yep, it's that bad.'

He went to the edge of the patio and Adelita joined him. She noticed his eyes were watery.

'Something tells me you are not the Respectico who discussed the shared water project at our Unity
Meeting years ago.'

He returned a wrinkly smile; 'That's for sure.'

'So, now I have to decide whether or not to do business with a corrupt emerald dealing hoodlum, or lose my beautiful forest.' She gazed ahead while pondering over the implications. 'But would Marshal Otiosum approve of thistle growing in Miser Terrace?'

Respectico made a 'Tch' 'Tch' sound. 'He still gets his cocaine, no problem.'

'Give me a few moments to think it over.' Walking onto the lawn, she sought the opinion of the bluebirds that had fluttered down to her from the helicopter. Satisfied, she then returned to Respectico.

'It makes sense.'

'Respectico always makes sense.'

She gave him a direct look. 'Then let's set out our stalls and do business.'

Doing business took less than five minutes, including the handshake.

'Strange,' she thought, as the helicopter rattled over the mansion and banked towards Miser Terrace. 'I even trust him.'

Following his return, Respectico had a bad night. It could have been festival time down below, but he knew he wasn't hearing firecrackers or smelling smoke from celebratory bonfires. Neither did the distant shouting and screaming which drifted up to him sound very celebratory.

This time the corpses were scattered over a wider area, and the smell from the smouldering remains of the settlements suggested a scant disregard for any trapped inhabitants. A tangle of copper pipes and molten sugar inside the blackened shells of several dwellings confirmed widespread booze making, but the nature of the carnage implied something more sinister than straightforward gang warfare.

'A lot more this time Boss,' reflected his chief henchman.

Respectico squinted into the rising sun. Spirals of smoke and red dust swirled upwards from different locations right up to the border of Fortunatus Viridis. He cursed because it was clear that about half of the defence force had been deployed, and Marshal

Otiosum was probably having doubts about his ability to manage the trouble.

Just visible at the head of a dust trail, a troop carrier and trailer had been making erratic progress towards them. Every so often it veered off to an excavation site where the soldiers disembarked to retrieve discarded weaponry, and report the location of injured survivors to the medical team. Jumping from the cab, the captain ushered his troops down from the carrier, and came over to Respectico.

'I didn't expect we'd collect quite so much ironmongery.'

He led them to the trailer and a large collection of weapons, ranging from cudgels and chains through to handguns and modern automatic rifles.

'They must have found some good supply lines for this lot,' he reasoned.

'Yep.' Sombre faced, Respectico agreed. This was all his mess-up.

'There's been trouble everywhere and around here looks like the worst.' The captain pointed to a distant white flag. 'We've set up a medical tent in the middle settlement which had the least trouble. Now it's getting packed with families. Some of them are in a bad way, and we're fixing them up as best we can. But there are burns, broken bones and all sorts.'

'You got enough medics?'

'They're whacked, and we're running low on bandages, splints, and pain killers.'

Respectico thought quickly.

'You guys tired?'

The captain shrugged. 'More like hungry, we missed breakfast.'

'OK, get me through to the Marshal if you can.'

The captain smiled wryly. 'Could still be in bed, he's not an early riser.'

As it happened, Marshal Otiosum was available, and having taken his special breakfast aperitif sounded quite attentive.

'It was noisy last night Respectico?' The words oscillated from bass to falsetto as his vocal cords settled down. Respectico avoided the implication that he might have something to answer for.

'Looks like we've had a turf war between booze barons Marshal, but something else is going on.'

'How so?'

'Too sudden; too many involved, and too nasty. There's been a lot of burning, and survivors are trying to make it to the middle settlement.'

Some crackly breathing followed.

'Any ideas?'

'We need to move fast.'

As he spoke, Respectico had been dipping into his personal reservoir of craftiness and guile, which had been refined in countless skirmishes over the years. He beckoned to the captain to come over and share the conversation.

'Your troops are doing great Marshal, but they need breakfast and rest, and we need some replacements.'

'How many do you need?'

'Your captain has been organising things. I'll pass him over. Best he reports directly to you, I don't want to get out of my boots. You're the boss.'

The captain did more nodding than reporting.

'The Marshal says he wants to leave it to you.'

'OK.' Respectico gave a diffident shrug while inwardly enjoying a surge of power.

He turned to the captain. 'Are you happy working with me Captain?'

'No problem with me.'

'Good.' Respectico went into organising mode. 'Get your troops to breakfast, and ask the medics to phone the office for the supplies they need. The chopper will collect them and ferry the worst casualties to Fortunatus.'

The captain checked his notes after phoning from the troop carrier.

'The medics keep hearing about trouble between two groups. There was some fighting in the medical tent, and it seems that a couple of ancient cults have started up again.'

Respectico turned to his senior henchman. 'Ask the office to find out what they can about any ancient cults living here.'

The captain continued.

'I'll arrange for the reserve troops to clear up the corpses, and we could take them north for identification. There are plenty of portable coffins at base, and if you got your diggers working, we could start extending the burial ground.'

'Good thinking. I'll try to get a priest from somewhere.'

They drove to the Villa for breakfast, and going straight to his office, Respectico ordered coffee and cornflakes before phoning Adelita. Her secretary asked him to hold on, and he finished his cornflakes as the sound of heels on a hard floor heralded her arrival.

'Respectico, so soon! You caught me unawares.'

'He pushed his luck. 'How they say? Chance would be the fine thing.'

'Try me after you've completed your etiquette training.'

'Ah! You give me hard words.'

'You sound busy?'

'Hoping for good out of trouble, but I need your pills and a priest.'

He briefed her on events, and asked for every pill that could be spared.

'Very well, but remember Respectico, this is our project, so we share the cost of the pills and the priest. You will also need the publicity team.'

'Publicity team…How so?'

'The publicity team will be making a documentary about the conflict, and how Sapiens Carduus will be used to bring about peace. There are only two in the team, and they will need transport and accommodation.'

'Right, I fix it. Tomorrow, we start burials and cleanup.'

'Send your helicopter for the pills first thing in the morning. Father Dududso and the publicity team will be waiting. And remember Respectico, this is a shared project.'

He lowered the phone as the jewelled hands placed some sheets of printed foolscap before him.

'There are several articles my Respectico, but this is the best researched.'

As he read, Respectico cursed himself for not bothering to look into the history of Miser Tellus before debasing a co-operative way of life which had evolved after centuries of primitive mayhem.

It seems there were several tribes with different belief systems who were all were fighting for more territory. The conflicts became increasingly intractable until a powerful El Niño caused widespread flooding, which in turn generated a climate of co-operation as the tribes got together with rescue and rebuilding. The flooding also provided breathing space for a courageous band of peacemakers to construct a fleet of sailed rafts which they used to navigate the flood waters while proclaiming the futility of war. Known as the 'Reconciliadors' they advocated co-operation and self-sufficiency as the only possible way to prevent conflict, and for a while, Miser Tellus settled down to relative peace with the exception of two tribes whose leaders continued to foment trouble towards each other.

An addendum to the article illustrated the tribal symbols, and Respectico snipped it off to use as a reference before driving to the middle settlement. Behind him, the helicopter swivelled over the roof of the villa and sped northwards to collect the casualties for treatment in Torrosus.

Amplified messages of support and reassurance sounded inside the middle settlement as a variety of vehicles and construction equipment zigzagged through the compounds. The second contingent of soldiers had been working efficiently, and had already erected some high poles numbered from one to ten to identify the assembly points. Scattered about the excavation sites were a selection of shelters improvised from lengths of timber and plastic sheeting, supplemented by bedroom only accommodation inside the scoops of dumper trucks.

The prefabricated coffins were being unloaded and assembled in the shade of the largest copse, and groups of relatives had already begun the grisly task of identifying loved ones who had been collected from the conflict areas and laid on stretchers. Again, the soldiers had worked efficiently, and plastic bags containing possessions were placed on the sheets that would be pulled over the bodies after identification and labelling. Beyond the copse, and producing thick clouds of red dust, diggers were noisily dumping conical piles of earth in rows as they prepared the burial ground. It was a scene of determined activity which somehow removed much of the wretchedness from the situation. At least something was being done, although a few sporadic crackles suggested that a number of scores were still being settled elsewhere.

Respectico entered a medical tent which had been improvised with poles and tarpaulin covers. A naked man was being treated for burns. The medic spoke wearily.

'He managed to get out.'

Respectico grunted. There was no need to ask what happened, but the man kept saying: 'Rabbits.'

'Rabbits?' repeated Respectico. Had he been sworn at?

The man screwed up his face with pain of talking. 'Rabbits do this.' He pointed to blisters on his lower torso.

'Yes, Rabbits.' confirmed the medic. 'Rabbits and Hares, they're the two sects that have started up again.'

'What's the difference?'

'There are more Rabbits, but the Hares are supposed to be tougher. The Rabbits don't like that of course.'

'Makes sense, hares get punchy and run faster.'

'This one didn't.' The medic grinned wryly.

Respectico spoke to the patient. 'Are you a Hare?'

He nodded and rasped: 'All my family Hares.' He beckoned Respectico to come closer and whispered, 'Once a Hare, always a Hare.'

The medic elaborated. 'It seems there were too many Rabbits making booze, so the Hares lost business and got nasty, which started up the old feud all over again. Anyway, that's what we've gathered so far.'

Respectico checked the symbols on the addendum he had removed from the article.

'I can't see any Rabbits and Hares on this.'

'It used to be Bears and Tigers. The Spanish made them change to Rabbits and Hares, in the hope they wouldn't be so aggressive to each other, but it didn't work.'

Respectico walked over to the nearest row of dwellings. Except for one blackened gap, the dwellings were scrawled over with images of rabbits, and the mattresses and cushions scattered outside were reserved exclusively for rabbit casualties.

Respectico questioned a man who had come from the eastern settlement for treatment. He had just been frisked and relieved of a handgun.

'OK, so what happened?'

'A big booze up and fighting, then shooting.'

'Who started it?'

'A Hare with an M15, and youths cheering him on.'

'Is it mostly Hares over there?'

'It's about fifty-fifty.'

'Who made the booze?'

'Everyone.'

'And what happened here?' Respectico angled his head towards the blackened gap between the dwellings.

The man half shrugged his shoulders. 'Same as happened to some of us.' he grinned…'Noisy for a bit.'

'You'll have to live together sometime.'

'You're joking.'

'You won't be fighting in the graveyard.'

The man laughed. 'You want to bet on it?'

An elderly lady who was limping, and clearly distressed, had been hurrying towards them from the copse where the bodies were being identified. She stopped and faced the line of Rabbit dwellings, then pointed a shaking finger at the burnt-out dwelling.

'So why you do that!' Crying and trembling, her voice split into a screech. 'They lovely people. Why you do that?' She half ran and half tripped into the dwelling. 'You pour petrol over me, eh? You laugh, you hear me scream!' Framed by the charred window frame, she placed her hands palms outwards on her head to simulate ears. 'I once Rabbit… now I Hare!

So, you kill me with your petrol or I live here. This now my home with Hares!' Stooping behind the window frame she picked up something just recognisable as an upper torso and hugged it like a baby. 'Now I live with them!'

She dropped behind the wall to a hubbub of self-justification and sniggers from the Rabbit dwellings, and Respectico clashed eyes with the man beside him just as his mobile rang.

It was Adelita.

'How are you managing Respectico?'

'We'll know better by morning. There's still some shooting going on.'

'The publicity team and Father Dududso will be with you soon. They all have experience of war zones, and Madge spent time in the Middle East.'

'There's a woman?'

'Why not Respectico?'

He jumped into acceptable mode. 'No reason…accommodation that's all.'

'The publicity team work together,' continued Adelita, 'There are only two of them and a shared room would suit them perfectly, but they need to be with the army to record the trouble. Can you arrange that?'

'No problem, they'll have a jeep and protection.'

'Good, they'll be coming and going at all hours.'

'I keep the kitchen open.'

He noticed the growing tally of stretchers in the copse. 'The priest will be busy.'

'Father Dududso will be a great help Respectico. He came to us from a diocese in Butkre.

'Butkre Eh?' Respectico understood.

'Try to start the pill distribution as soon as possible. Father Dududso won't object even though his church is against their use. 'You should notice subtle changes within a few days.'

'When it happens Respectico believes it.'

'I did say 'subtle', Respectico, but I'm impressed with your speed and efficiency.

He nearly blushed. 'Awe, old habits Adelita. It's fix or get fixed in my world.'

'Your feral lifestyle is serving you well.'

'Could be…what's feral mean?'

'No matter. Are you continuing with emerald extraction?'

'We tidy up and keep going. Work should hold off trouble.'

'When can you start preparing for planting?

'After the burials. We'll need help and training.'

'You'll get both. The agricultural team can start surveying anytime. Just supply the labour when the trouble has calmed down.'

'Sounds good. So, I just pay the labour.'

'Correction Respectico. 'We' pay the labour.'

He grunted affably. 'Yeah, OK. OK. 'We' pay the labour, or Respectico gets put in corner with hat on, eh?'

'Exactly,' she laughed. 'So don't let me remind you again.'

He lowered the phone knowing that he was second in command, but somehow it didn't matter anymore. With a shrug of acceptance, he walked across to the burnt-out dwelling and peered through the charcoaled window frame. Flat down and face up, the woman had merged into the cinders and the dead. She noticed him but didn't move.

'You've got courage, lady.'

'I must atone.'

'For what?'

'For the evil I have bred,'

'That won't work. You'll just be one more dead.' She insisted. 'I make this my tomb.'

'Why make it a tomb when it could be a monument of hope?'

'This?' She flicked her head disbelievingly from side to side. 'This hope?'

'Lady, the dead you have chosen to live with in this dwelling need to be taken to the graveyard for a decent burial, so this can be made into a place for flowers and peace.'

Confusion rippled her features as she rose onto her elbows. 'Here?'

'Yes, here, but I can't do it with you in the way.'

She trembled with the effort of rising, then slipped on something and fell back again. He hurried round and lifted her to her feet by which time she was crying.

'You give me hope?' Snuffling and shaking, she hugged him as tightly as she could. The stench was overpowering, but he returned her hugs.

'Things will change. Just keep living lady, Miser Tellus needs your courage.'

Later, during dinner in the Villa, there was a guarded feeling of optimism. Down below all was calm. The army was doing a good job, and a more relaxed Respectico was at the table.

The publicity team had returned from their first patrol, and Father Dududso was curious to know how they had been affected by their experiences as reporters in different parts of the world.

Madge spoke with resignation.

'It's making us quite cynical now.'

Father Dududso raised his eyebrows: 'In the UK as well?'

'We've had some good moments, but it's changing.'

'Really?' You surprise me.'

She smoothed the surface of the table as if laying out her thoughts.

'It's not grown up anymore.'

'How do you mean?'

'It's the only way I can put it.' She looked up. 'I could give a hundred reasons why, and you might see it differently if you went there, but I don't much like going home these days.'

'I try to avoid Manchester as well,' grinned Ben.

Madge prodded him. 'He's trying to wind me up because I come from Manchester.' Switching on her tablet, she placed their first report on the table before Father Dududso. 'This is a bit strong in places and sorry for my language at times.'

She gave Ben another prod. 'Get that cake down you Clever Clogs. It's time for the next patrol.' Father Dududso rose to bless them, then turned his attention back to the tablet and grimaced.

'Well timed Madge.' chided Ben as they climbed into the patrol vehicle, 'Just after desserts.'

Next morning in the graveyard, Respectico stood with the woman who was prepared to sacrifice herself in the burnt-out hare dwelling. They watched as her as her son was lowered into a grave ready for Father Dududso to give the last rites. The ceremonial scattering of earth had shifted the sheet, revealing a crudely tattooed whisker on his forehead.

She spoke flatly. 'I have no feeling for him.'

Respectico placed a comforting hand on her shoulder.

'Give it time lady, maybe he just had to go along with the crowd.'

She remained impassive, and in her face Respectico saw his mother's expression after his early recruitment into gangland.

Outside the medical tent, two patients were being stretchered into the helicopter for further treatment in Fortunatus Viridis hospital. Soon biodegradable leaflets proclaiming a new dawn for Miser Tellus would be floating down from the same helicopter, and nice pills would be supplementing the vitamin intake of the residents as part of a compulsory healthcare programme

Respectico watched the lady walking back to her settlement. All the rabbit images had been cleaned off the dwellings, and sensing a spark of satisfaction, he once again thought of his mother.

4. A Place to Call Home.

A royal hand pinned the medal onto Jim's tunic.

As he stepped back and saluted, he felt a genuine surge of pride, coupled with the emptiness of lost comradeship. The floaty detached sensation which had been barely noticeable in the month since leaving hospital, had returned during the ceremony, and the palace carpet pressed upwards as he walked back to his small group of army pals who were seated with Dawn, and a bored Shaun.

The bulge below Dawn's waistline would soon present a challenge to young Shaun. So: 'All Hail' to Gary her new partner, who, as the latest resident, was currently applying his DIY expertise and parental skills in her small semi. This came as a welcome relief to Jim, who had accepted ward sister Beryl's totally unprofessional offer of a flat share even before he was released as a patient.

The flat provided simple accommodation above a flower shop in the high street, and was entered from the street through a bottom side door and up a flight of concrete steps. The hospital was in easy walking distance, so there was no need for Beryl to own a car or even a cycle.

Jim's position as a paying guest, quickly progressed to one of being a cohabitant, since they were soon sharing everything, including each other. Being independent suited them. He wasn't sure about Beryl, and although she proclaimed her love for him in moments of high passion, he sensed that he was regarded as damaged goods, to be replaced once she had slimmed down to more attractive proportions by curbing the desire for anything chocolate.

She followed his programme of tests for telepathy with interest. Bit by bit he developed the skill of ignoring oddities in their conversations before commenting on them, but not all the oddities came with a buzz, so it was very unpredictable. Beryl played games with him by pretending to be angry or expressing desire, but soon it became clear that pretence didn't work. Only genuine unspoken emotion triggered her voice in his head, and even that was inconsistent. So, he concluded that his telepathy came with faulty circuitry, along with the floaty feeling and sense of being pressed upwards. The test results were inconclusive, although conversations outside the testing programme had caused some surprises. One of the researchers at the Benton Institute buzzed: 'Something's going on up there Jim, but there's no way we can prove it, so bang goes my research grant!'

As a result, paramedic training had to be put on hold, and he found work at a local supermarket while waiting for a clean bill of health. The work was undemanding; even mildly enjoyable. But as the year moved on, he became ever more despondent about his adopted neighbourhood and general way of the world.

Following a late dinner after Beryl's Saturday shift they watched yet more reportage about increased hostilities in the Middle East and Eastern Europe; starvation in Africa, oppression of women, and local knife crime. Sensing his despondency, she snuggled up to him. 'You've done your bit Jim. You can't solve everything.'

She was always a comfort in his despairing moments, but silly or not, he couldn't shake off a nagging belief that somehow, he had been landed with the awesome task of solving the horrors perpetrated by humankind.

'But it never stops. I should do something.'

As he spoke his voice was overlaid by a sound picture of sexual improbabilities drifting up from the street below.

'Sorting out this street would be a good start.'

The casual swearing and coarse laughing had already begun, and it wasn't even pub turn-out time.

'But it's not up to you to sort it out, so please don't try.' He dropped sharply as Beryl rose from the sofa to close the window. 'I just wish it wouldn't get to you so much.'

She secured the window, then 'Grrrd!' and shook him by the shoulders. 'If only I could just shake it out of you!'

'I wish you could.' He bobbed up again as she swivelled down beside him.

'I get upset as well,' she continued. 'It's been dreadful in the wards recently, but I've got a box in my head where I hide the nasties while I'm working.' She stopped. 'But you've seen much worse.'

He thought about this.

'Maybe, but I get more upset by that sludge down there because we produce it. The army probably saved me from getting like them, but I know how they think, and it's everywhere now.'

'Yes, and Wendy doesn't put her eldest on the school bus anymore. But life would be impossible if we went into despair at everything we hear.'

He managed a wry smile. 'You'll just have to give me your box for nasties.'

'Why not? I'll make one especially for you.' She ruffled his hair. 'And that's not all you're going to get if I have my way.'

The second offer came with a buzz, so he kissed her and accepted it.

But the despondency deepened. He didn't need to hear the world news for his spirits to drop. What he saw and heard in the supermarket was bad enough. Altercations were commonplace, and occasionally members of staff were assaulted. Then there was the 'kids will be kids' amnesty at confectionary thefts in 'Kids Corner' during school holidays. And so it went on. The tattooed tough who jabbed a finger at the elderly attendant while driving into a disabled slot probably reversed out only because he saw something beyond anger in Jim's expression.

The modest get-togethers with Dawn, and second husband Gary were enjoyable though. Dawn couldn't have chosen a better replacement for Darren, and in any other situation Jim would have embraced Gary as a much needed soul-mate. But conversation always defaulted to tiny Penny gurgling in her cot. Everyone went into high voice mode at her minor squawks of discomfort. Nappy changes and open breast feeding brought forth 'Oooh's and 'Aaah's' which usually left little time for anything else to be talked about. It was unclear what Shaun thought of it all, but Gary confided to Jim that Shaun had bitten a pupil in the school playground, and a brand new 'Z Deck' was on offer only if he maintained good behaviour and completed his homework.

'It's been uphill with Shaun Jim,' confided Gary. 'But I have to be careful, so I'm trying the carrot approach first. I daren't risk him disliking me at this stage, it could make life very difficult.'

'You're doing a good job Gary.' Jim felt gratitude on Dawns behalf, but did wonder just how much support Gary was getting from her.

Beryl usually went broody, after their get-togethers.

'It's just the way I'm made. I feel guilty because I'm denying a life to someone. That's the way others and the media make me feel these days. Then the loneliness cuts in because I'm denying myself love as well.'

At this point she would usually open up to him.

'But I couldn't do it, not to someone that was part of me; not to someone I would bring up to be kind and considerate. I really couldn't do it Jim.'

There was no need for elaboration or questioning. It was Beryl's decision, based on her experience of life at work; in the borough, and probably during her childhood. Sometimes he held her until the tears stopped. They were usually brief, and she always followed them up by polishing her favourite vase from the small display cabinet in the corner of the end wall.

So, Jim adjusted to work in the supermarket and living with Beryl, occasionally enhanced by outings to restaurants and places of interest in company with her friends. They were a likeable bunch, and while they shared little in common, he was readily accepted as Beryl's new man and was content to settle into a bland routine, which was about the best he could hope for in the circumstances. Yet the despondency and anger at what he observed in that small urban patch wouldn't let go. He wanted to ignore the graffiti; the casual indifference, and rubbish on the street as he went to work each morning. Most of all he wanted to erase his own hypocrisy. But his head wouldn't open up to pleasant things, and one Monday morning in that frame of mind, he picked up a scattering of soft drinks cans from the pavement, and holding them pointedly aloft for all to see, made a show of dropping them one by one into the supermarket rubbish bin before reporting for work.

The ceiling speakers were already sighing with synthesised love, which added emotive falsity to his black mood as he wheeled his replenishment cart to the tinned vegetable shelves. From the opposite end of the row, a dummy-sucking child in a trolley loaded with sweetie pops was being pushed towards him by an obese couple. It was a common sight, but this time he went into incendiary mode. He wanted to shout 'Child abusers!' while pushing an image of a young diabetic amputee in their faces, but the fear in their eyes was directed beyond him towards the checkouts. From behind came a shout of pain, then fast padding footsteps, and someone with a serious knife swerved round his trolley straight towards them.

Unleashing his fury into a run and flying jump, Jim sailed feet first onto the assailant's rib cage sending them sliding along the floor and into the trolley, which knocked the woman down and sent the pop bottles hard onto the child. He applied a shoulder lock firm enough for the knife to be released, while the father grabbed his screaming infant and pulled his partner to her feet. They made it to the exit by almost running, and as he watched them go, Jim conceded to a flaw in his own personality by trying to understand why he loathed them as much as the knifer beneath him.

One of the security staff ran up to him. 'Are you OK Jim?'

'Yes, He won't move.'

'Right; the police are on the way. Sure you can manage? I'm the only first aider.'

Jim nodded towards his supervisor who was curled up by a checkout.

'Get to Phil, I can manage.'

The shoppers grouped round taking pictures with smartphones and giving profane advice about what he should do to the knifer, while his captive snorted out a diatribe at the floor which didn't make sense. At last, the police arrived, and hurried the assailant away from more injuries inflicted by vegetable cans. Jim was awarded backslaps and cries of 'Top man!' as he made it through the crowd to the storeroom. But once inside, he let off steam by hammering his fists on a stack of rubber mats while waiting for the crowd to disperse.

Word quickly spread that the knifer had only recently been released from care, and Phil the supervisor was in hospital - but would survive. That at least, was good news, but it was a fair bet that more incidents were brewing up, given the problems in the area.

From start to finish the whole episode took about ten minutes, and the local media caught up with him well before the store closed. It should have been a straightforward interview, but he started to boil up the moment he was introduced.

'Well, it's not the first time you've saved lives Jim, and this time it was a child.'

It was an accolade, and he would have liked to reply in spirit, but he just couldn't play the reluctant hero.

'It would be good to believe that.'

'But you brought down the attacker before he got to the child.'

'Yes, but I wouldn't like to bet on that child having much of a life anyway.'

Susan, the interviewer, signalled for the recording to be stopped.

'Could you say more about that Jim? I need to be clear about it before we start recording again.

'If I said what I felt, it wouldn't go down very well on air.'

She angled her head perceptively. 'You don't have to of course, but it won't go beyond this room unless you say so, and I'm intrigued, so try me.'

The camera operator moved to go out, but Jim palmed him back.

'It's not confidential. It's just that I can't pretend to be the big hero over this one. 'That child was a ball of fat in a trolley full of sweetie pops. How long before it waddles into hospital with diabetes? That's the sort of child abuse I see every day in this store, and the nutter with the knife got my anger. He would have probably gone for the adults anyway. But I can't tell it like that can I?'

'It would cause a stir, but I don't see why not.' She gave him another perceptive glance. 'Anything else?'

Do I need to spell it out? Drugs, bag snatchers, car theft, domestic abuse. He pointed to himself. 'Maybe it's just me being a misery, and yes, it isn't bad everywhere, but I don't see much joy in this place.'

'And are you prepared to say so.'

'It would be honest.'

'So, can you offer a solution?'

'My solutions would be unacceptable, although for what it's worth, I did hear talk about a nice pill?'

'Just what I need for the mother-in-law.' grinned the camera operator.

Susan gave him a black look and returned to Jim. 'Yes, a nice pill was mentioned in the news recently. Are you serious?'

'If it works, why not? What else is there?'

'But surely you are thinking globally, not just here?'

'Here might be a good place to start.'

She became thoughtful, and then compressed her lips decisively.

'It might cause you some aggro Jim, but are you prepared to go on air with that?

'Yes'

'Very well, let's go for it then.'

The interview took about five minutes, and aggro or not, he felt better for it.

Back at the flat he received a mixed reception.

'You brave boy.' Beryl hugged him hard, then released him with a look of reproach.

'You were right about the child, but I didn't like what you said about overweight people. They can't always help being overweight you know.'

'Those two could have rolled round the store. One nearly did.'

'But there's usually something wrong in their lives, so they eat to get comfort. It must be really distressing to be called a fatty.'

Then she caught his look.

'Oh, you rotten stinker, you deserve to be rolled around this floor!'

She pulled him down, and they rolled on the floor for some time.

At work next morning he was called to the manager's office.

'It's your chance for fame Jim.' The manager passed over the phone.

'Jim Kettle?'

'Yes?'

'Jim, I'm the producer for 'Brian and Beverley's Bright and Breezy Breakfast Show' and we'd like you to join them on the show tomorrow if you can make it…can you?'

'Yes.'

'Have you seen the show?'

'I watch it occasionally.'

'Good. So, I don't need to explain the format. Brian and Beverley want to discuss some of the issues you raised on 'Neighbourhood Focus' after you brought down that knifer in your store. Is that alright with you?'

'Yes, but I'm not bright and breezy.'

'No problem, just be yourself. We'll give you an early call, and a car will be round to collect you.'

The studio was laid out like a sitting room with comfortable armchairs and a large sofa for Brian and Beverley. Two actors and a rising tennis star, had already primed the air with laughter and bubbly banter, well before Jim was introduced as a war hero, and the man who had downed the supermarket knife attacker. He was received with enthusiasm, but there was no way he could tailor his mood to blend in with the prevailing bonhomie. After all, this was a chat show; not a seminar about Doomsday, and given his previous rant about crime in the locality, and the general way of humanity, he was heading to be a lack-lustre party pooper if asked why he thought nice pills might be a good idea.

His confidence dropped to rock bottom as Beverley put just that question to him.

'So, Jim, you've experienced the horrors of war, and of course tackling that child attacker in your supermarket. Has it been those experiences, or something like them that has led you to believe we all have to be nicer, even if it means taking something like a nice pill?'

Some incredulity and a touch of amusement ensued, so Beverley outlined what she knew about the nice pill and added a supplement to her question.

'And you seem to be very despondent about the troubles in your home borough?'

He hesitated, but Brian gave him a pointed look and a buzz. 'Just say it how you feel Jim. I'm stuffed to the nostrils with the trivial tosh we push out each day. You've lived. So, give it welly your way!"

It was a strong buzz, and Jim's self-constraint vanished in the wake of some bemused expressions from the other guests.

He turned to Beverley.

'Yes, and we've got acid squirters, drug dealers, and bag snatchers. Not much love in our high street during weekends either. Try living above the leglessness; fights, and swearing and you'll know what I mean. Should I care about a friend's daughter bullied into watching mobile horrors at her primary school, and family abuse like never before?'

'Gee!' He rocked his head in his hands. 'And should I be surprised that we produce the unhappiest children in Europe?'

Beverley made some concurring 'Mnn's.'

'And am I supposed to care about the millions of diseased and starving in bombed and barren lands, or try to imagine what it's like to be slow burned alive by ISIS so called? Or should I care about devastated rainforests, polluted oceans, and the earth being sucked dry for never ending industrialisation!'

He clenched his hands and looked up, while Beverley anxiously cast her eyes towards Brian.

'Well, yes I do care! My head's bursting with it. I care about it even more than Norma having rumpy-pumpy with her boss in 'Wet Ends!'

He took a breath.

'And if nice pills, kindly pies or whatever else can make things better, then bring them on. Nice pills or not, do we really have to spread our greed, muck, and violence all over this beautiful planet?'

He made a mess of blowing his nose and wiping his eyes, and following some uncertain applause

Beverley waited a few moments before lowering her voice.

'Well…thank you Jim. 'Perhaps now we should pause, and take a deep breath before asking Lenny Bean about his new role in '*Precious Star*' at the Drury Lane 'Cosmo.'

After the show, Jim received a warm handshake from Brian.

'Thanks Jim, the show needed that, even if I do get the boot.'

Back at work, Jenny in Customer Service said, 'I knew what you were getting at Jim, but deep-down people just need love you know.' Bob in the stores said: 'Nice one Jim, and if there weren't so many foreigners streaming over here, we wouldn't be having all this trouble.'

That evening on Beryl's insistence, he watched a repeat of the show, and squirmed at his tear wiping and nose blowing finale, but Beryl was full of praise.

'You came over so naturally, and everyone on the shift agreed that you told it just the way things are.'

He dropped sharply as she left the couch to resume sewing a button on her uniform. and without looking up she said, 'And I really like you being here.'

There was a flavour of impending loss in her voice and he responded to it.

'It's the same with me. I'm a willing lodger you know.'

'But you won't want to stay at the supermarket now, will you?'

'I shouldn't think my moment of fame on the Brian and Beverley Show will change that. Anyway, I hardly received a standing ovation, did I?'

Her hands concentrated on getting the button in place, but her expression didn't match.

'No, but you'd like it to lead to something better, wouldn't you?'

'Something to stop us messing up ourselves and world you mean? Yes, I'd go with that.'

'And you've made good start.'

He looked around the room while she was sewing. It was an oblong box, divided into living and sleeping areas by a double plasterboard partition. A doorway at one end of the partition opened into a short corridor leading to the bedroom and ensuite. The front of the partition supported some kitchen cabinets, and on a ledge above the sink, a photo of a slim Beryl smiled down from a group of nurses holding certificates. From the sink, and supporting some African carvings, a high shelf ran the full length of the long wall to the bottom door which opened onto the concrete steps leading down to the exit. A window in the end wall looked over to Ali's hardware store, and along the High Street towards the hospital roundabout, and the cabinet displaying Beryl's favourite vase marked the corner of the other long wall leading back to the partition. Secondary glazing sealed the narrow window recesses, so there were no windowsills, and the relaxation area included the couch, a TV on a small table, and a black and white photo of Beryl's parents in a sailing dinghy. There were no knick-knacks from holiday resorts, or pictures of Beryl with friends on fun nights out. It was a room devoid of excitement.

She finished sewing on the button.

'I really hope you find what you want Jim, but I'll miss you.'

'What makes you think I want to leave? Anyway, if I did find what I wanted, it wouldn't have to mean saying goodbye.'

'But working in that supermarket and living here with me isn't really you is it?'

He walked over and held her.

'I wish I knew who really is me. Right now, I don't have a clue.'

5. Green

An eagle circled above the regular green plateau which now spread to the border of Fortunatus Viridis. Intent on dastardly business, it made several false swoops, but had arrived too soon to benefit from a life cycle of creatures plentiful enough to be worth hunting among the thistles. Wisps of dust still curled upwards from the remaining excavation sites, but they didn't float as far in the increased humidity. The Fortunatus Viridis agricultural team had done a thorough job, and as Respectico looked out from his terrace, the rotary sprayers started up again and hazed over the view.

Legitimising the emerald business and tidying up any trails that might point to dodgy dealings was expensive, but Adelita had insisted that Miser Terrace had to avoid becoming vulnerable to vested interests exploiting bad publicity.

'We have to be squeaky clean, Respectico,' she had demanded, and Respectico was left in no doubt as to who required the squeaky cleaning.

Life down below had improved enormously, and he viewed the changes with satisfaction. The old settlements had been cleared, and new settlements had been arranged in quadrangles with central pergolas that could be reached by paths leading from each back door. Vegetable patches, flowers, and trees enhanced the frontage of the dwellings, and neighbourly co-operation was now evident in most of the settlements.

Without doubt Miser Terrace had been transformed. The pills were doing their job, and while some animosity persisted in the aftermath of the troubles, it rarely came to more than verbal abuse and rude gestures. There had been no formal reconciliations, and Father Dududso had advised against topping the memorial with an embracing rabbit and hare.

'Raising icons to remind us of past divisions will only give them credence,' he had insisted. 'We have to trust that a new maturity will arise from these troubles, and that we can dispense with such potentially divisive symbols.'

Respectico wasn't sure what Father Dududso meant. But as a small concession to the prevailing mood, he decked out his henchmen with rose patterned uniforms and quick release covers over their M15's.

Adelita had engaged Bogota and Lima Universities to conduct independent surveys on the health and well-being of the population following the first six months of the pill programme. As with previous studies, the findings confirmed there were no adverse health effects, and laboratory sampling tests found the pills were high in vitamins C and D along with beneficial trace elements. Individuals were also asked to give reasons why they felt happier since taking the pills. Typical responses were:

'Our children don't shout so much.'

'I've stopped swearing.'

'Our marriage has improved, because I don't get pissed so often since taking the pills.'

The publicity team had included the findings in their documentary of events before and after the troubles, and soon everything was set for the large-scale production of pills and several varieties of soup. So, now it was time for the big decision.

Adelita walked out to the patio and onto the lawn where she was circled by the bluebirds. She had done her thinking, and had already arranged a brainstorming session to consider the way forward. Now it was up to her team to decide the next step towards a dream that she had nurtured since childhood. Promising to inform the birds of the result, she scattered some seeds and went into the conference room to lead the session.

Wine was served, and she motioned everyone to stand and raise their glasses.

'At last Miser Terrace has settled down, so congratulations everyone. It has been a whopping achievement in such a short time, so let's drink to that, before considering our next move.'

Glasses were raised, and Adelita continued. 'This is an informal meeting because we have now reached the moment where each of us must think very carefully before deciding if we should continue simply as a profit-making business, or how I say? Go both feet in' and strive for a better world.' She scanned the table for reactions. So, over to you. Do we go global or not?' She cupped her hands together as if making a wish.

Madge spoke first.

'I'm for both feet in. We're running out of time, and there's no other way to stop all the warring and shitty mess we're making of the world.'

The production manager agreed: 'It would be quite wrong to think purely in business terms now that we have the means to try for a peaceful and healthy world. We must give it a chance.'

Adelita turned to Father Dududso. 'But using Sapiens Carduus on such a scale would put you in a dilemma surely Father?'

Father Dududso rose to his feet.

'Yes, it would, and indeed it does. My fellow priests would almost certainly consider the use of any substance to modify human behaviour as being inconsistent with their beliefs, and I agree that ideally human enlightenment should come from within. However, the diffident official reaction to some of the evils uncovered in my own church has led me to question its consistency in matters of morality, and I have of course, witnessed the calming effects of Sapiens Carduus in Miser Terrace. So, because of that, and regardless of my dilemma, I am prepared to endorse such a mission.'

'Too many fancy words,' grunted Respectico. 'Hands up for Yes.'

All hands went up, and Adelita felt a surge of relief as the first building block for her vision slid into place. But there was something amiss in Father Dududso's demeanour.

'Are you comfortable with that, Father?'

His answer was vague.

'I am prepared to answer for my actions, and will endeavour to ensure that the qualities of Sapiens

Carduus can also be employed to calm the growing hostilities between our neighbours.'

Adelita replied wearily. 'Yes, it's happening all over again, and in your old diocese Father. It was on the early news. It seems that Butkre has imported mercenaries to stir up trouble on the borders of Flandora in readiness for its army to attack.'

Groans circled the table. The ill-defined boundaries of both countries traversed the lumpy terrain of the eastern foothills, and hostility between the different Butkre sects and disputed ownership of mineral deposits had simmered for years. Full blown hostilities would almost certainly create a refugee crisis in the neighbouring states including Miser Terrace and Fortunatus Viridis.

Adelita continued, 'Currently our only option is to persist with diplomacy. We are trading with our close neighbours, but importing soup or pills to Butkre would be too dangerous.'

Father Dududso again rose to his feet. 'Which is why my duty is to represent our mission in Butkre.'

There were utterances of disbelief.

'Don't do it Father!' exclaimed Madge. 'The Butkre hierarchy are just a bunch of thugs.'

He nodded. 'So it seems, but if I can make them kinder with soup as well as prayers, I will have achieved some good.'

'Try the soup first,' advised Ben.

Respectico raised a finger. 'We play crafty. I write 'Flandora Health Aid' on big bag of pills and drop them on Butkre mercenary base to fool mercenaries. They eat them and go nice. I drop them in helicopter...Yes?'

Adelita shook her head. 'No Respectico. It's a good plan but we can't have you risking your life either. Goodness, we can't afford to lose any of you - especially now.'

Respectico winked grotesquely and bobbed his eyebrows. 'OK so I save myself, just for you, my Adelita.'

Adelita gave an exaggerated grimace and returned to Father Dududso.

'And it would be terrible to lose you Father. Our mission is global, so why confine yourself to this conflict? '

Father Dududso became ill at ease.

'I am defying the authority of my church, and the developing conflict in Butkre is calling me to demonstrate the courage of my convictions.'

'But you will be risking your life for a local conflict by turning your back on a world riven with conflict. A scream next door may sound louder than a million distant screams, but now the world is screaming. We need you for a global mission Father. Please don't sacrifice yourself for a family dispute.'

She looked at him intently. 'If we can get our pills to the mercenaries, would you really have to go?'

He answered carefully.

'Perhaps not, but I must be the one to drop the pills from the helicopter.'

Respectico disagreed. 'Waste of pills. You no good at dropping pills Father, they go everywhere. I pay someone to drop pills, OK?'

Adelita kept her eyes on Father Dududso as she spoke.

'We will have to see how the situation develops before risking any lives. But Father, surely there are many ways of doing what you feel is right? There can be no one better than you to challenge those who oppose our mission, including those in your church. Surely that would take courage?'

He appeared resolute. 'It would, but that is not where my courage is taking me.'

She acknowledged Father Dududso's stubborn streak with a shake of the head. Nothing more she could say would change his mind, but at last her vision for a better world had become a possibility, so she announced it was time for a small celebration, and ushered everyone outside onto the patio for drinks and nibbles.

The Production Manager joined Ben and Madge.

'Now all we need is an overseas representative. He'll need to be very committed. Do you have any suggestions?'

'Or maybe 'she' will need to be very committed,' corrected Madge.'

'No, Miss supersensitive politically correct person,' countered Ben. 'You may remember Jake at UBC getting excited about a bloke.' he prodded her. 'I repeat 'bloke' who'd been ranting about the need for a nice pill or something like it?'

Madge snapped her fingers. 'Yes, you're right. It was on one of those cheery chatty shows. Try and get hold of Jake to find out if he knows who it is.' She had a further thought. 'Better still; ask him to send a podcast of the show if he can.'

She explained.

'It's a long shot, but we might have come across a good candidate. Ben's trying to find out more.'

After an animated chat on his mobile, Ben nodded and raised both thumbs.

'That was lucky. Jake's sending a text and the podcast.'

The text came in quickly, and Ben read from it.

'Ben. Your person is 'Jim Kettle,' a war hero who went ballistic on UBC about crime in his borough, and the damage we're doing to the earth. He said we should all be forced to take a nice pill or something like it before totally mucking up the planet.'

'Sounds like a top man.' announced Ben.

Soon everyone was grouped round the patio table applauding a tinny reproduction of Jim's rant on 'Brian and Beverley's Bright and Breezy Breakfast Show.'

Respectico raised a clenched fist. 'He got pugna. We get him, yes?'

Ben gave Adelita Jim's contact details, and after the meeting she took her wine onto the patio and watched a huge murmuration of blue birds entertain her with their ever-changing aerial patterns. She scattered more seeds, and dropping down onto the lawn the birds encircled her with their heads tilted sideways in listening mode for her report.

'Well birds,' she announced. 'We have decided in your favour, and with luck, a Mr Jim Kettle might just be the key to your future.

6. Maybe

The phone rang mid-way through breakfast, and it was for Jim. Normally Beryl would have given him privacy by finding something to do elsewhere. But he was looking at her as he spoke, and broke off at one point to ask for a pen and something to write on. It was a long call, and she had gathered enough to know that a flight would be involved; that it was linked to his broadcast, and that she had been mentioned.

Her heart sank. She knew something like this was inevitable, but it was much sooner than expected. Then he said, 'Of course.' and gave her the phone.

'Beryl, you are Jim Kettles partner…yes?'

'Yes.'

'Good, and I am Adelita Justica. So please, we shake hands over the phone.'

Beryl shook hands in mid-air. 'I've just shaken hands, Adelita.'

There was a faint clink at the other end, and following a short delay Adelita said: 'I just shake my glass of water… how silly.'

They both laughed, and Adelita continued. 'I am Governor of Fortunatus Viridis which is a small state in South America, but your Jim will give you the detail. I have invited him over to meet our team to discuss doing business in the UK. He needs, how I say it? To be happy with us, and we need to be happy with him…yes?'

'I understand.' The sinking feeling remained, but Beryl had an instinctive liking for the person she was talking to.

'What would he be doing Adelita?'

'He would be marketing our soup in the UK. But it would be more than marketing. We need someone unusual…' She corrected herself and laughed apologetically. 'No, I say that wrong. We need someone special who believes in our mission. We heard his broadcast on your UBC programme which is why we have invited him over to Fortunatus to meet us.'

'Is your soup something like the nice pill Jim talked about?'

'Yes, we grow a special thistle which we add to many eatables. They were in family meals all over these parts of South America before the drugs came along. Thistle soup is still on the menu here in Fortunatus Viridis. People become kinder to each other in communities where it is eaten, and now it being used to calm down troubles in the country next door to us.' She sighed. But making money is, how you say?... 'All the rage' now. So calming trouble might not go well for some businesses, and they could try to damage our mission by saying our soup is drugged.'

Beryl considered this.'

'You mean some businesses would be against it because they wouldn't make so much money if everyone was nicer towards each other?'

'Quite so, lots of businesses would lose money, like those who profit from mistrust and those who make weapons.'

'We wouldn't be so overworked in our hospital if everyone was nicer.'

'So, you are a doctor or a nurse and are, how you say?... at the sharp end?'

'Yes, I'm a nurse Adelita. Here, we need the strongest soup you can make.'

'Then maybe we try where you live first.'

'Please do. We get most trouble during the weekends.'

Beryl then asked the question uppermost in her mind.

'When would you like Jim to fly over to meet you?'

Adelita detected something in Beryl's voice.

'You worry about him going?'

'Well yes, but he must go, Adelita.' She concentrated on Jim as she spoke. 'He'll burn up if he can't do something about the damage and horridness in the world. This could be just what he needs, - I couldn't stop him anyway.'

'Very well. We would like to meet him as soon as possible, and could book him on the late flight from London to Bogota tomorrow, or is that too soon?'

Beryl hugged him while still holding the phone.

'That's fine Adelita. Tonight, I'll make sure he sleeps like a log on the plane.'

Adelita laughed. 'Goodness, La pasion! OK, so I book him business class with recliner. One of our team will meet him at Bogota Airport and accompany him on the flight here.'

Beryl put the phone down while struggling with mixed feelings.

'This is just what you must be hoping for Jim. And fancy flying business class with recliner and a private escort to an exotic land to meet an exotic woman. What more could you want?'

He feigned self-importance by pretending a plummy voice and giving an effete flick of the wrist.

'I am merely acknowledging my coming status as Souperman.'

The following evening, they waited for the taxi at the pull-in beside Ali's hardware shop. Jim had pared his packing down to bare essentials in a rucksack which he hoped would pass for hand-luggage.

Beryl gripped his hand.

'I so want you to get that job Jim. If you don't get it, you'll be impossible to live with, and if you do get it, I'll probably lose you.' There was no after buzz; she was saying it just the way she felt.

He replied matter-of-factly. 'And I'll be gutted if you get another bloke, so it isn't that one sided.' He regarded her carefully. 'It's not love though, is it?'

'I don't know what it is, Jim. Come to that I don't know what love is. These days it's just a word that's spread over anything from dogs to teddy bears. It's more a big need I suppose.'

He nodded. 'I'll go with that. But if you get the perfect bloke, promise to keep me as first reserve.'

'You do the same.'

He grinned. 'I promise, but not much chance of that after last night. I'll probably be back by the time I'm topped up.'

She kissed him hard. 'Well, that's something to look forward to.'

A black London Cab came towards them from the hospital roundabout, and dressed in jeans, with a rucksack, he felt like a disrespectful youth cocking a snoot at the mannerisms of its age. The last time he travelled in a London cab was with Dawn, and wealthy aunty Brenda who treated them to afternoon tea at 'Claridges.' Oozing national pride, she died wearing her Ascot hat. It would have been beyond her comprehension to fly first class to a foreign land dressed in jeans, and chastised by her memory, he decided to scan the duty-free shops at the airport for something more suitable.

'Get that job!' commanded Beryl as he entered the cab.

They exchanged waves, and as she slid away from the window, he received a buzzy 'Dammit! and it's no chocolates for me from now on.'

Greeted by the smell of burnt aviation fuel and rumble of jet engines, revived in Jim the anticipation of adventure. It was rather like walking to the coach for his first school outing. He'd flown plenty of times with the army, but this was different, and the lighting and bustle of a night time Heathrow Airport added to his sense of adventure. Soon he would be blasted over the Atlantic into a country he'd never visited, and his anticipation increased as he arrived at the check in on the escalator, and booked in for the night flight to Bogota, and possibility of a new lifestyle.

He slept solidly between meals on the Avianca Airbus.

He hadn't slept so comfortably since his time in hospital, and would sleep more soundly in the flat if he could avoid sliding into the hollow formed around Beryl. So, a firm mattress was on the shopping list when he returned.

Dozily raising his seat upright as the undercarriage clunked into the landing position, he watched the rocky terrain tip sideways on the approach to Bogota Airport. Then the plane swung into line with the runway, and through the windows on the other side of the cabin he caught a glimpse of distant glaciers before a smooth touch down and the roar of reverse thrust.

By-passing the baggage conveyor, he went straight to passport control through a crowd of dishevelled families carrying strapped bundles of possessions and fatigued children. The smell of unwashed bodies was intense, and he was relieved to see someone skirting round a similar crowd with a placard bearing his name. As they drew closer, he could see she had wiry ginger hair and at least one heavily tattooed arm.

Formalities were brief.

'Jim Kettle?'

'Yes.'

They shook hands

'I'm Madge from the Fortunatus Viridis publicity team.' She led him along a corridor to a gated kiosk 'We have to clear this checkpoint to get onto our plane, then it takes about an hour from here.'

'Where do the crowds come from?'

'Flandora; escaping before the trouble gets serious. They're the lucky ones.

'They don't look very lucky.'

'They are, believe me, and you know about troubles, Jim.'

'Yes, but I missed this on the news. What's it about?'

'It might not have made the UK news, with all the commotion going on about that pop star making millions on the dark web. But it's the usual stuff. An ancient border dispute; drug gangs, clashing beliefs, paid rebels, and corrupt regimes. That's about it.'

They cleared security, and walked through a small reception area onto the airfield and boarded an executive jet.

'So will it affect Fortunatus Viridis?' He spoke over the whinny of small turbo jets.

'It could do. They're smallish countries but densely populated. Flandora is close to us, so we could get refugees. They're both run by a couple of crap-heads. If they had a neuron between them, they could sort it out over a couple of beers.'

The jet levelled out just above the lumpy inland slopes of the Andes, and glimpsed through cloud breaks, the irregular bare blackish patches at the lower levels indicated acres of forest clearance.

A second tattooed arm directed his attention to a ribbon of smoke creeping over the higher foothills.

'They're probably burning forests for palm oil, or something else that the big money boys have dreamt up for our supermarket shelves. They don't give a pig's shit for the creatures they burn alive, and the importers aren't too bothered either.'

'Is there enough land for the special thistles to make us nicer?'

'Plenty, although we may need to increase production if you can get London soup crazy.'

'First I want to be sure it does what it says on the tin.'

'The tin won't say anything about making you nice.'

'That makes sense. Being nice could be a lost cause where I live. Do you have the soup at mealtimes?'

'Of course; we all have it.'

'So has it made you nicer?'

'Maybe?' her forehead wrinkled quizzically. 'Well, not exactly nicer, but now I think twice before mouthing off.'

'What's special about Fortunatus Viridis?'

'It's friendly. Everyone gets on well together, and there are all sorts of community things going on.'

'What about jobs?'

'Mainly horticulture, small industries, and recycling. There's also high tech, and medical research. Health care is good. They sorted my arm in no time.'

She showed him a faint scar traversing a tattooed scorpion just above her wrist.

'Was it a clean break?'

'Luckily it was. I fell out of a tree trying to video a rare parrot.'

'Was it worth the pain?'

'No, and it broke my camera.'

'So, are you making a documentary now?'

'We started by making a documentary about life in Fortunatus Viridis, but a year ago Miser Terrace erupted into a nasty bust up between two sects, and we've been covering that ever since. You'll learn all about it after you've kipped and met the team.'

Banking sharply over a patchwork of varied greens they dropped onto a landing strip between a wide corridor of trees which ran alongside the Governor's Residence.

A wooden rickshaw was waiting for them to disembark from the plane, and they were pedalled along the frontage of the residence to the entrance steps where Adelita was waiting to meet them.

'Welcome to Fortunatus Viridis, Jim.' Her smile contained a hint of intimacy as she ushered them inside. 'Presumably you slept well on the flight.'

He smiled back. 'Like a log, Adelita.'

Slim, and in a long whitish dress, Jim's telephone image of Adelita was uncannily like the person before him, and it seemed that he was conveying a similar impression to her.

'It's so good to meet you, Jim.' She regarded him with approval and hint of puzzlement. 'It's almost as if we have known each other for years.'

She led him up the main staircase to his room, and invited him for coffee and eats on the patio as soon as he felt ready.

First taking full advantage of the luxury shower, he changed, and went over to the large sash window to view the surroundings. Facing him in glistening rows, tiers of solar panels covered the land which sloped above the industrial estate. Wide palm tree avenues separated the buildings, and alpacas grazed freely on the grassed areas. The largest structure was the soup production unit, and he watched as two escalators loaded thistles into its giant hopper. Beside it, a second unit was under construction and he noticed that the feeder warehouse was already up to capacity.

Without a doubt Fortunatus Viridis was in serious production mode, and assuming he got the job, he would have to be in very serious selling mode to keep up with it.

Later, over coffee and biscuits at the patio table, Adelita gave him a brief history of Fortunatus Viridis. Brushed with a faint American drawl and some quirky phrasing, her spoken English was otherwise impeccable.

She summarised. 'So, our history is messy, and we certainly haven't created a paradise here. It's simply that the climate, and a community founded on co-operation with a good level of education has made this a pleasant place to live.'

'And your thistles?'

'Of course. Our thistles have played a key role in the way our state has evolved. Roughly translated they are our 'Wise Thistles' and have been on the family menu for centuries. They have shaped our way of life, and even if we stopped consuming them, I doubt if we would wish to change anything.'

'You must have some crime here?'

'Not much. We do have domestic flare ups every so often, and once had a double murder resulting from a love triangle, but theft and violence is uncommon because there's very little to motivate it.'

A group of school children waved as they crossed the lawn, and chatting animatedly, entered the building and walked up the stairway to the library.

'They seem happy enough.'

'We get teeny troubles, but it's rarely bad enough to cause much worry.'

'No bullying?'

'Not often, and other children usually stop it. Parents are expected to bring up their children to know right from wrong, and they usually do.'

'Is education and health care free?'

'Education is free including higher education. Health and social care are also free, but no one is paid for having children. Having children is considered a joy; not something others have to pay for.'

She smiled ironically. 'As a small state, we have to keep a balanced population, and I have to set a good example.'

'So, you don't have a child of your own?'

'At this time in our history it would be selfish. Our population is already too high.'

'Even though there is no family assistance?'

'No, it's because we have a bulge of elderly people from previous generations when our welfare provision was tailored to encourage larger families. Now we are struggling to cater for the infirmities of age.'

Jim spoke half to himself. 'Well, that's something we have in common'

'You have the same problem in UK?'

'Yes, although it's not seen as a problem.'

'But surely, many of your beautiful green areas have to be taken for crop growing and house building?'

'There are usually objections, and our green areas are becoming scarcer by the day, but housing and developments must go somewhere.'

'And here in Torrosus we could lose our forests for palm oil or cattle ranching, although we are now hopeful that the profits from our soup sales will discourage the government selling out to the big interests.'

'How are sales developing so far?'

'Better than expected. And if our soup proves popular in the UK, it will give us a platform to launch our mission into Europe and beyond.'

A round of applause came from the children in the library, and she looked upwards.

'My goodness we have to try.'

Seen in profile, her features were sharply defined, and the streaky ash blond hair hinted at something north European in her make up, but he was unable to guess at any heredity influence that might have nurtured such a natural air of authority. She rose and walked over to the terrace, which prompted the resident flock of blue birds to flutter onto the lawn and parade before her. He followed, and together they took in the natural beauty of the scene in silence.

Without turning she said quietly.

'Do you believe in God, Jim?'

Her question blended into the mood of the moment.

'I'd like to, but there are too many versions to choose from and that puts me off. I think there's something, but that's the only way I can put it.'

'And would it seem strange to you, if the logic of the natural world stopped short of moral judgement?'

'Yes, it would, but I'm not sure, and that's a big one to think over, Adelita.'

She laughed. 'Sorry, and just after your flight.'

He would have liked to continue on the same theme, but the children had come down from the library and were waving to them as they crossed the lawn.

'We wouldn't expect waves like that from our children.'

She turned to him.

'You really are despondent about your own country Jim.'

'Our children are brought up to be suspicious of adults they don't know.

'That's almost sinister.'

'It's a climate produced by good intentions I suppose.'

He tried to lighten the mood.

'But I keep latching onto bad things. Just tell me to wind my neck in when I start being a misery.'

'Ah you give me an idiom; I must learn more. 'Winding the neck in'… like a tortoise you mean?'

'It's a way of saying: 'I've heard enough from you, so be quiet.'

'So, if you are a still a misery after visiting Miser Terrace with Madge and Respectico, I can tell you to: 'Wind your neck in, Jim.' She thought of something else. 'Oh, and I should have told you that Respectico was a big-time gangster and drug dealer.'

He managed a smile.

'I'm trying very hard not to be a misery, Adelita.'

The following morning, he joined Madge on Respectico's helicopter, and watched the video of the Rabbits and Hares conflict as they flew over to Miser Terrace.

He returned the tablet as the grey flanks of the escarpment slid past.

'I'm glad I had breakfast before looking at that. So, what's life like there now?'

'It's not all hugs and kisses yet, but the pills are doing their stuff. If you're lucky you might even see some smiles.'

They hovered over Respectico's villa, and looked down to a carpet of thistles interspersed with settlements bordered with young trees.

'OK, so it's not a rain forest.' continued Madge, 'but it was a barren mess about eighteen months ago, and now they've started a tree planting programme. Respectico is sorting out this place faster than any of us expected.'

They settled onto the rooftop landing pad, and oozing big time gangster, Respectico waited for the rotor blades to stop before greeting them with two bear hugs and directing them into the rooftop lift and onto the veranda for coffee.

'I welcome you to our team, Mr Jim. 'He pointed to the thistles stretching before them. 'Soon you get these down British throats…eh?' He raised his cup and made a gulping noise.

'I'll do my best if get the job Respectico.'

Respectico gestured dismissively. 'You get job, no problem.'

After coffee Respectico ushered them into his Humvee and drove to the nearest settlement.

A few residents were tending their front gardens, and the sound of guitars drifted across the courtyard as they walked to the central pagoda. A teacher signalled the class to stop playing and stand up, but Respectico palmed them down. 'No, you play music, we listen as we walk, or maybe we sing.' He grunted a few notes. 'Music make me better and make Miser Terrace better.'

They came to a fenced area where a workforce was assembling an array of solar panels.

'Each home gets a storage battery,' explained Respectico. 'Enough heat for a shower and wash, and…' He ushered them to a large tank in the ground fed by pipes from the dwellings. 'This will be treatment plant for changing shit to fertiliser.'

Jim was impressed. 'And you've done all this since they were slaughtering each other.'

Respectico beamed. 'Gracias Jim, but with guidance from boss…you say: 'She who must be obeyed.' like in the army, eh?' He stood to attention and saluted towards Fortunatus Viridis.

Madge prodded him. 'You wouldn't have it any other way.'

'Ah so,' he muttered sheepishly.

Back in the Humvee, the large wing mirrors reflected a blurry white line of glaciers, and straight ahead, uniform rows of purplish-blue thistles added another dimension to the view. The climate was perfect, with a few puffy clouds and light breeze. With, or without a nice pill, it seemed worthwhile taking the trouble to get along with the neighbours, if only to ensure that nothing got in the way of enjoying such an environment.

Jim thought back to the borough. But where was the joy in traffic snarled streets; crammed terraces and tenements, - not to mention toxic air? He checked his watch, making allowance for the time difference. By now Beryl would be in the flat after the late afternoon shift and preparing dinner for herself in time for the usual Saturday night kerfuffle in the street below. Would nice pills or the soup really change all that?

He turned to Respectico. 'Does everyone have to take the pills?'

'They get paid in their homes. No pills, no pay.'

'They get nice or go hungry.' added Madge.

Jim voiced his doubts. 'I'd like to be sure the pills would work where I live.'

Madge was optimistic. 'They should work. We tested a family of Rabbits by giving them dummy pills, and it wasn't long before they were getting stroppy with the Hares. Once we put them back on the real pills, they stopped the aggro.'

'But would nice pills work in the rough parts of Manchester?'

He caught a change of mood buzz as Madge flashed back to the constant school bullying because of her hair colour.

'Alright,' she conceded. 'So, nastiness is more sophisticated in the UK.'

'You said that from experience.'

'Yip, I had a choice. Top myself, or get tough - I got tough.'

'And you survived.'

'It was close. Like always, the cruds got the attention, and decent kids got the bullying in my school.'

'The same in my school, but I was one of the cruds.'

'So, you joined the army and got un-crudded?'

He was doubtful. 'Not completely, but we were talking about you. I'll take a guess that you got into making documentaries by taking gritty pictures around Manchester.'

'Good guess. I went round with my cheapie camera taking snaps of the grot areas near home, and giving them to the local paper who took me on as a trainee.'

They stopped and backed up to the burial ground. The copse where the bodies had been laid for identification had been landscaped and planted with flowers, and a simple wooden archway now fronted the entrance.

'We check for graffiti,' announced Respectico.

Madge elaborated. 'At first, we found scorched toy rabbits and hares on top of the mounds. Then graffiti was scrawled on the new gravestones. There's not so much of it now.'

The mounds were fuzzy with grass and wild flowers selectively managed by a few alpacas. There were no glittering trinkets or emotive messages, and the plain round-topped headstones were identical. It was clear that personalised decorations had been forfeited in favour of creating a communal area of warmth and maturity. Mourners moved between the mounds reading inscriptions, while others knelt before the headstones of those they had known or loved.

Waiting inside the entrance arch was the elderly woman who had been prepared to sacrifice herself in the burnt-out Hares dwelling. She took them to a burial mound and pointed to the faded blue residue of something scrawled over a headstone.

'Usually, young ones do this at night with marker pens my Respectico. Only this one done since camera put up.'

'We caught two,' explained Respectico. 'Now they wear hoods, but we still catch them.'

'What happens when they are caught?'

'We stop pay, or parents' pay - it works.'

He patted the lady on the shoulder.

'You're doing a grand job Depurador, are you happy?'

'You gave me life and work my Respectico, so yes, I'm happy. But why Father Dududso leave us?'

She spoke with concern.

'Respectico laid a comforting hand on her shoulder. Maybe one day we see him back. You pray for him, eh?'

She consented with a dip of the head, and walked with them to the memorial which had been erected on the site of the burnt-out dwelling. Fashioned from the smoothed and polished trunk of a Giant Cedar, only the names of the dead were carved into the wood, and the stone plinth simply said: 'In Memory.'

'My son not there,' announced the woman. 'I don't remember him.'

Respectico described how she was black with soot as he helped her from the dwelling.

'Now she scrub everything; fences, paths, the memorial plinth. She known as the 'Old Scrubber'. We give new brushes with her pay.'

He pointed to a recently built settlement. There we mix up Rabbits and Hares; all Father Dududso's idea. No problems yet, but we wait before building community hall and football pitches.'

'What about booze?'

'No booze. Maybe later we allow wine with meals.'

They returned to the villa, and onto the helicopter pad.

Jim thanked Respectico. 'You've worked wonders here, Respectico.'

Respectico slapped him on the shoulder. 'How you say: 'Better late than never?' He looked upwards. 'Now maybe I get to Heaven… before, no chance.'

Holding the cabin door for them to embark, he shook hands firmly with Jim, and above the increasing swish of the rotor blades came a buzzy: 'Eres el hombre correcto.'

On the way back, Madge told him what she knew about Respectico. Then he enquired about Adelita.

'Pass.' Madge shook her head. 'I doubt if anyone knows much about Adelita. She's got more natural authority than anyone else I've known, and I've never heard anything said against her. But there's always that distance, you know? I don't think there's a man around, and I daren't try it on with her. Could be there was someone once, and she turned herself off when it went wrong.'

Jim wanted to know more about Father Dududso.

'How about the priest that the old lady mentioned. Does he approve of pills to make people nicer?'

Madge replied carefully.

'Father Dududso's always been in a tizzy about that, because his church is against nice pills. But he's seen how effective they've been in Miser Terrace, and like us, I'm guessing that he's come across enough nastiness to decide that the world won't get any better with humans the way they are. The aggro between Butkre and Flandora is forcing him to prove the courage of his convictions, so now he's back in his old Butkre diocese serving up our soup and getting the locals to grow thistle eatables against the wishes of his church.

'He's got to be in big danger.'

'You can bet on it. He's a stubborn so and so, but it would be the pits if we lost him.'

They approached the Governor's Residence from a different direction, and looked down on acres of green-houses as the helicopter dropped onto the lawn.

'Has everyone decided on the next move?' he asked as they disembarked.

'Well, we're all set for a big production run, and everyone agreed to save the world at the last meeting.' She took a deep breath. 'So how about that Jim? Yes, we're on a mission to save the world.' She drew his attention to the rain forest. 'Anyway, we might as well save the world, because all that could be chopped down for palm oil and meat production if the money barons get their way.'

'Which means if I get the job, Sales had better pick up quickly?'

He received the Madge prod as they walked towards the Residence.

'What do you mean: 'If I get the job?' She raised her voice as the helicopter took off and banked towards Miser Terrace. 'There'll be a rumpus from me if you don't get it.'

They stopped to watch the blue birds flutter back onto the lawn and her hair waxed and waned hypnotically as Jim fought his red/green colour deficiency to separate her from the green of the forest. In the same instant came the familiar oddity of feeling pressed upwards, which, coupled with a perfumed breeze caused him to sense that he had fleetingly edged into something wonderful, but currently beyond reach.

She came back into focus as he caught the tail end of more she was saying.

'…and we all heard your rant on that breakfast show. You nailed it, Jim!' She noticed his vacant expression. 'But if we're going to save the world, you'd better charge up your batteries by snatching some shut-eye before the meeting.'

Adelita opened the Meeting.

'There are plenty of encouraging developments to report, but first let me introduce Mr Jim Kettle, who has flown over from London at short notice to meet us in time for the launch of our mission.'

She extended a hand of welcome to Jim, who stood up and bowed to sounds of approval.

'We've all heard Jim's outburst on the radio,' smiled Adelita, 'and those of us who have had the opportunity to meet him in person, will hold no doubts about his commitment to our mission. So welcome Jim, and welcome to our team. We all hope that by the end of your stay you'll feel happy to work with us as our UK representative.'

A round of applause followed, and it dawned on Jim that the job was his, unless he refused it.

Adelita continued. 'This morning Jim toured Miser Terrace with Madge and Respectico, so he knows about the troubles, and how our pills have been used in helping to bring peace to the area. Tomorrow he will be shown round our production and research facilities.' She turned to him. 'And Jim, please ask as many questions as you wish, we want you to feel confident about the work we are doing here.'

She then handed over to the Production Manager, who placed a tray containing three small bowls of soup and a questionnaire before everyone.

'These are the varieties we will be marketing. You wouldn't believe the hassle we've had deciding on the flavours, but we're sticking to these for the moment. Try them while they're hot, then tick your favourite, and please use the comment box because we need feedback at this stage.'

Jim recalled his mind-shift after an early puff of marijuana, and worried that wise thistle soup might add another oddity to all the other oddities flying round in his head. Half filling his spoon, he sampled the plain unflavoured variety, which tasted as if it was making up for some of his dietary shortcomings. So, throwing caution to the wind, he filled his spoon with the other flavours without experiencing any strange reactions. The avocado and orange was the sweetest, and probably best suited to young tastes, while the blackberry and apple might arouse nostalgia in older scrumping generations.

No clear favourite emerged from the tasting session, so it was decided to market them in equal quantities until early sales figures gave a guide.

The Production Manager then handed out some rectangular green containers for inspection.

'At this point I must thank Malami and the production team for devising a brilliant method to process the thistles while producing these tough eco containers from the stalks. It's all done in one continuous operation, and has dramatically reduced our production costs by saving us the expense of building and operating a separate canning facility.

The containers should be popular with retailers because their rectangular shape makes for good displays, and should also attract customers because the containers and lids can be clicked together to make all sorts of useful items.' He smiled at Malami. 'Show them, Malami.'

Malami held up a row of plant pots; a bug house, and some simple children's toys.

Adelita was impressed. 'Excellent! You have given us a big competitive advantage, Malami.' She started a round of clapping. 'Please pass on our congratulations to your team.' She tapped the table for attention. 'Who can give me an idiom for: 'very pleased'?'

'Chuffed!' chorused Ben and Madge. 'Ah, yes. So, we're all chuffed with you, Malami.'

Next, the Marketing Manager outlined the sales plan.

'We hope to make a start in Jim's part of London, because it's an ethnically mixed borough and densely populated with plenty of deprivation and crime. There are also some wealthy areas, so it should be an ideal testing ground. Once we are satisfied that our soup is improving those communities, we plan to extend our operation to the whole of the UK, and into Europe. Jim will be assisted by the publicity team, who will also be producing a documentary about life in the Borough, and recording any positive effects our soup may have made. The documentary will also include the results of laboratory tests, which should head off any accusations about the soup containing mind changing drugs.'

The Administration Manager was optimistic.

'We are all set to go. Sales to our near neighbours have increased, which should give us enough financial support for the early stages of our operation in the UK. All the documentation is complete, and the three varieties of soup are ready to be shipped over for warehousing. We must prepare for losses until the UK market is established, but we have good reason to be hopeful. The Food Standards Agency have approved our soup as a low-calorie health product, and sales could be boosted because of increasing concern about obesity in the UK.'

Ben raised a warning finger.

'But we need to be careful. If London suddenly goes all lovey-dovey, we'd better stick to the natural health angle. Once the peculiar brigade thinks they've got tags on something dodgy, we'll get nothing but trouble.'

Adelita agreed. 'Yes, we had better keep - how you say? - 'mum' about our soup causing niceness. It will come out sooner or later, but we need to avoid controversy in the early days of our mission.'

'Do we know why the thistles make people nicer?' asked Jim.

'Not yet, although our research team have uncovered some ancient drawings with smiling thistles inside tribal warriors, and they show that thistles with the biggest smiles are inside the fiercest looking warriors.'

'So, the fiercer you are, the more niceness you get from the thistles?' suggested Ben.

'Possibly, but we can't be sure. It may simply be a reaction to high testosterone levels, so more research is needed. We may have the answer when our soup is being served in homes and restaurants across Jim's part of London.'

She stood up, and asking everyone to rise, again extended the hand of welcome to Jim.

'So, once again welcome, Jim. You've joined a team with an awesome task.'

'Ah so! Respectico came forward with open arms. 'Respectico reward you with kiss and a hug!'

Amid predictable cries of 'Ugh!' and 'Gruesome!' Jim endured Respectico's slobbery attention and, for the first time since leaving the army, experienced the camaraderie of being in a team.

He had been accepted, and wiping his eyes, on the pretence of removing Respectico's kiss, said: 'If I can survive that, then saving the world should be a doddle. But thanks for having me, and I know I've joined a great team.'

It was later, after the champaign had been downed, and Jim was on his way to Bogota airport, that Adelita went onto the patio to inform the blue birds that the final building block for her vision had been put into place.

7. Friends & Neighbours

Beryl was happy and relieved.

'When you phoned I thought you were going to say that you wouldn't be back because you had decided to stay with your exotic woman.' She tweaked his nose. 'And fancy asking if your lodgings were still free after being away for only four days.'

Jim hung up his anorak and found a place for his wet shoes by the door.

'I did stay with my exotic woman, and for all I knew, you could have taken in some exotic bloke. I couldn't wait too long before checking my options in case I'd been thrown out.'

'After two night shifts and a call-out what chance do you think I had of snaring another bloke?'

'Pretty good! After all you snared me when I was on a bedpan.'

He avoided an assault.

'Rotter! Anyway, you were lucky to have made it here. Flights are being diverted everywhere because of the flooding.'

'I thought so. The Bogota flight must have been one of the last to land at Heathrow. All was quiet when I cleared customs.'

He moved to the window. 'It's getting to be a river down there. I was hoping we could have something in that half decent restaurant, but nothing's open.'

Unzipping the wet rucksack, he took out the alpaca gown that Adelita had asked him to give to Beryl as a special gift from Fortunatus Viridis.

'It's not for wet weather, but the exotic woman suggested it would be just the thing for you to settle into after a long shift.'

She unrolled the gown and tried it on. It was loose enough to hide her girth, and almost swirled gracefully as she pirouetted before him.

'It's just perfect Jim. Your exotic woman couldn't have chosen better, there's even room for expansion.'

'I was hoping for some contraction.'

'Well, I haven't touched any chocolates since you left.'

He examined her at arm's length. 'That's five days of deprivation. Would life still be worth living if you kept it up?'

'I might have to keep it up. Some of us have been told to lose weight because we're setting bad examples to our patients.'

'And were you one of the: 'some of us'?'

'Alright…yes.'

He was about to say, 'and about time too,' but suddenly she was hugging him.

'Oh Jim, I know we agreed it's not love, but for me it's just about everything else. I'm so pleased you're back.'

She had voiced what he felt. Beryl's absence during his stay had caused him to think of her in the same way. She had become home. It wasn't the flat, and certainly not their whereabouts, it was just Beryl.

He returned the hug. 'Once the world has been put to rights, I'll ask my exotic woman if we can live in beautiful Fortunatus Viridis - how's that?'

'It would be wonderful. So, hurry up and put the world to rights, I don't want to wait too long.'

They listened to the rain.

'Do you remember? We had rain like this when you first came onto the ward and there was that rush of patients from the traffic pile up.'

'You all coped really well.'

'There was just one who didn't make it, and he didn't want to anyway.' She opened the refrigerator and took out a tray of mushrooms. 'I'm just hoping I don't get called out tonight.'

'Couldn't you refuse because you had company?'

'Yes, but I'd feel bad about it.'

Jim helped her prepare dinner, then remembered the soup he had brought with him, and walking over to the rucksack, returned with an avocado and orange which he placed on the draining board.

'Let's have this for starters. It's low calorie, and I should soon be selling it.'

She examined the container.

'So, if I like this soup, we could have it regularly.'

'We could. Be careful though, it might make you nice.'

'Then I'd better have some quickly before you get thumped.'

He opened the container and put it straight into the microwave while Beryl lit a candle and pushed it into the neck of a wine bottle.

'We'll just have to celebrate here.'

She tried the soup. 'It tastes as if it's good for me.'

Jim added some pepper. 'I prefer the natural flavour which is earthy without the sweetness.'

'But would everyone like an earthy flavour?'

'Maybe not, but that's what I'll have to find out. It won't be long before hundreds of gallons will be at the docks waiting to be popped into saucepans and microwaves.'

'Shall I try the hospital catering company?'

'Good idea. It might even make your patients nicer.'

She served up the mushrooms.

'I knew you would get the job Jim. You were made for it.'

'Thanks, although saving the world could be difficult.'

She was about to say something else when the phone rang, and picking it up, she nodded glumly and swore.

'It's an emergency. There's been another big pile up on the ring road. I'll have to go in.'

He insisted on walking with her to the hospital. Water was lapping over the pavement and they were splashed by speeding ambulances at the roundabout. From everywhere came an ominous smell of sewage.

He released her hand. 'Call me when you've finished. I'll have something ready when you return.'

'I'll hold you that.' She winked, waved, and waddled off.

Back in the flat he completed the washing up, and settled onto the sofa, just as a flash and crash of thunder combined with the rain rivulets on the windows to jolt him back to the sparkly clubby sequence in the hospital ward during the last ring road pile up.

It wasn't fair. He wanted time to adjust after the warmth and beauty of Fortunatus Viridis. Standing up, he angrily personalised the developing atmosphere and shouted at the windows.

'No thanks, I don't want you back. Not now anyway, so get lost!'

There had been something indefinable about that stay in hospital. Despite his session with the psychologist and all the tests, he still couldn't shake off the impression that something had been hidden from him, and like a crucial word half remembered, it retained its power, yet eluded recognition.

II

The first consignment of Sapiens Carduus Original couldn't have arrived at a better time. National concern about obesity, and its burden on an already overstretched Health Service was tailor-made for marketing healthy cuisine, and Jim took full advantage of the government campaign to assist with the advertising.

He arranged tasting sessions in superstores, and travelled round in his rented van to retailers with samples and batches for display on a sale or return basis. As anticipated, the rectangular eco containers proved popular with retailers and sales picked up faster than expected. It was exhausting work though, and he looked forward to the time when he could return the van and leave deliveries to an agency.

Customers who came back for more soup, consistently mentioned the earthy flavour, and food bank volunteers gave the same reason for its popularity. Comments like: 'It tasted as if it was hitting all the right spots.' And: 'Like... it was rough and raunchy,' from a younger customer, were repeated to him by retailers and, as he had anticipated, there seemed to be a strong preference for the plain variety.

The publicity team arrived in early March.

Jim met them in the bar of their modest hotel, and Madge introduced him to a vaguely familiar character.

'Jim, meet Brinod, who has tarted himself up and joined us by courtesy of Respectico.'

Brinod gave Jim a crinkly grin and became instantly recognisable as Respectico's senior henchman. Pulling a face in mock regret he said. 'I leave my M15 in Miser Terrace… how I cope here?'

'He'll cope,' declared Madge. 'He coped pretty well as one of Respectico's naughty boys, and that was well before they took over Miser Terrace.' She patted him on the cheek and he fluttered a burly hand.

'You honour me, my Madge.'

'And he's gay,' added Madge. 'So, in a sense we're soul mates.'

Ben, who had been rolling his eyes at the ceiling, received a warning glance from Madge, who went on to explain Brinod's role.

'He's here for our protection in case someone starts hiring nasties to make life difficult for us.'

'I suppose that's reassuring.' Jim gave Brinod a closer look. 'Here's hoping you don't have go into action.'

Brinod shrugged. 'No action, Brinod gets bored.'

Jim ordered three beers and a cherry liquor, and passed round his early sales graphs.

'Sales are going better than expected, and that's just me in a van. The agency will be taking over soon and I've already told them to double the order for the plain variety. But can Torrosus production manage that amount?'

'Don't worry about that,' Madge assured him. 'It's gone frantic back there, but they're managing. They've been on twenty-four-hour shifts since completing the new production unit, and Respectico's pill drop onto the Butkre mercenaries got us more thistles.' She poured her beer. 'The mercenaries just lost the will to fight, and the army mutinied for more pay because the mercenaries were useless. I've forgotten the Butkre dictator's name, except he was a complete pillock. Seems they stuck his head on a post, and once the Flandoran's realized the pills were made from Sapiens Carduus their Dictator…' 'Who was slightly less of a pillock,' cut in Ben, 'came to an agreement for us to harvest thistles on the northern hills of Flandora.'

'Are they just growing wild?'

'They're everywhere. There are more on those hills than in Fortunatus and Miser Terrace put together,'

Madge praised Adelita. 'Adelita's a cool negotiator. She used the contract to encourage stability in the region by signing it only if Flandora and the new regime in Butkre came to a formal agreement to end hostilities.'

'Have they?'

'They have, as far as pillocks like that can be trusted to agree on anything, and now production is going full chat day and night to cope with the influx of thistles.'

She reached for the paper on the bar top. 'Now let's see what's happening here?'

Tut-tutting noises came from behind the paper.

'Well, if you don't believe that nastiness is more sophisticated in the UK, then listen to this.' She read out some of the headlines.

'Pensioner scams at all-time high.'

'Head bans parents from football matches because of behaviour.'

'Depression and anxiety spiralling in UK.

'Donkey blinded by youths.'

'Continued assaults on paramedics.'

'Schoolgirls terrorise sheltered housing tenants in Manchester.'

'Must be your old school chums.' remarked Ben.

He caught the paper, and read from the TV programme schedule.

'And how's this for fun viewing? *Car crash Britain. Fights in fast food restaurants. Nightmare neighbours. Digital Porn Barons.* Just right for settling down with the family over chicken and chips I hear you say.' He flicked over to the back page which depicted a night street scene fronted by two brutal looking men.

'And what about this?'

The caption read: *'Alley Men. You won't forget it!'*

He handed the paper to Brinod who bared his teeth and held it under his chin for comment.

Ben shielded his eyes. 'Suddenly those alley men look beautiful.'

'The film isn't so beautiful,' remarked Jim. 'Toughs on social media are already acting it out, and this place is ripe for it.'

Madge placed her phone on the bar stool and spoke to it with feeling.

'Listen, phone. We've only just arrived in the UK, and I'm depressed already. It's about time we heard something pleasant from you.' The phone beeped obediently, and picking it up, her expression changed to bemusement. 'Strange? We were just talking about that.'

She relayed the conversation.

'That was Jake Barrow. He's just got word that a crowd of Ironside residents are outside the Regent

Cinema making a fuss about that Alley Men film we've been discussing. He thought we'd be interested.'

'It's about ten minutes' walk away,' said Jim. 'Let's see what it's all about.'

The Regent was a large Art Deco cinema doubling as a bingo hall. It was well set back from the pavement on a stepped terrace which led upwards to a line of swing doors. The Alley Men film was advertised as a coming attraction on a large banner which spanned the frontage of the cinema. Beneath it, a group holding placards were standing either side of a formidable black lady who was making her views very clear.

She was nearing the end of a tirade, and her voice shook with emotion.

'Look, we've been trying. We've been trying bloody hard. We've been clearing up the mess. Oh yes, and the needles, and we've even got some of the kids onside with us. But we don't need this!' She shook her microphone at the banner to whoops of agreement, and the crowd split up into impromptu discussion groups.

Madge asked a man what it was all about.

'If that film's shown we'll get copycat yob trouble.'

'So, you want it stopped.'

'You bet. It's about gangs with all the gang-speak and violence. It's a gang turning itself into a business by getting street hard nuts to fight in empty warehouses for money, and one of the hard nuts becomes a street fight champion worth millions. They've just had big trouble up north with local yobs acting it out, and it'll be the same here.' He did a backward nod to three youths who had been noisily kicking a ball around behind the crowd.

Madge walked down to them and pointed to the banner.

'Who's seen that that film?' One smirked, and gave it a thumbs up while the other two continued noisily kicking the ball at each other until Brinod captured it in a lightning tackle and challenged them to take it from him. 'You tough guys Eh? You tough like Alley Men Eh? You take ball from me Eh?'

Unchallenged, he flicked the ball from his foot to his knee and headed it with impressive speed onto the side wall, then, to some applause, turned his back on the youths with a dismissive wave.

They returned to the group who were holding placards, and Madge asked a lady why she wanted the film banned.

'See over there?' The lady directed her attention towards rows of large accommodation blocks fronted by plain iron balconies. 'They're our homes, but we get trouble, and most of it comes from outside. We tried living with all the noise and nasty behaviour, but it got so unpleasant that we formed a group to start doing something about it, and went round asking residents to join us for a big clean up.' She raised her voice skywards. 'God, it bloody well needed it! We'd tried before, but this time more turned up, and we bandied about ideas on how to get our kids involved as well. Things have started to get a bite friendlier now.'

She beckoned to the speaker. 'Our block's better now wouldn't you say Mabel?'

Mabel nodded and joined them. 'We're starting to get together at last… well, some of us are. We were up to our tits trying to improve things, and I say that because it's been mostly us women doing the work.'

'How bad was it?' asked Madge.

'Bad, believe me. Druggies, graffiti, rubbish, swearing… all sorts.'

'You never knew what was going to happen,' added someone else. 'If anyone did anything nice, like plant flowers, they'd get trashed.'

'What about the police?'

They shrugged in unison.

'They do their best.' added Mabel, 'but a lot of the trouble is kids, and they don't like touching kids these days.' She looked angrily over Madge's shoulder. 'And right now, we can do without that!' She directed a string of expletives at a nearby Alley Men poster, and then put a hand to her mouth with an expression of dismay. 'You're not from the UBC are you?'

'No, and don't worry, I'll cut them out,' promised Ben.

'We'll try to get your protest in the news,' added Madge. 'But we're just a small unit recording what life is like for the population of this borough.'

'Don't mention population!' Mabel generated more steam. 'That's half the trouble here. My kids can't run around in the playground for all the portable classrooms they're putting on it, and we're jammed in here like sardines.' She pointed to the distance beyond the accommodation blocks. 'But they won't clear that precious green belt to build homes for young families will they?' She shouted into the camera. 'So how about that, council!'

After a collective 'Phew!' Jim made his way to the flat, while Madge and Ben went off in search of more local flavour by exploring Ironside and its locality.

As he walked through the hospital underpass, he noticed that most of the graffiti had been cleaned from the sides of the walk-way, and further along the high street, the window box over Pegs Cake Shop had been planted with daffodils in Sapiens Carduus containers. Could these be the early signs of the soup doing its stuff?'

The carpet was rolled up when he entered the flat, and he was greeted by the sound of vacuum cleaning and fresh smell of beeswax polish.

Beryl had been on day shift, but had somehow found time to give the flat a thorough going over. She moved a dustbin bag towards the door, and giving him a light kiss, warned, 'Don't get too close. I've been going at it cats and dogs since coming back, and could be a bit whiffy.'

He helped her to unroll the carpet and put the table in place. A bulb from the centre light was lying on a pile of 'Swish Home' magazines which had long been destined for the charity shop.

'I took it out to clean the shade,' she explained. 'But the bayonet bit wouldn't twist back in.'

He could see it was one of the old filament bulbs and going black.

'I'll get another from 'Ali's.' He pulled the carpet straight, 'Any particular reason why you've been so hard at it?'

'Work didn't get me so bushed today because there wasn't the usual hassle. I think the soup is having an effect. Anyway, this place was a tip, so I set to and lost some weight.'

By the time he had taken the magazines to the charity shop and returned with a new bulb, the table had been laid, and airlock noises were coming from the plumbing while Beryl was showering. He fitted the bulb, and some different bumpy noises later, she came into the room wearing the Alpaca gown.

Swirling round she launched herself onto him with considerable energy.

'I love this gown Jim. It's so comfortable.'

'And it seems to be swirling more freely. Maybe there's not so much of you holding it back?'

He received a warning glance and an ear tweak, but continued as before.

'You were saying that work wasn't such a hassle.'

'I didn't get as tense and edgy as I usually do, and it wasn't just me. The team weren't so edgy either. I almost enjoyed work today, and we were at full stretch with some difficult arrivals. Could it really be the soup?'

'I'd like to think so. Give it another week. By then we should know for sure.'

'Well, you'll soon be getting a bigger order, because the patients like it, and now it's being served in the staff canteen.'

'Have any of the patients said why they like it?'

'They give the same reasons as we do. It's the earthy flavour. The older ones said it took them back to sweet rationing, when they ate all sorts of things from the hedgerows. She pulled a face. 'One said it reminded him of his younger days because it was nice and salty like his nose pickings; he sounded serious.'

'No wonder it's popular. Let's hope it stays that way.'

They had the avocado and orange for dinner, and in keeping with her exercise regime, Beryl insisted on maintaining a good posture by watching the news from her chair at the table instead of slumping onto the sofa.

Local coverage of events included snippets from their video of the cinema protest, and the interview with big Mabel. It came across well, followed by some probing questions to the cinema manager and a local councillor who agreed to make a case for cancelling the showing of 'Alley Men'.

The presenter then went on to introduce a party of schoolchildren who were seated in two rows with their teacher.

'This week, some of you may have noticed pupils carrying litter sticks and bags on their way to and from school.' She scanned the front row. 'Who can tell me more about that?'

'So…' a girl in the front row oozed confidence. 'We're starting a school campaign to raise awareness about all the plastic litter in the borough and the damage it's doing.'

A boy raised his hand. 'Like… and we've got a website with a map showing where we'll be picking it up, and there's an idea's box.'

'Can adults contribute?'

'Yes, but it's our campaign. We don't want adults taking over.'

'Or fawning over us just because we're young,' added the girl. 'We've had enough of adults treating us as if we're somehow, well, cute…you know?'

The boy stood up. 'And it's adults making all this plastic and letting it get dumped everywhere and killing wildlife and sea creatures. They're not doing much about it are they?'

He received a chorus of whoops.

'But we rely on plastic don't we? The presenter waved her pen as an example. 'Plastic is made into all sorts of things; just think of all the plastic needed to make the items we use at home.'

Another boy piped up. 'That sort of plastic should be made so it can be recycled, because we know that lots of plastic isn't recycled. Anyway, we could do without most of it, and we don't have to wrap everything up in it do we?' He pointed to her pen. 'Your pen is two colours isn't it?'

'It is why?'

'All plastic should be the same colour for easier recycling. It's only coloured like that to sell better.'

'And we shouldn't be putting plastic into clothes.' added the girl. 'When clothes are washed, lots of fibres come out and get swallowed by creatures that live in our rivers and the sea.'

'So, what material has been used to make the uniforms are you wearing?' enquired the presenter.

'We're not sure about our school uniforms, but I'll stop wearing one if it's got plastic in it.' said the boy.

The presenter turned to the teacher. 'Do their uniforms contain plastic fibres?'

The teacher was doubtful. 'We are checking, but if they do, it's going to be expensive to replace them.'

The presenter put on a sombre face. 'And that could mean some hard bargaining at home kids.' She encompassed them with a wave and concluded. 'So, there you have it viewers, 'Kids against plastic.'

The girl interjected, 'Our slogan is: 'Young people against plastic.' Calling us 'kids' is demeaning.'

'Oops! Apologies for that, 'Young people against plastic it is.' corrected the presenter. 'And I'm sure we'll be hearing more from our young campaigners in the future. So, let's applaud them for raising awareness, and helping to clean up our Borough.'

Beryl, reached for the remote control.

'Do you want to see anything else, Jim?'

'No, but I enjoyed that. So far it's been a good news day.'

He opened the end door, and taking the rubbish bag down the steps to the bin, made sure the street entrance was tight shut by pushing the securing bolts fully home. But the mustiness from the drains followed him back up the steps into the room, and no amount of air freshener was going to disguise that.

Even so, there was cause for some optimism. Towards the northern end of the high street, plastic wrapping caught in the lower supports of the advertisement hoardings still trailed onto the pavement, but at last the obscene graffiti had been cleaned from the boards. Then Beryl gave an excited girlie clap of the hands and drew his attention to a hedgehog poster in the antiques shop window.

'Look Jim, they've started up the hedgehog sanctuary again. I'm so pleased. Things really must be looking up.'

He agreed. It had been a day full of promising signs, and after a long absence it sounded as if enough bell ringers had at last been recruited to practise ringing the changes in St Michael's Church. Their roundelays mingled with the rumble of a take-off from the airport, and Jim asked Beryl if she had ever taken an overseas holiday break.

'I did once, with a group to Ibiza.' She didn't elaborate.

'Sounds as if you didn't enjoy it.'

'I didn't. They were drunk most of the time. I was ashamed to be British.'

'The Spanish will have learned how to live with that by now. Some of the older ones might even remember when we were among the best-behaved visitors in their resorts. Maybe if I can get Britain well souped, we'll be able to go to somewhere for a sunny break without feeling apologetic.'

They scanned the street for more positive signs. The pub had been open for some time, but only a few cans and chicken wrappers vied for space in Ali's shop doorway, and down below, all was quiet. He allowed his spirits to rise for a few seconds. After all it was Friday evening, and something other than mustiness really did seem to be in the air.

8. Getting Better

Following the Council's decision to ban 'Alley Men' from being shown at the Regal, Big Mabel was keen for the publicity team to record how the Ironside residents were increasingly working together as a community.

'This place has had a bad name for yonks,' she sighed. 'But with you putting us on the news, others came to help, and now, a lot more of our neighbours have started to pull their fingers out.'

'Being on the news made us feel we mattered at last,' added a lady with a bucket.

An elderly man, who was introduced as Bob, waved his finger across the stark frontage of the building.

'Mind you, there's some here who still don't give a monkey's for anyone.'

'Yeah, they start peeking at us behind their windows when we're working,' said a tall lady. She laughed. 'You should see them disappear when Mabel throws them a kiss.'

Mabel made a sucking sound, and pouting her lips, lathered Bob with kisses on both cheeks.

'You've earned those, Bob,' she grinned, and turned to Jim. 'He stood up to a bunch of turds who were kicking our bins around, and he's not well.'

Bob shrugged, 'So I'm eighty with the big 'C', I could have died like a hero.'

'You're too precious to die like that, Bob.'

'Better than being forced to gasp my lot looking like a rotten turnip.'

He diverted their attention to a large pile of black plastic bin bags. 'They need collecting, before some kid cuts them open.'

'Is that what you'd expect?' asked Jim.

'It's what we used to expect,' corrected the lady with a bucket. 'Now it doesn't happen so often. But there's a solid day's worth of clearing up in those sacks, so we still have a watch rota until the special collection comes round.'

'It's all deprivation round here,' declared Bob. 'A bit like wartime, but worse. At least I didn't have to get fat then.'

'Watch it, you're heading for a kiss,' warned the tall lady.

'So, is it still youngsters causing most of the trouble?' asked Madge.

Mabel replied warily. 'Not so much now, but talk gets round, and there are some things you can't say. But what is there here for kids?' She waved her arms around. 'Look at it! Home here is being squashed up, looking out at traffic and concrete. They can't run around much, and we daren't let them go far on their own. Kids want excitement and there's not a lot of excitement for them here.'

Jim was nudged by snippets from his childhood. 'And boredom makes for trouble.'

'You could say that again.' Mabel paused. 'OK, so I admit I've had problems with my four, but I've kept them from gangs.'

'Must have been difficult for you?'

'Yes, it's a big struggle for parents round here. Some just give up on their kids.'

'She's right…straight after nooky,' added Bob.'

Mabel went for him with pursed lips but continued with her theme.

'Trouble is, a lot of boys want to find excitement by getting in with the wrong mates, and a lot of the girls have babies because that's a way they can feel wanted and loved.'

'But is that so bad?' The tall lady smiled in recollection. 'Being a young mum means you can share your baby with other young mums and learn from each other.'

Bob raised his eyebrows. 'And guess what? They don't even have to buy prams. Prams get handed down from their unloved mums. You can't get into 'Starbucks' for antique prams these days.'

'Yes well.' The tall lady tucked her chin in. 'There's nothing wrong with that. You were a baby once weren't you?'

'Yes, until I got hairy and went for unloved girls.'

Mabel spoke with feeling. 'It's not just this end of the borough; it's the same in Spikewell and Brandon's Heath.'

'Have you tried getting together with them to improve things and share ideas?' asked Madge.

'We're starting to.' Mabel explained what was being done as she walked them over to a portable cabin in a corner of the courtyard. 'After we got 'Alley Men' cancelled, Brandon Heath asked if we were interested in something they'd got going for their kids.'

They entered the cabin which was fitted out with benches and some basic hand tools. She introduced them to a youngish man in a dustcoat.

'Show them what you're hoping to start up here, Sami.'

'Sure.' Sami took them to a workbench. 'They've got a group of crafts people together at Brandons Heath, and they're training kids to use tools so they can make simple things out of items that can be recycled. It's popular there, and I'm planning to start up something like it. They don't have time to teach enough practical stuff in schools round here, and practical work is what a lot of our kids want. Trouble is you've got to be careful working with kids these days.'

'Big risk,' warned Bob. 'Nowadays they're all wised up and waiting to nail you.'

'With two of us here we should be safe enough, but we need parents to support what we're doing.' stressed Sami. 'Most parents are keen, but some don't want to be bothered, and they're mostly the ones we want to get involved.'

He showed them a photo of two girls with a grinning snake constructed from plastic cream pots which had been threaded together. In the background a boy was straddling a lorry made from Avocado and Orange containers.

'Is it all their own work?' asked Madge.

'They get help, but mostly it's all their own work which gives them confidence, and that's what they need.'

'And that's what a lot of the kids round here don't get,' affirmed Mabel.

'So, has life in Ironside improved since we last came?' asked Madge.

'It's got better,' agreed Mabel. 'There's a long way to go, but we're working together, which is the main thing.'

'Somehow there's a friendlier feeling in the air,' added the bucket lady.

'And I saw a smile yesterday.' said Bob.

'But we need more homes!' declared Mabel, and gesturing towards a nearby cluster of young mums she looked straight into the camera, then swung her arm round to a line of trees marking the green belt and repeated her previous mantra. 'And they need homes, so give us more homes, council!'

'Well, you win some and you lose some,' remarked Ben as they walked into the park.

Madge closed the gate. 'You mean Mabel's plans for the green belt?'

'She'll get her way. Back home we've been fighting the developers for years. Even Great Crested Newts couldn't stop them. We can't see the church for all the boxy new builds, and the primary school they're planning will take up most of the old cricket ground.'

'Serves you right for living in a cutie snooty little village.' said Madge. 'Maybe you haven't noticed that life is still a struggle for normal people. Not everyone gets afternoon crumpets and cakes on the Vicar's lawn you know.' She prodded him. 'Sorry Mr Hoity Toity but you'd better learn to live with those boxy new builds and more kids …Oop's, children.'

'But I like living in my cutie snooty little village.'

'Tough. It's called growth, and you'd better get used to it. So, what's your answer to that?'

Jim grinned provocatively. 'How about our soup?'

Ben feigned excitement.

'You beat me to it Jim. I never thought of it quite that way. No more land grabbing; wars or climate changing. Just a great big global 'love in' with hundreds of different 'isms' and boxy new builds recycling themselves into a sort of spiritual compost, for forests; goodwill and all things green.'

Madge eyed him suspiciously.

'He's still pushing it Jim. It's his usual clever dick and graduate uppityness stuff, just because he got a first in comparative philosophy at Wissell.'

'Well, let's hope our soup does its job.' said Jim. 'But right now, I'd jump into one of those boxy new builds if I had the chance - we don't even have room for a window box.'

On approaching the exit gates, they noticed a bench displaying a large blue sticker circled round with *'Our World, Our Business,'* and a website address to *'Youthsense'* with an assurance that the sticker was biodegradable. They sat on the bench and tapped in the address on their mobiles.

'Could be back to the seventies, if anyone knows their social history,' remarked Ben.

'Madge was enthusiastic, but could see that Jim had doubts. 'You don't look so sure, Jim?'

He prodded the ground with a twig to focus his thoughts.

'Not so long ago it was children skiving off lessons to parade against climate change. Surprise, surprise, they got more fawning publicity and hype than any experienced environmentalist could wish for, and it was soon forgotten. Yesterday on the TV, we had schoolchildren making a fuss about plastic, and now this. We need fired-up youth, but it has to be well informed and I want to know a lot more about this campaign than it says here.'

From the road side of the fence came the scream of emergency sirens, and a stream of flashing blue lights. Hurriedly shielding their ears, they waited until a queue of loaded transporters had clattered back into life before walking out of the park gates and onto the pavement into a mist of fumes. Passing alongside a gallery of angry faces mouthing exasperation behind windscreens, they left the traffic jam, and continued onto a scaffold-board bridge, which took them over a trench being laid with drainage pipes, and into the hospital underpass. Placed at intervals along the underpass were more *'Our World, our Business'* stickers and some tombstone shaped *'In Memoriam'* posters which listed recently extinct wildlife.'

Madge stopped before an *'In Memoriam'* poster, and voiced her approval.

'Someone's been doing a lot of research. This shows thirty creatures that became extinct just last month.'

She placed her finger on a bird. 'This one's a Cozumal Thrasher from the West Indies.'

'Better not tell Mabel,' grinned Ben. 'She'll be straight onto the council about that.'

Madge slid her finger over some close-ups of lizards. 'There's something hopeful about all this. I would have thought everyone round here would be too stressed up to give a bat's poo about anything outside their front doors. Yet someone has cared enough to put this up.'

But hopeful thinking was cut short as they emerged from the underpass and into the cause of the traffic jam. Ambulances and police cars were wailing into the hospital forecourt parking bays, and armed police were fanning out as patients were stretchered through the entrance.

'Cozumel Thrashers won't be in the news this evening,' said Jim.

It was later reported that two stolen vans had been driven towards each other from opposite ends of a pedestrian zone, causing death and injury to a number of shoppers. The perpetrators were shot while trying to sustain the attack with knives, and rumours that a terrorist group had planned the attack were quickly de-bunked by a police statement describing the perpetrators as dressed like characters in a violent 1980's film. 'They were really enjoying it,' said a witness. 'One was still laughing as the police shot him. He just shouted: 'I'll be remembered now!'

It came as a pleasant surprise to Jim that in the days following the attack, the local Mosque had not been vandalised, and there had been no assaults or peer bullying of Muslim school pupils. Later enquiries about the motives of the killers revealed that both had troubled family backgrounds, but neither had any previous convictions, and one had made it to university. Of greater concern were the nihilistic web pages on their smartphones, and it was thought that these could have been a big influence.

'What does nihilistic mean?' asked Beryl.

'I'm not sure.' Jim consulted his phone and read out slowly: *'Nihilism is a viewpoint that traditional values and beliefs are unfounded, and existence is senseless. A true nihilist would believe in nothing; have no loyalties, and no purpose.'*

He settled back. 'That sounds about right.'

Beryl took his phone and read it for herself. 'There wouldn't be many of us alive if everyone was like that.'

'Maybe it's worth asking why they get like that in the first place.'

'You mean kill lots of people for no purpose?'

'Seems it gave them enough purpose. Now they'll be remembered instead of being just nothings, and that checks out what one of them said.'

'But they must be hated. I bet they wouldn't have done it if they believed in Hell.'

'Maybe, but Hell's not trendy anymore, and being hated would be a reward. They were after notoriety, and as usual, the media's given them buckets-full of that.'

Beryl sighed. 'You really are such a miserable cynic Jim.'

They laughed together.

'Make me happy then?'

She closed up to him. 'Well, I'm happy if it helps.'

'Tell me more.'

'It's because I feel part of a team again. The chief executive has been running around praising everyone for the way we coped with the last emergency, and for the hospital meeting its targets. The whole mood has changed. We're worked silly with all the extra patients, but everyone's been pulling together, and the managers have chipped in when we've been really short. There's a lot more mickey-taking as well, which is a sure sign things are getting better.' She grinned mischievously. 'And the patients who have your soup get fresh faster than those who don't.'

He moved away. 'I'm surprised they're not exhausted since you've been having it.'

He dodged her backhand.

She continued. 'Anyway, my team say it's also become much friendlier where they live. Wendy was going to take her son out of junior school, but said that most of the bullying has stopped, so she's keeping him there now. She was really surprised how many turned up for the last parents evening, and the form teacher told her that more children get breakfast at home now.'

'Has anyone mentioned our soup?'

'Not yet, the teachers think it's because family support was upped recently.'

'What about the senior schools?'

'They seem to be improving. You must remember Connie who attended to you when you first came to the ward.'

'You mean the blonde attractive one before you got your hands on me?'

'Stinker!' She connected with her backhand this time. 'Yes Connie. She was really worried about her daughter going secretive and spending hours alone on her iPad. But suddenly it's been all work and talk about university. The staff put it down to the new headmaster introducing careers guidance, but Connie thinks her daughter has been encouraged to learn by a campaign called something like: 'It's Our World and …'

'Our World, Our Business.' cut in Jim.

'That's the one. She wants to study environmental science. So you know about that campaign?

'I've seen their website. What's Connie told you?'

'She says it's a campaign and a research project about the damage big business and governments are doing to our planet.'

'The politicians will need a lot of soup before doing anything about that.'

'I think it's good. It's given lots of young people something worthwhile to aim for. Connie says it's as if her daughter has come back to life.'

Jim worried. Those youngsters could be heading for danger.

9. Too Soon

The weather had been unpredictable from summer through to early autumn. Yet again, harvesting was affected. Yet again, flooding had returned to valleys. Untreated sewage had been discharged into rivers and the sea, and yet again the government and local authorities were blamed for providing inadequate flood protection.

After a delayed arrival at Kings Cross, and a dank trip on the underground, Jim walked from the station into a stinging deluge of rain and water bubbling up through the road grids. But work on the sewage outflow at the hospital underpass had at last been completed, so there was no need to sponge his shoes in the bucket of disinfectant on the top step before entering the flat.

His trip to the North had been encouraging. Soup sales were on the rise, and the northern agency had negotiated contracts with two prisons and a detention centre. Setting up free soup kitchens in the badly flooded areas had reduced profits, but Jim had correctly reasoned that the good publicity would further raise the profile of the soup and expand the local market.

Trying to assess any improvement in the social climate had left unwanted memories of paramedics and police being spat at; weekend leglessness in town centres, and a particularly nasty brawl egged on by a mixed audience. On the bonus side, he had met an engaging young priest who had the ability to attract the attention of those enjoying the late street life amid the mayhem and profanities outside a disco. Voluntary groups such as the 'Street Clean Squad' were working closely with some hard-pressed local authorities to remove graffiti and rubbish in several towns, and the 'Green Our Town' group were constructing plant stands from discarded pallets for shop owners who were willing to decorate them with flowers. Small garden and window box clubs were increasingly popular in poor urban areas and special interest groups like the, 'Gash Street Bog Mint Preservation Trust' were encouraging their communities to protect rare plant species.

Clearly there was some way to go, but it really did seem as if as if a mood of congeniality was seeping into the population centres of the north, and he smiled while popping the pasta bake into the oven for the evening meal.

Then the phone rang, and he returned to his default condition.

'Jim?' The inflection in that single word, told him that Adelita had something important to say.

'Jim, you never had the opportunity to meet our wonderful Father Dududso. He did so much to settle the community in Miser Terrace, but he was murdered in his Butkre diocese only yesterday. It's so sad, and he will be missed terribly. I have informed Ben and Madge who both knew him very well of course.'

'Dammit!' I wish I'd known him. Madge told me he had gone back to his old diocese to encourage the locals to split from the drug gangs and return to their traditional lifestyles and thistle farming. He must have been brave.'

'Yes, very brave, Jim, and he paid with his life because of it. He was shot during a 'Soup and Praise' service in his church. It was brutal.'

'It must have been a gang.'

'Yes, they killed him like that to frighten the congregation back to cocaine farming. I hated him going to Butkre, but he insisted on practising what he preached, even though it went against the principles of his church.'

'And the gangs are forcing the locals back to cocaine production I suppose?'

'That's what they intended, but they made a big mistake. His community is now seeking revenge for his murder, so they are going for the gangs, and it's spreading across Butkre because the new regime also wants to get rid of the gangs.'

'Let's hope some good comes from it.'

'I'm sure it will, but his community is also angry with the church, because the bishop denounced the 'Soup and Praise' services, and they think of Father Dududso as a martyr.'

'His church isn't helping much then?'

'No, and they have formidable leadership.'

Bishop Pocklington loomed large in Jim's mind.

'Yes we've got one here who's against nice pills, and he's impressive as well. It comes from having a strong belief I suppose.'

She caught the note of regret in his voice. 'Just keep trying Jim…how you say? 'Rome wasn't built in a day."

Just in time, he removed the pasta bake from the oven, and straightway arranged a working lunch at the Chantcel Restaurant overlooking Chantcel Square. It was a quality eatery, and the team had worked hard, so he would foot the bill. The murder of Father Dududso would be uppermost in their minds of course, but a focal point was needed to prevent thoughts straying too far from their mission, and he struggled to think what it could be. He finished slicing the vegetables, and was about to put them in the saucepan, when the large inflatable globe in the stationary shop window came to mind.

Twelve chimes from the Catholic Church clock tower echoed over Chantcel Square, and heads bowed, the team stood in respectful memory of Father Dududso.

'Strange?' Madge was thoughtful as they sat down at a table dominated by the globe. 'I felt he was with us.'

'Like a Father Dududso breeze?' suggested Ben.

'Yes, well, sort of.' Madge eyed Ben warily, but could see he was serious.

'He with us!' Brinod was adamant. Waggling his head up and down he repeatedly pointed at himself. 'I know Father Dududso ambassador in Heaven. I feel him …yes?"

'Jim?' Madge waited for his reaction.

Jim hesitated. He might have felt something, but he was already up to his ears with telepathic buzzes and floaty feelings. Trying to cope with ethereal priestly supervision would be a sensation too far, and he'd never met Father Dududso.

'I wish I had known Father Dududso, but you have all worked with him during the troubles in Miser Terrace, so it's hardly surprising you all felt something, because you knew him so well.'

They settled into a few more moments of reflective silence as a waiter handed out the menus, then Jim set the scene.

'If the media latches onto Father Dududso's murder and his work in Butkre, we're bound to get questions about mind changing soup.'

'OK, I'll make a start,' proposed Ben. 'So, why should everyone have our soup?'

Madge answered forcefully, 'Because we are a nasty selfish lot, and don't care what we do to get what we want. We've got to take something to make us nicer - there's no other way.'

'Speak for yourself,' insisted Ben. 'There must be plenty of exceptions. My grandma was very nice, and she didn't like soup.'

'Neither did mine.' retorted Madge. 'But if she'd had some, she might not have been in such a hurry to ditch Grandpa and shack up with a football pools winner.'

'We'd better make a stronger case than that for our mission,' advised Jim. 'The bishop has already spoken out against nice pills, and he's is bound to make a fuss about our soup once he knows it contains the same ingredients.'

'Then why not ask the church how it would go about saving the world?' suggested Madge.

'You're joking,' said Ben. 'They'll soon throw that one back at us. Even you should know that the church has a comprehensive manual to deal with that.'

'Alright, I'd forgotten,' she admitted. 'But it isn't very clear. I tried reading it once and got lost.'

Jim went back to his early attempts to seek wisdom from the Bible.

'It's not very clear to me either. We should try harder to understand it I suppose, but there's no time for that now.'

He laid a hand on the globe. 'If we have to make a case for our mission, we need to be sure we've got our facts right. So, let's start from the top and work down.' He placed a finger on the North Pole. 'Up here ice is melting fast, and the glaciers are breaking up causing rising sea levels and stranding polar wildlife. I also read something about plans for more mineral extraction once the polar ice gets thinner - anything else?'

Ben had been squinting at his phone. 'Plenty more. There's all sorts of industrial pollution and toxic run off around the top of Greenland and Russia, and a lot of deforestation caused by logging. They've even had wild fires in Greenland because so much ice has melted, and trawlers are still drag-fishing by scraping up everything from the seabed. And listen to this.' He read from his phone. *'Warm current flow that has historically caused dramatic changes in the climate has slowed down to its weakest in 1,600 years and could collapse the Gulf Stream leading to extreme winters in Western Europe.'* Which means we could freeze and flood, while everywhere else is sunning it up.'

'So, what's to be done?'

'I didn't say anything should be done about it'.' Ben distanced himself from Madge. 'My uncle Sid has shares in most of those things, and I could be a beneficiary. Why should I lose money because of a few polar bears?'

'That just about says it all!' exclaimed Madge.

'Fair enough,' conceded Jim. 'It's Uncle Sid versus polar bears, so I'm not going to bet on who's going to win that one.'

He slid his hand further down the globe.

'As it starts to get warmer, pesticides, manufacturing, and huge infrastructure growth over green areas are causing all sorts of eco damage and loss of natural habitats.' He looked round. 'Anything else?'

'Traffic pollution, plastic pollution, and water pollution, added Madge.' She laid a hand over the America's. 'And here they're cutting down rain forests for all sorts, including cattle farms to produce thousands of tons of cheap meat which we're quite happy to gobble down.' She broke off to wave Brinod's attention away from a youngish waiter who was clearing a nearby table.

'And let's not forget the billions of cattle burps and farts being pushed into the atmosphere,' added Ben.

'Yours don't help either.' grimaced Madge.

Jim circled his hand over Northern Europe; the Middle East, and top of Africa.

'Now we're into serious war zones – not to forget the nasty one just starting up, and it's getting to be more of the same as we go down'

Ben stood up and sang: 'Because we're: 'Happy,Happy,Happy!' He then bowed and sat down. '…Sorry, I just wanted to cheer us up for a moment.'

Madge prodded him. 'As usual you've been pushing it ever since we started.' Then she had a second thought. 'No wait a jiff, you're right. We need to hear some good things as well. It can't all be bad.' She stood aside for a waitress to take their orders, and asked Jim to continue.

'Cheer us up with some good news Jim.'

'Well, if you don't mind going back to those casualties being rushed into accident and emergency, you may remember the poster in the hospital underpass which listed all those extinct species. He pressed his finger onto the West Indies. So, cheer up because a nesting pair of Cozumal Thrashers have been found right here near Santo Domingo.'

'Madge whooped.'

'Mind blowing,' said Ben.

'There were a couple of lizards as well,' added Jim, 'although I don't want to cause too much excitement. Anyway, let's try to stay cheerful by flying over most of this and landing near the equator.' He slid his hand downwards. 'I haven't come across any happy wars yet, but maybe we should be content with a good try. He placed his hand over the Congo and Uganda. 'Down here a guerrilla campaign started up which called itself the 'Lord's Resistance Army.' It sounded hopeful because the leader claimed he was a spokesman for God, and was fighting to set up a government based on the Ten Commandments. His followers killed thousands, but after some outside opposition, the campaign split up into lots of smaller conflicts and he disappeared. It was all done with the best intentions I suppose.'

Jim thought back to an early army training detachment in Central Africa, and the incredible wildlife he saw on the high peaks bordering the Congo and Uganda. 'I just hope that hellfire is automatically awarded to those who use mountain gorillas for target practice.'

'Could our soup prevent that type of cruelty?' asked Madge.

Jim pondered the question. 'That's difficult. If someone honestly believes they have to kill thousands to make a better country, are they worse than someone who kills rare wild creatures for so-called fun, or scammers and nasties on social media, who don't give a damn about the distress they inflict?' He shrugged. 'I'll have to pass on that.'

The youngish waiter arrived with the first course, and giving Brinod a wide berth, aroused the displeasure of other diners who viewed him as a source of flatulence while Ben was deflating the globe.

Madge tried to summarise what had been covered. 'So, it's wars and big business causing most of the damage, right?'

Ben raised a hand. 'Bags I defend big business.'

Madge pulled a face, 'Does he have to?'

'It might help to make the issues clearer,' said Jim, 'so let's give it a go.'

Madge reluctantly agreed. 'Alright if we must.'

Jim gave her his phone and pointed to an article. 'Ask Mr Big Business if he feels any responsibility for this.'

Close to disbelief at what she had read, Madge addressed Mr Big Business.

'Did you know Mr Big Business, that the UK has lost over half its wildlife in the last fifty years?'

Mr Big Business kept his distance. 'Perhaps, but you can't have everything. Producing what we need for this modern age is a national priority, and both require land and raw materials. Like it or not, you should bear in mind that this is for people, not birds or hedgehogs, and all this green talk is holding things up. According to my phone which is a 'Hiwi 8 Universe,' he waved it provocatively at Madge, 'most countries don't have all this trouble finding land and raw materials for development, so they're growing much faster than us, and we'll be way behind if we don't get a spurt on.'

She sighed with exasperation. 'So it's concrete or wildlife.'

'Concrete or wildlife indeed. You must know that's a gross overstatement. There will always be wildlife.'

'But you've killed nearly half of it already.'

'You mustn't believe everything you find on that phone. People, and I mean 'real' people, have to be our main concern.'

'So anything else that lives and breathes doesn't matter! That's what you're saying isn't it?'

'Oh you really are exaggerating young lady. Anyway, we will be greening our new towns with trees and roof gardens, and investing billions in developing clean energy and electric transport.'

'Yes, while you are grabbing more land, making billions of tons of concrete, and messing up more wild places while you're grabbing the stuff to do it.'

'Again, you are exaggerating young lady, and anyway, you must be well aware that your concerns are represented on many international environmental bodies.'

'Yes, and it's all talk while hardly anything gets done, which suits you perfectly doesn't it?'

'I can only repeat that your concerns are well represented on international bodies.' Mr Big Business dismissively removed his glasses. 'So off you trot to seek out the answers you are so determined to find elsewhere.'

He just avoided a clout.

Jim summarised: 'So there you are, and while we can grind up enough trees to turn into billions of loo rolls, don't expect homeless sloths and orang-utans to get much sympathy either.'

Madge vented her exasperation by prodding Brinod who had been winking at the youngish waiter on the far side of the restaurant, then Jim's phone vibrated with a text message.

It was good news.

'Well at last here's something we can smile about!' He topped up their wine glasses. 'They've doubled our bonuses because of soaring sales, and,' he raised his glass, 'they're backdated from July.'

The sound of an approaching bass drum, and blare of a badly played trumpet had been intruding into their celebration for some time, and now the window frames had begun to rattle.

Moving to the windows, they watched a drummer and trumpeter lead a column of young marchers to the centre of the square. The column halted, and banners were raised displaying caricatures of politicians and big business leaders. It then moved round to form a semi-circle behind a girl holding a large megaphone. Two other marchers unfurled an *'Our World Our Business'* banner while the trumpet nearly played a fanfare as the girl swept round with the megaphone and spoke angrily to the caricatures.

'You are ravaging our world! You call it growth - we call it destruction. Destruction of our forests, poisoning of our rivers, and pollution of our seas!' You are sucking and hacking our wonderful planet to death, and for what? We demand you answer that. What are you doing it for? Is it for happiness? We don't get it. All we get is a trashed world after you've stuffed yourselves with money and power, and that's the world we'll be left with after you've gone!'

Jim swore. 'This is too soon, they're starting the street stuff too soon Dammit!' He cursed himself for not squeezing in enough time to meet them before his sales trip to the North.

'Why?' chorused Madge and Ben.'

'Because they're just heading into trouble.'

He broke off just as a crowd of hoody's rushed into the square with clubs. They were fast and efficient, leaving many of the demonstrators injured and motionless. A few attempted to fight back with disastrous results, and the remainder scattered in all directions, pursued by the hoody's.

Jim swore again. 'Professionals and right on cue!'

Alarmed faces in the restaurant turned to the sound of footsteps pounding up the stairs as Jim and Brinod made for the entrance. Bursting through the swing doors, the megaphone girl ran straight into a party of shocked diners as she sprawled over the first table, and in the same instant, Brinod had slammed together, and frisked the two hoody's chasing her, while Jim neck-locked a third who had clubbed a young man unconscious. Pulling the hood down with his teeth, Jim revealed the tattooed head of an adult.

'Contracted?'

The grunted denial could have been East European, then he tried a sudden move, and Jim dropped him hard to the floor.

Brinod had retrieved a knife, and Jim nodded at his captive as Ben ran up.

'Frisk him!'

'Snap!' Ben found a knife and a phone.

'Keep the phone,' said Jim, 'and get your techie mates to check it, before we hand it in.'

The young man had fallen awkwardly under the reception desk, and remained motionless with his face flat against the carpet. Madge had rushed over to turn his head sufficiently for him to breathe. But he wasn't breathing, and the desk was hurriedly moved by a customer and the youngish waiter for her to apply artificial respiration.

The mood of the restaurant had abruptly changed from cosy to hostile. Conversations had been cut short; eating had ceased, and diners sat before newly served or half eaten meals while others tried to decide whether to leave, or pay their bills. The only noise came from three children who had been playing tag round their table throughout the episode, and were now watching the emergency services from the windows, while their parents yelled at them to return.

A buzz of desperation, and a sideways jerk came from Jim's captive.

'Tough!' Jim dug in his knees to a gasped expletive, and hoped the police would arrive soon.

Smeared with dessert, the megaphone girl was looking down to the young man in a state of distress.

'Please, please, come round Strummy.'

She knelt down close to him and wept, but Madge could give her no comfort, and, when at last the paramedics arrived, neither could they.

In the days following, and enhanced by mobile phone images, the violent aftermath of the demonstration was widely reported across the media. In addition to Strummy's death, twelve demonstrators had been injured; some seriously. It was clear that the attack had been carried out by organised thugs, and not by an opportunistic youth gang looking for trouble, although early official reactions seemed to infer otherwise. If the purpose of the attack was to stifle the campaign, then it had just the reverse effect, and regardless of police warnings, more campaigners went ahead with a second *'Our World our Business'* demonstration in Birmingham to increased public support.

Tearful and angry in the Birmingham UBC studio, the megaphone girl responded to the presenter's first question as the camera closed in to capture an emotive facial shot.

'Yes, I loved Strummy so much.' Her nose streamed and her lips quivered as she fumbled for a tissue. 'He was a wonderful person. Why is it that people like Strummy get hurt or killed, while the horrible ones get so much attention and help?'

The presenter lowered her voice and spoke with practised empathy. 'Do you wish to continue?'

The girl nodded vigorously. 'I've got to continue for Strummy, and for the others who were injured. That's why we went ahead with this second demonstration.'

'It must have been terribly difficult for you.'

'I had to do it. Why should those thugs stop us? Our demonstrations are about the beautiful world we are trashing, and big business and governments grabbing everything they can from the land and oceans, and politicians just letting it happen. They've killed half the creatures my mum remembers. Creatures I'll never see, and the insects as well. That's the world they are leaving to our generation. That's what our demonstrations are about, and that's what Strummy was all about.'

'But we must have economic growth, surely? People need jobs and homes.'

'So, when will it stop? When will we stop spreading more roads, more railways, and buildings over the countryside? And how many jobs will there be when the robots come along and there's millions more of us? Will working ourselves stupid to make more and more stuff create happiness? Is that really the idea? Will it really stop all the conflicts and cruelty?'

Her tears and anger grew. 'Where is the hope in a world like that?'

'But sadly, we've always had conflict.'

'Yes, and now millions more of us, are killing millions more creatures, and the planet as well.'

'But Emma there is still love in the world, and millions of lovely people. It isn't that bad surely?'

'Isn't it?' She became distraught. 'Then why can't they give our beautiful world and its creatures some love! Why is it always people?' Clenching both fists she pressed them hard onto her forehead. 'Please, please, answer that for me and Strummy. And please give me some hope by telling me why I'm wrong!'

She repeated it: 'Why am I wrong?'

'Emma, I can't say whether you are right or wrong.' The presenter moved over to her. 'I can only give you a cuddle.'

The cuddle caused a stir, and attracted a speedy reaction from the Prime Minister, who expressed: 'heart-going-out-sympathy.' to Strummy's friends and family, with an assurance that the police were treating the incident as a top priority investigation.'

Yet right from the beginning, Jim suspected a downplaying of the attack. There were reports of police interviewing suspects in the following two weeks - but no arrests. Neither were Ben's techie friends able to unlock the hoody's phone, which suggested some sophisticated blocking. He suspected that the attack was motivated by one or more powerful corporates, but the brutality of the attack was probably a blunder which sent those connected to it scurrying into boltholes. And why hadn't he or

Bridon been called up for a police interview? They could have easily gathered something of interest, yet hadn't even been acknowledged for their actions.'

A few days after Emma's interview, Strummy's ecological burial was attended by a large *'Our World Our Business'* cortège, but questions about the lack of progress in the investigation soon faded in the wake of the pre-Christmas hype.

10. It's Here There & Everywhere.

Jim looked down onto the high street from the flat window. It was rushing home time, and the usual late afternoon traffic fumes were filtering into the room. Shop front decorations mirrored on the wet vehicles produced iridescent bands of colour rippling down to the hospital roundabout, and close-by on the roof of his old superstore workplace, an unconvincing Santa Claus leaned over a sack bulging with gifts. Changing from red to white in the beams of switched spotlights, it proclaimed Christmas with more dazzle and panache than the grey spire of St Michael's Church would ever permit. It was the essence of modern Christmas: tinselly, commercial, and trivial.

As a boy he was required to attend the Christmas Eve service in the village church with Dawn and their parents. It was the proper thing to do in the village at that time. Everyone wore smart coats. The pews were hard, and the carols were sung too slowly. He didn't really enjoy being there, but the flickering candles, the sub-bass of the organ, and even the boring service was somehow solid and reassuring. After exchanging greetings with the Vicar, they usually shared joggling torch lights with the neighbours on the crunchy footpath home. The conversation was always light hearted and confined to niceties, but somehow the evening conveyed a depth which resonated through the years.

But he wasn't looking forward to Christmas at Dawn's. There would be garish parcels under the family tree, and at least one hyperactive child repeatedly screeching 'I want!' to one of Gary's sisters. Beryl would be fighting off her own broodiness by making insincere cooing noises to little Penny, and he would be trying to avoid Shaun and baby chat, by seeking refuge with the dog.

Then there would be parcel opening time. Unrecyclable wrapping would be ripped away from big plastic Spidermen with exaggerated American accents, and there would be girly dolls with makeup packs and plastic assault rifles firing foam bullets. Worst of all would be the frilly adornables emblazoned with something like 'Jim's special' over a strategic place for later compulsory wearing.

'How's it going Jim?' could be the beginnings of a tolerable conversation with Gary, but it was usually cut short with a shouted demand from Shaun, or Dawn spotting an imminent nappy change for Penny. Then there was the walk back with a preoccupied Beryl through a gauntlet of legless high street celebrations up to the flat. They were daft not to have taken a Christmas hotel break. Beryl was off duty and with Jim's pay rise they could have easily afforded one.

He grimaced as he conveyed his thoughts towards the roof top Santa.

Yet something was odd about Santa. For a start, where was the beard? And why was he stooping over that sack of presents like Dawn fawning over baby Penny? Jim wondered if his frame of mind had become so jaundiced, that it wouldn't even allow him to recognise a well-crafted model of Mary gazing down to baby Jesus, and it took some moments of disbelief for him to realize that, yes, it was his frame of mind. He was indeed looking at Mary gazing down to baby Jesus. Forget Santa Claus and his sledge topped with garish parcels, this was the real thing, and there it was of all places, bang on top of his old supermarket workplace. Something cosy welled up from deep inside, but cynicism was still fighting optimism. His old workplace - surely not? Most likely it was a ploy from head office to attract a better class of customer.

He had to find out, and donning his anorak, left the flat and hurried alongside the traffic to the supermarket entrance foyer. Once inside he was greeted by carols playing softly from the ceiling speakers and a faint aroma of incense.

It seemed a bit over the top, as did the pinkish shades clipped over the fluorescent lighting tubes. But a welcoming feel pervaded the store, and he reasoned that it would probably pay off at the expense of more pilfering. Whatever the intention, sales had been good enough to thin out the items on the shelves.

He took a hand basket in hope of finding something worthwhile in the vegetable racks, where he reluctantly dropped a plastic encased cucumber, and some plastic wrapped salad into his basket, before meeting up with Phil, his former supervisor. Phil, who had received no lasting damage from his stabbing, was a master of false bonhomie, and had to speak loudly and finish with a laugh, but still managed to achieve a score of 'alright' on Jim's sliding scale of approval.

'Giving 'Harrods' a miss today then Jim?' They shook hands during the laugh.'

Jim continued along Phil's theme. 'Yes, and it's about time you started catering for class customers. But what's this plastic cucumber doing in my basket?'

Phil became nearly sincere.

'It's gone crazy these last few weeks. Everyone's gone for loose veg recently, and purchasing can't keep up with it.' He pointed to a member of staff brandishing a pair of scissors beneath a notice which read, 'Plastic removal here.'

'Staff idea,' explained Phil. 'We set it up because we've had so many complaints about plastic recently. She'll sort out your cucumber before you can say onions.'

'And why the Nativity model on the roof?'

'Staff idea again, and head office agreed. They forked out enough for it to be made in that new adult training centre; the shoppers really like it.'

He removed the plastic covering from a beetroot and laid it thoughtfully on a display rack.

'It's a bit of a mystery to me Jim, but recently things have got a lot better round here. Everyone say's so, and it's still the same management.' Then something occurred to him. 'Ah...but wait a minute!' He slapped a hand on his forehead and reverted to type. 'Come to think of it, how long has it been since you left?'

The sound of laughter followed Jim to the soup shelves where he put the remaining two containers of Sapiens Carduus Natural in his basket and reported the shortage to the checkout operator. She held a container aloft, and called Phil.

'More of these needed Phil!'

He came over and angled his head at Jim.

'Watch that one Donna.' He used to work here, but now he gets commission on that soup, so we've got trouble already!'

Phil's laughter followed him to the plastic removal corner; through the foyer, and out onto the street where the Christmas traffic was moving hesitantly from the hospital roundabout.

Taking short breaths in the fumy air, he walked up to the Baptist Church Hall where a disabled man was struggling up the entrance steps. He supported the man up the steps and into part of the hall which had been set aside as a sleeping area with a row of camp beds.

The minister greeted them, and helping the man onto a seat, asked him to wait until the shower was available and he could be kitted out with some donated clothes.

'What about drugs?' enquired Jim.

'It's an open shower with two volunteer attendants.'

'No room for ingenuity then?'

'We have had problems, although not with syringes, I hasten to add.'

Jim dropped some loose change into the collection tub.

'Thank you.' The minister smiled his appreciation. 'I must say our community has been unusually generous this Christmas and that was evident well before the new revelation.

'New revelation?'

'Yes, haven't you heard? Science has at last decided, that there is indeed a heaven and a hell, or something very like them.'

'You mean up there?' Jim looked upwards.

'Not just up there. Apparently, it's all around us. 'It was on the news this morning, and more details have been coming in since then. As you can imagine, the explanation is quite complex since it involves new findings about dark matter, but scientists and mathematicians, with very few exceptions, have concluded that morality must be accounted for in the universe.'

'Good and evil you mean?'

'Yes, although they avoid such terms.'

'So, science is saying that we are continually being judged for our behaviour?'

'It seems so.' The minister conveyed his satisfaction. 'It is reassuringly close to our own concept of God of course.'

'Do they say it's God?'

'They say there is a system of adjudication; it's not personalized.'

'Good news then?'

The minister was cagey.

'It simply confirms my belief, and the belief of many others, although some traditions may not see it quite like that.'

'Why?'

'Because many venerate highly personalized deities, and they would find it difficult to believe in anything outside the human construct. If moral judgement is thought to be an inseparable part of the space around us, they may not wish to accept it.'

'They want faces and human expressions I suppose?'

'Well yes, expressions they can relate to of course.' The minister shrugged. 'Frankly it is difficult to conceive it in any other way.'

Back on the high street Jim pondered over his conversation with the minister.

So, the existence of something like Heaven or Hell had been given scientific credence. Was it just possible that morality could sweep over the world and everyone will soon be jumping over themselves to do the right thing? It really seemed too good to be true, and probably was too good to be true. After all, would scammers and drug dealers be frantically trying to find ways to redeem themselves by making up for all their criminal gains? And what would murderers do?

The Ten Commandments had laid down some pretty clear do's and don'ts, but they didn't cover everything, and the god who dictated them to Moses seemed to have too much attitude to be just part of the ether. A general command which said: 'Only do what you know is right.' could have been useful, but somehow it seemed a bit tame. It was all getting very confusing, although bringing back Heaven and Hell had to be a good thing, even if everyone became nicer purely through self-interest.

As Jim continued down the high street, he noticed sprigs of mistletoe dangling from the windowsills, and a banner extending along several shop fronts reminded everyone that: 'Christmas is also for the lonely.' And there were smiles - lots of smiles, and even hugs and dancy steps after the hugs. Someone was even apologetically cleaning his dog's poo from the pavement, and the aggressive bass boom of gang rap was absent from the crawling line of traffic.

Was this just the soup, or could it be that the Christmas season had been given an extra boost by science as well?

First popping into the antique shop to give a donation to the hedgehog charity, he went onto Ali's hardware store, and bought a roll of string for parcelling up the presents. He had agreed with Beryl that it was to be a recyclable Christmas, and whether he liked it or not, Shaun would get a book wrapped in string and brown paper. Feeling almost buoyant, Jim exchanged greetings with Ali, and crossed over to the flat to prepare dinner and begin wrapping the presents.

Christmas Eve at Dawn's was surprisingly enjoyable. Tiny Penny was allowed to simmer in her cot, and Dawn almost became the sister he had known when they used to make mud pies and share imaginations. As expected, there were too many presents in garish wrappings, but nothing pointy or shooty for Shaun to brandish, and he seemed sufficiently pleased with his book to say, 'Thanks Uncle Jim,' which came as an even greater surprise. Clearly Gary had been a good second dad, and whatever the reason, Shaun had undergone a transformation since the last time Jim had tried to avoid him.

Beryl had clearly enjoyed the company of Gary's loud sisters who, after noisily sharing their dodgy life experiences, had decided that all of them, including Beryl, should just about qualify for heaven, or at least be permitted to scramble onto neutral ground while the jury was out. So, with the outspoken intention of bettering their heavenly chances, everyone, including an uncomplaining Shaun, walked to the local church for the candlelight service.

Rainwater had filled up a dip in the road, and was rippling over the pavement onto the church entrance steps when they arrived. Action was required, and rolling up their trousers, Jim and Gary removed their shoes and socks, and joined two others who were already probing elbow deep into the water to drag out the accumulated rubbish from the road grids. After completing their task, and on Jim's command, they lined up and bowed to an appreciative audience as the water drained off.

Leaving their shoes and socks in the porch, they entered the church barefoot, and were each given a candle by the verger who apologised for the lack of towels and under floor heating. But once inside, all was glowing and sparkly. Two large firs, strung with baubles and topped with golden stars fronted the choir stalls, and dominating the chancel, an elaborately embroidered alter cloth twinkled metallically in the light from two pillar mounted candles. The age of the building added an aura of historical authority to the service, and it was all cosily reassuring.

Beryl sensed the ambience, and squeezed his hand. 'This is lovely Jim - so Christmassy.' The elderly couple seated next to them agreed. 'Yes, just like old times.'

The man took their candle, and passing it to the candle lighter in the aisle, grinned knowingly and, said, 'It's been ages since we've had this many here.' It was almost a question, and taking the hint, Jim replied, 'Yes and we decided to come as soon as we heard the news.'

Some amused faces turned to them from the pew in front. 'It's a race against time for me as well,' agreed someone, and the theme developed into light hearted speculation about their likely places in dark matter, until the Vicar took her place behind the lectern.

It was the deep pedal tones from the bass organ pipes that affected Jim. The singing was good, yet it was the bass notes that gave the carols a depth and vibrancy that resonated exactly with his mood. It was like coming home, but an elusive home without structure or location; a home full of sensations, and pleasant events from the past that he could never fully recapture. Then came the familiar buzzy sensation brought on by the flickering mass of candles, and rivulets of rain on the stained glass windows. He'd experienced something like it in the hospital of course, but this time the sensation came with buzzes of kinship and sharing, which were strong enough to divert his attention away from the rest of the service, until he was aware of Beryl nudging him to leave.

They thanked the Vicar, and Jim re-joined the voluntary water drainage team in the porch to put on his socks and shoes, before walking back to Dawn's semi with a crowd of suddenly closer neighbours. Goodbyes and hugs were shared in the rain, and everyone made firm promises to meet again in the New Year. Then it was coffee with rum, and Gary drove them through saturated streets to the flat.

Jim turned on the electric fire and closed the curtains while Beryl put on the kettle and collected a modest array of cards from the shelf above the television. He had received a few cards from his old regiment pals, but most were for Beryl. She joined him on the couch and showed him a confident scrawl wishing her a 'Bonza Christmas from Ally and the Aussie tribe.'

'We trained together,' explained Beryl. 'Then Ally got a job in Brisbane. They wanted nurses in Australia at that time.'

'Weren't you tempted?'

'Yes, I wanted to go, but it would have been difficult because Mum needed me then.'

She continued uncertainly.

'I used to read my cards again and again on Christmas Day.' Selecting a card, she laid it flat down on the coffee table. 'I'd put them on the table like this, and read the messages aloud to pretend my friends were speaking to me.' She became sheepish. 'Sometimes we'd have a get together, and sometimes, well… we got blotto."

'You got blotto,' corrected Jim.

She compressed her lips and nodded. 'Yes, and how sad was that?' Her cheeks were wet, and she shook a little as she closed up to him. 'But this is the happiest Christmas I can remember, and the love in church took me to somewhere I once knew before loneliness came along.'

'He gently palmed away the wetness. 'And you know what? I'm almost happy as well.'

She laughed and shook him by the shoulders. 'Oh! You lovely miserable old moaner, let's have you into that bedroom pronto!'

11. Together

Jim reasoned it was unlikely that the, *'Our World Our Business'* campaigners would receive any more attacks in the immediate future, but he worried that the media would continue to probe the megaphone girl about Strummy's murder. Seasoned presenters chasing emotional credit points could easily push her over the top, which wouldn't go down well with mature viewers, and could in turn have a negative effect on the mission. She had to be thoroughly briefed if the mission and her campaign were to support each other, so he was pleased to receive a prompt reply to his email.

Dear Mr Kettle.

Thank you for contacting me. I will never be able to thank you enough for saving me from injury or death during that horrible attack in the Chantcel Restaurant, and I welcome the opportunity to thank you and your brave friends personally for trying to save Strummy.

I also heard your broadcast on Brian and Beverley's Breakfast Show which is another reason I would be pleased to meet you and your team.

So grateful.

Emma Dowty.

They met in their usual hotel lounge venue, where Emma described how Strummy's passion for the natural world had led him to study ecology and conservation, which later spurred him on towards environmental campaigning.

'I first met him after he had taken a year out from university to work with overseas groups who were protecting endangered species and their habitats. What he saw fired him up so much, that he could think of nothing more important than protecting the natural environment, which pushed him to do something about it, rather than just going for qualifications.'

'Where did you meet him?' asked Madge.

'We first met on a boat tour of the Great Barrier Reef while I was on holiday with my cousin in Australia. At the time he had been assisting with the rescue of injured Koala bears during those dreadful wild fires on the East coast, but he needed to earn some money, and found temporary work as a guide on one of the tours. He couldn't hide his frustration that so little had been done to protect the reef over so many years. I shared his frustration of course, but he could speak with authority because of his considerable knowledge. Anyway, we met a few times during my holiday, and got together to form our campaign once we had both returned home. Chantcel Square was our first public demonstration.' Her voice quavered. 'He was a wonderful person.'

Madge rose to comfort her, but Emma palmed her back.

'No, sorry, I'm upset, but keep asking me questions.'

'What about the thugs who killed him?'

'They deny it of course, and the one that Jim captured managed to get away.'

Jim stopped short of an expletive. The police weren't daft enough to just let that happen, and with

Strummy's DNA on the club they had all the evidence they needed. The whole episode stank of high level connivance, but he kept quiet to avoid more distress to Emma.

'How about those who were injured?'

'The four in hospital should be released soon, but one has a brain injury which affects his balance. I visit them weekly and meet their relatives, but we've heard nothing about the investigation since Christmas, even though the police keep telling us it's a priority.'

'Dammit!' exclaimed Jim. 'We should have met before your demonstration.'

'Why?' Emma was puzzled.

'Because you are young and well informed. Your campaign will have a huge emotional sway with the public, and the powerful interests responsible for damaging our planet will see you as a much greater threat than any number of impartial experts.'

'But that's what we wanted.'

'And that's almost certainly why you were attacked.'

'We knew we could be in danger, because Strummy had worked in countries where villagers who were trying to protect their forests were attacked by paid gangs. But we had been planning the demonstration for ages; nothing would have stopped Strummy from going ahead with it.'

'Well, perhaps not, but I wish we had met before you marched onto that square. Right now, it's important for you to know what our mission is all about, so we can combine forces and work together.'

Jim described how the co-operative lifestyle of Torrosus Viridis had been the incentive for the launch of a worldwide mission, and how success in calming the trouble in Miser Terrace had led to the decision to introduce Sapiens Carduus, or 'Wise Thistle' soup into the borough as the first step towards achieving it.'

'All this may seem far-fetched,' he continued, 'And you might have doubts about the rights and wrongs of such a mission, but we can think of no other way to prevent our species from perpetuating a never-ending cycle of cruelty and death upon each other, and the natural world.'

'Put simply,' added Ben, 'We concluded that it's everyone for themselves unless souped.'

'So, you don't believe that persuasion will ever stop wars or damage to our planet?'

Jim answered. 'Maybe it will, but persuasion hasn't worked yet, and how long have we got?'

'Not long I suppose,' Emma sighed morosely. 'And countries always put their interests first, so something must be done quickly or it will be too late.'

Madge laid her tablet on the table for Emma to view the Rabbits and Hares conflict. 'It's not pleasant viewing,' she warned, 'but you'll see the difference the thistle pills made. Even now it's hardly hugs and kisses, but they are talking to each other.'

Emma was clearly disturbed by what she saw, but expressed admiration.

'I so admire your courage for recording it all, and it explains why there's less litter in our street, and why Mum and Dad keep on about our neighbours being friendlier.'

Ben raised a cautionary finger.

'But bear in mind that Miser Terrace is only a tiny country. Billions of people will have to become very nice before the whole world is saved. Remember Emma, even thistles have limitations.'

Madge tweaked his ear as she sought Emma's confidence. 'We want to keep our mission hush-hush for as long as possible so we can sell lots of soup before its contents stir up controversy. We've been lucky so far and if the soup really takes on, it will be harder for the big interests to start lobbying against us.'

'By which time,' added Ben, 'the borough will be nicely souped up and ready for your campaign.'

'Yes of course.' Emma was enthusiastic. ' That should make both of our campaigns more effective.' She turned to Jim. 'You were right Jim. Now I wish we had met before going to Chantcel Square, but please don't feel bad about Strummy's death. I can't say for sure, but I still think he was too fired up to cancel our demonstration.'

She crossed her heart. 'I promise not to mention your soup or mission to anyone, and I'll be really careful at interviews because it doesn't take much to get me upset since Strummy was killed.' She paused to think. 'We don't have soup at home, but If had some, do you think it would help to calm me down before I go on the radio or TV?'

'It should help, but you've good reason to be upset, so speak as you feel. Just try not to blow your top.'

'It was wonderful when you blew your top on the breakfast show.'

'Possibly, but once is enough. I have our soup, although it doesn't prevent me from getting angry.'

Emma nodded as she cast her thoughts back.

'Strummy got angry because so many know about the damage we are causing. The news is always on about it, but politicians are too scared to risk losing votes by doing what needs to be done.' Her voice changed pitch. 'We can't go on like this forever, but they just let it happen and ruin the world for us!' She emphasised 'us' while jabbing a finger energetically into her chest, then registered acute embarrassment and apologised.

'Oh, I'm so sorry. You didn't need a tirade like that from me.' She covered her face in her hands. 'That was so rude, and you've heard it all before.'

Jim shrugged. 'You're just being yourself, and saying how it is, and yes, we've heard it all before. Mostly it's wrapped up in doomsday bundles before being dumped onto the scrapheap.' He looked pointedly at the familiar rivulets of rain on the lounge window. 'And we don't need experts to tell us what's happening. Any thickhead can see the weather's gone bonkers, and half our birds have already chirruped their last chirrup.' He felt like a father lecturing a child he would never have, and unsure how to continue, paused for a moment while Emma filled the space.

'So, the politicians have to do something about it.'

Ben pointedly cleared his throat, and lowering his glasses, announced he was an eminent politician.

'I certainly don't intend to: 'do something about it,' young lady, unless you can say what I'm supposed to do.'

Madge groaned.

'Not again!' He keeps coming it on with his, 'Clever Dick pretend stuff. just ignore him, Emma.'

But Emma was intrigued, and replied.

'We want you to stop building industrial estates, airports, and roads all over the countryside, and killing wildlife and insects with pesticides and destroying their habitat. And that's just for a start.'

'So, you don't want jobs?'

'Not those type of jobs, and we won't have them anyway, when you bring in all this advanced technology and robots.'

'Well if you weren't breeding like rabbits, there wouldn't be these problems would there?'

'So why don't you stop paying us to have babies then?'

'Because I'm a politician and not a masochist young lady.'

She sighed with acceptance.

'I suppose it all comes down to that. But will people ever consider other living things before having more and more of themselves?'

'Putting it that way is hardly likely to get you any support.'

'That's what it's all about though isn't it?' She dipped her head. 'Anyway, I won't have a baby.'

She shuffled through her shoulder bag and produced something akin to a small camera.

'Strummy said this was his baby.' She smiled. 'It saved me from the pain of childbirth I suppose.'

She laid it on the table. 'It's a camera and keypad for children, and can be linked to a database of products which are either good or bad for the environment. He made it to encourage children to protect the world of their future.'

'How far did he get with it?' asked Jim.

'He found a company to produce it, but they dropped out at the last minute and wouldn't say why.'

Ben came in again.

'I can guess why. Children have power these days. If you were a big meat mogul, how would you like children screaming at you for burning down rainforests for intensive cattle breeding?'

'Yes, that's why he made it. Strummy wanted children to put pressure on businesses to get on the good list, because they'd have to take notice of children.'

Jim pressed the top button and took a picture of his cheese waffle.' 'I like the idea.'

'I did wonder if it could be developed to fit in with your mission?' asked Emma

Jim sensed her buzz of anticipation, because the camera would be Strummy's heritage, but he was wary of raising false hope. 'It's worth a try. The boffins in Fortunatus Viridis are building up a database and it might link in with that.'

'It would be wonderful if they could use it.'

He raised his voice above the rattle of hailstones on the windows. 'I can't promise anything Emma, but right now our planet could use some child-power.'

12 Blue Skies

New Year progressed through a saturated January, and stormy March into a steamy April. America was getting stroppy with Russia for trying hack into their security systems. China had commandeered some islands in the Pacific that weren't really hers, and once again, India and Pakistan were making horrid noises at each other. So, the big national gangs were taking off their gloves for fresh disputes, while religious conflict, power struggles, and border disputes continued to stir up death, starvation and cluster bombs in the Middle East, and an assortment of other countries.

Jim inflated the globe so he could position the what's and where's of current worldwide events. Not much had changed since he had been popping off those who were trying to pop him off, and he wondered if the global death toll had overtaken the global birth rate. Apparently not, so the international arms trade would continue to profit, providing the pool of belligerents could be sustained.

All this was a big come-down since the Christmas revelation of something like judgement existing in dark matter. He naively thought that it should have been the cause of jubilation or at least earnest discussion, but all had remained quiet on the belief front. Perhaps even more time was needed for science to achieve credibility.

He patted the globe, and telling it to cheer up, left the flat for the distribution agency.

The agency was roughly a mile from the flat, and absorbed in his gloomy musings, he hadn't noticed the strength of the sun until he crossed over the steaming yard to the manager's office.

'All the vans are out,' reported the manager. 'We've two larger vehicles being tarted up in the spray shop, but we need more, and I'm looking to rent a bigger yard.'

'So new customers are pouring in?'

'Yes, and by the thousand. We're getting bigger orders from the existing ones, especially for the original flavour, and customers are telling us that the original flavour containers are better for pot plants, because there's not so much coloured lettering to scrape off.'

He pointed to some sharp upward curves on his sales graphs. 'We've got two big buyers here.'

His finger rested on the first curve. This is Burnbush Hospital Catering Service and the other...' He smiled and dropped his finger onto the second curve. 'That's our second delivery to the Parliamentary Catering Service. So, how's that for good targeting?'

'Bull's eye!' agreed Jim. 'Just the customers we need.'

The manager thought of something else. 'More and more customers are saying that the soup is doing them good, and we've had reports of improved prisoner behaviour from the two prisons up North?'

'I was hoping for that. What are they saying?'

'They've had a big drop in trouble, and staff assaults since our soup came on the menu. I'm guessing that the Governors suspected that it could have been doctored. Anyway, they asked for the bumph from 'Food Standards,' and just to be sure, they sent samples for independent lab tests, which found nothing suspicious. Mind you, I'll be surprised if anything could make a difference to the nasty tykes they've got in Hitisham.'

'It could do. We're not sure yet, but the research team found evidence that Sapiens Cardus is more effective with more nastiness. So, we could be supplying prisons across the country.'

'Here's hoping then.' The manager crossed his fingers as Jim rose to leave. 'With luck, it'll soup some sense into Parliament as well!'

And as Jim walked back, someone was indeed having a very big effect on Parliament.

That someone was the Secretary of State for International Trade, who, and without notes or a hint of ambiguity, had unexpectedly announced his resignation to a hushed chamber.

It came as a complete surprise, and the opposition should have had a field day. But his speech of resignation was an earnest confession of guilt for successfully negotiating two Chinese multi-billion-pound heavy engineering contracts, which would guarantee thousands of jobs in the North.

'My success in negotiating these contracts,' he confessed, 'was not just a betrayal of my conscience, but a cowardly acceptance of our hypocritical industrial policies, which if continued, will blight the future of generations to come.'

He gave no further explanation, and bowing to the speaker, departed from the chamber which quickly erupted into the chatter of bewildered MP's.

It made no sense. He was respected as a highly competent minister by all sides of the house. A minister with an unimpaired track record of bringing business to the UK, and forging solid trade relationships across the world. Yet there he was, denouncing himself for boosting jobs and securing long term prospects for engineering companies.

Plenty of colourful speculation fluttered between MPs and journalists, but nothing remotely scandalous could be dragged up. So, it had to be assumed that his resignation was entirely consistent with an honest belief that current industrial policies were heading towards ecological disaster, and that he could no longer bear the hypocrisy of continuing as a minister.

Shortly afterwards on *Brian and Beverley's Bright and Breezy Breakfast Show* he admitted that a desire for ambition and money, had overridden his conscience in persuading him to go for a ministerial position. But his success in negotiating lucrative deals for British business, regardless of ethical considerations, were overcome by guilt, and the brutal attack on the *Our world Our Business* Campaigners, and killing of Strummy became the catalyst for his resignation.

'And that attack,' he added, 'came as no surprise.'

'Came as no surprise?' queried Brian.

'Of course. Why should it come as a surprise? Powerful commercial interests are bound to see them as a threat because they are young and attractive to the media. My own life is also in danger because n I am also of interest to the media.'

'Because of your resignation?'

'Yes, because I have aligned myself with the increasing concern being expressed about our damaging industrial policies.'

'And you genuinely feel that your life is in danger?'

'Certainly I do, but at last I don't have to endure the torment of being a coward and a liar by perpetuating a system which is destroying so much of the natural world, and ultimately many of us.'

'Do you know of other MP's who are thinking the same way?'

'Yes, but I'm certainly not going to name them.'

'But how can we possibly change our industrial policies without losing thousands of jobs?'

'I wish I could give you a quick-fix answer to that, but I doubt if anyone has a quick-fix answer now. It's too late for quick-fix answers.'

'So what can be done, or should I say 'how' can it be done?'

'Yes, 'how' can it be done?' is the big question. There's more than enough blather about 'what' should be done.'

'Very well,' probed Beverley, 'then tell us how it can be done. You must have thought about it.'

The ex-minister shed what remained of his formality in a heartfelt sigh directed at the ceiling.

'You can be very sure I've thought about it. I've thought about it day and night, and have only one suggestion.'

He shook his head in apparent disbelief at what he was about to suggest, then registered panic.

'No, no, forget I said that.'

'You can't stop now!' chorused Brian and Bev.

'No please it was a just a …'

'You have to tell us.'

Brian and Bev shared anxious glances while emotional credit points hung in the balance.

'I'm really going to regret this.'

'Then you must go on,' urged Brian.

'I don't wish to.'

'You can't let our viewers down now,' chided Bev.

'They won't like it.'

'Try them.'

'Very well.' The ex-minister fidgeted on his chair amid contradictory signs of embarrassment and suppressed mirth.

'We have to have a national debate about moving towards sustainability and then…'

'Yes? Yes?' The camera closed up.

'You are making this very difficult.'

'But please go on,' urged Bev.

'Followed by a National Referendum of course!'

The interview ended in bursts of laughter.

'Well, that's really shot my reputation.'

'He smoothed his suit and wiped his eyes. 'Still, there must be some hope if we can find humour along the road to oblivion.'

The following week, it was the Shadow Secretary of State for Business and Industry, who was facing the commons in confessional mode, while giving similar reasons for his resignation.

'Sincerity,' he concluded, 'must be at the heart of political representation, and in the light of the minister's resignation it would be duplicitous of me to continue.'

Lowering his notes, he straightened up and turned to both benches.

'I put it to this house that tackling the damage we are doing to the earth is so fundamental to the future of all of us, that we now have to cast aside party politics.'

A new Secretary, and a new Shadow Secretary of State for International Trade were hurriedly appointed with enhanced briefs for tackling climate change, and it wasn't long before an overweight figure would be shuffling across the central lobby to prompt for a change of mood in the second chamber.

The overweight figure was wealthy financier and veteran peer Lord Gannon, who, after soup and a snooze in the Peers' Dining room, shuffled to his seat and addressed his fellow peers.

His speech was to be the culmination of a lifetime of astute negotiations, and profiting from the unexpected. But high finance, and deals in fancy restaurants had lost their allure. Something else had always been trying to get out, but a million here and a million there had stifled the urge for a career change. Now at the age of eighty-four it was reflection time, and his reflections weren't giving him much pleasure.

After all, what had he really achieved? Money? Yes. Power? Yes. A big house, a private jet, helicopter and yacht? Yes. A knighthood? Yes... and very nice too, but somehow even that missed the nub. Like everything else, it was mostly about money. He hadn't found a cure for cancer, or solved the mysteries of space and time, and his investments into short use clothing production were still poisoning rivers in the Far East.

None of this used to bother him, but a few weeks ago he had picked up that fledgling house martin from the patio of his mansion and hadn't been the same since. It should have been well outside his sphere of interest, yet he viewed it with wonder. Nearly weightless, but with enough attitude to peck at his thumb and poo in his hand, this tiny creature would soon be self-navigating all the way to Africa.

The gardener returned it to its nest, and once down the ladder, remarked: 'We can say we're clever when we can make something like that.' But to his shame, Lord Gannon knew the small bird would soon be flying into the Africa of his pesticide control investments. So what to do? If moral judgement did indeed exist in dark matter, then he was on a short lease, and had better start making amends very quickly.

Rising before his fellow peers, he opened a magazine that he had taken into the house, and read: *'The growth of free market economies in an increasingly populous world has, in recent years, led to a massive acceleration of international infrastructure and industrial activity, which, under globalisation, has led to an unprecedented rush to acquire raw materials, regardless of the ecological and atmospheric damage done to the fabric of the earth.'*

He raised the magazine.

'My lords, This 'Green Globe' magazine has been in my home library since 1980. So should we be surprised at the amount of damage that has been done to the earth in the years since that frontispiece was written?'

He pointed to a small greenish-yellow bird featured on the front cover.

'Has anyone seen one of these recently?' A ripple of head shaking confirmed a majority of no's.

'No, and neither have I. It's a yellowhammer, and clouds of them used to fly out of hedgerows when most of us wore short pants.'

He opened the magazine, and turned it round to show the illustration of a giant panda spread across the centre pages.

'These were in grave danger way back when this photograph was taken. A doting auntie gave my grandson a plastic one this Christmas. It's at least five feet tall, morbidly obese, speaks American slang, and is unrecyclable.'

He leaned forward.

'I've seen them in department store windows. They're on the internet and would have come over in their thousands on container ships from China.' He waved the magazine for emphasis. 'Just one example of the sort of garbage waiting to be jammed into bins and thrown into ditches a couple of weeks after Christmas, yet it's something we applaud as international trade!'

'Yet over there,' He turned and pointed the magazine accusingly in the direction of the Commons, 'they could only muster thirty members for the recent debate on climate change, and that, despite the ministerial resignations.'

A tone of contriteness entered his voice.

'My Lords, I have benefitted more than most in this race for economic growth, so am one of many who have unwittingly led us further along the path to a global wasteland. Successive generations will never forgive us for knowingly presiding over the destruction of their natural heritage, and I for one will try to make amends for it.'

He raised the magazine in one hand as if taking an oath.

'I therefore pledge before this house that I will devote all my remaining wealth to the cause of environmental protection, and the promotion of a way of life to sustain it.'

He allowed time for a few grunts of approval to subside.

'Be under no illusion my lords. The challenge we face is formidable, but as a nation we are unsurpassed in overcoming formidable challenges. So, given our history and mature democracy, I can think of no other country better placed to lead the world out of this environmental madness.'

Outside in Parliament Square, and drifting into the chamber over an uncertain spattering of 'Hear-Hear's,' a chorus of sixth form students sang 'Here Comes the Sun' with doomsday inspired lyrics.

13. Conundrum.

The temperatures achieved in mid-April were the hottest since records began, and in the confines of the High Street, facemasks were now commonplace. Having been slated for inadequate drainage, the borough council was now being slated for traffic hold ups while construction work was in progress to improve run-off capacity. Respiratory ailments, especially among children, had accelerated the process of obtaining planning permission for first time homes on the green belt, and as Big Mabel put it, 'About bloody time too!'

Jim leaned forward with his hands on the windowsill, and looked along the High Street towards the sound of a siren. This time it was the fire engine zigzagging towards him through the chaos of traffic below, and belching black fumes from a vertical exhaust pipe, a dumper truck mounted the pavement by Ali's store to give the fire engine clearance. Faces screwed up, a line of pedestrians squeezed into the entrance until the truck moved on, then, after some confused joggling, returned to the crowded pavement and their intended destinations.

This was crazy. He was looking down on stress: traffic stress, driving stress, noise and fume stress, probably work stress, and much the same was being repeated across the nation in urbanised villages, market towns and crowded highways.

Flaps down and pushing out more fumes, an airbus whinnied overhead on its descent to the airport, and he watched it arc downwards and disappear behind the Ironside residential blocks before shaking his head at the absurdity of the scene. Was this really the lifestyle that everyone was striving for? He eased himself up from the window to check that the new air purifiers were switched on. They were the expensive fine filtration type, and made quite a difference, but the fumy smell persisted, and would probably do so until the old street entrance door had been replaced and re-sealed.

Away from the urban sprawls, moorland and forest fires were a constant worry, and rivers, including many that had flooded only weeks before, were draining rapidly since developments and intensive agriculture had reduced the permeability of so many marshy areas. Now muddy streams and lifeless channels, they were being tramped over by curious visitors and metal detectorists seeking relics from the past. Seasonal weather could no longer be expected. Billions of tons of water sucked from the earth during a month of heat were likely to be returned in a week, or even days of ferocious downpours, and European weather patterns were just as worrying. The melting of the Greenland ice fields continued apace and permafrost softening in northern latitudes was already causing wobbly settlements.

Not so far away in Parliament, the arguments raged. Compared with many countries, Britain hadn't done too badly in curbing emissions, but the action demanded by *'Our World Our Business'* and similar campaigns would create mayhem should an attempt be made to impose them. Even so, it didn't prevent many MP's fishing for media popularity by fawning over young campaigners after paying lip service to the experts for years. Yet, as they emerged from the shade of their debating chambers, it was abundantly clear that no amount of party-political jabber would prevent the sun from behaving like the sun. So, bit by bit, party politics were reluctantly cast aside as MP's confronted the enormity of the problem.

Jim spoke to the globe. 'Well, what do think of it so far Globe?'

It buzzed back an obscenity as the phone rang.

It was Adelita.

'Jim? We may need a video meeting soon, but now I give the bare bones, and send everyone an email. Are you hearing talk about our soup?'

'There's a rumour that it might be responsible for pleasantness spreading through the borough.'

'So good results with you, and I phone to tell you that the Butkre Government are subsidising Sapiens Carduus farming to encourage well-being and social harmony as part of their: 'Building a Better Nation' programme. They make no secret about it, so you may get, how I say - a grilling on your UBC.'

'Thanks for the warning Adelita, I'll prepare for hostility. Social harmony doesn't always make for good business here.'

She laughed. 'You give me a very 'Jim' comment, but just keep selling the soup, you are doing wonderfully well. I also phone to tell you that we are extending our range of healthy eatables to include biscuits and cereals. We will be starting with a cereal, and linking with *Conbran* because they have spare production capacity and a worldwide distribution network.'

'Will we be selling it here?'

'You'll have a consignment soon, but first we want to extend sales into Europe, and *Conbran* will do the marketing there.' Something else came to her. 'Oh, and if you get accused about selling mind changing soup, we are one hundred percent squeaky clean now. *Conbran* has its products tested by all importing countries, and they told us that the thistles remove a lot of bad things we take in from modern foodstuffs.'

'So they make us nice by giving us a good flush out then?'

'Yes, if you must put it that way Jim, but keep up the good work, and I finish with an idiom because production is going 'bananas' here.'

He returned the phone as Beryl arrived from her shift with a copy of the 'Sunday Truth'.

She laid it on the table and pointed to the headline, which shouted: *'Doped Britain?'*

The introduction claimed that Britain was acquiring a taste for a brand of soup which could have mind-changing properties, and it went on to repeat the concerns voiced by many behavioural experts and religious leaders. Jim noticed that the headline ended with a question mark which left room for doubt, but on first reading, his customers could be misled into thinking that thistle soup was good for wild raves in warehouses.

The main report described the 'Building a Better Nation' programme in Butkre, and that the new government had re-introduced Sapiens Carduus or Wise Thistle farming to reduce drug crime and promote social harmony. It went on to explain that thistles had long been common fare in parts of Latin America, and were thought to encourage stable communities where they were consumed.

In considering the effects of the soup in Britain, the report included speculation that it may have contributed to the reduction of violence and anti-social behaviour, and a rise in voluntary support groups and community activities.

So, regardless of the misleading headline, it was a relief to Jim that the main body of the report was well balanced. All he could do was await further developments.

'We'd better start practicing answers to the questions you'll be getting on the *Breakfast Show*,' advised Beryl.

He reluctantly agreed. 'I suppose so. I was hoping to keep a low profile after my first appearance, but this could be the end of anonymity for me. 'The Truth' is being careful because it knows we can afford a top litigation team. But I'm not keen to go on that show again.'

'You'd be good on it. You were really good on the last one.'

'I nearly swore. Anyway, there's so much happening right now that the media will be in a tizzy on what to shout about first. With the big climate debate coming up I doubt if our soup will be top of the agenda.'

He folded the paper as an image of Bishop Pocklington flashed before him. Surely it was about time he started making a fuss about the soup?'

And at that moment, soup was very high on Bishop Pocklington's agenda. Church attendances in the diocese had risen considerably during the year, and that was well before the ridiculous claim of judgement existing in dark matter was made. It would of course be wonderful if he could attribute the larger congregations to the performance of his clergy, but having attended many services, he had long since discarded that as the reason. Services had lacked punch in the years since Hell had been downplayed, and he wasn't aware of any inspiring new initiatives. Yet, along with the rising numbers of new churchgoers had come fresh energy, and demands for less ambiguity in matters of morality. Conversations with fellow bishops had also revealed similar trends in their dioceses.

This was welcome of course, but it was also perplexing, and only while enjoying the afterglow of his lunchtime Merlot and settling down with 'The Truth', did he link the doped soup report to the unaccountable spread of pleasantness in the locality, and fewer syringes and condoms littering the churchyard?

Doped soup! He should have thought of it before. It may even have found its way into church food banks, and goodness - some of his clergy might even be consuming it!

Perhaps the lawlessness in Butkre could justify such an extreme measure, but this was social engineering of the worst kind. In a nation with so many finely graded services catering to our emotional needs, it was surely an affront to debase our natural humanity with artificial pleasantness. Something had to be done, and done quickly. This was a mass assault on our very being, and had to be challenged.

He half ran the short distance from the diocesan office to St Mary's Church to clear his head and seek out any suspicious containers that might be in the food bank.

Dust was in the air, and brushes were rattling in the pews as he hurried towards the food bank unknowingly followed by a dishevelled man who swerved past the surprised cleaners, and dropped to his knees with his hands pressed together in supplication.

It was abundantly clear that the man had not rushed into the church for quiet communion with God.

'I make confession Please! Please!' He looked frantically around. 'I make confession before soon I am killed!'

'But you are safe in church.'

'No, I soon be killed, then no chance of heaven.'

With drugged soup steaming in his head, a rushed confession was the last thing the bishop wanted. But here was someone in torment; someone in urgent need of counselling.

'You are perfectly safe here.'

The man shook his head vigorously. 'No, I soon be killed, maybe outside. But please I confess to you now!'

The bishop ushered him into the privacy of the vestry and attempted a sensitive listening stance.

The man again dropped to his knees. 'I confess now to killing the boy, Strummy.

'Strummy? You mean the young man in the protest march?'

'Yes, I now confess before I am silenced.'

'But you must tell the police before I can absolve you.'

'Then maybe I lose chance for penance, and go to Hell.'

'But Strummy was killed weeks ago. Why have you only just confessed?'

'Because now there is certain judgement in dark matter.'

'You mean what the scientists have said?'

'Oh yes.'

The bishop cursed. He was only half way through setting down his position on the 'Judgment in Dark Matter' nonsense, and here was somebody who had the brass neck to burst into his church in hope of getting absolution in it. But the man was distraught. There was no way he could be made to understand the rights and wrongs of making a confession.

'I try running to the police before they kill me.' He clasped his hands together, 'But please-please you give me absolution?'

The tension built up as the bishop juggled his ethical duty against the frantic pleading of the stranger before him and, with the stress of trying to reconcile one with the other, he dipped his head to relieve the growing tightness of his clerical collar. It could have been a nod, and he was instantly rewarded with hugs and kisses.'

'I am blessing you! Yes, I bless you!' The man opened the vestry door, and peeking warily into the church, rushed out promising to say he was: 'Sorry like anything.' to Strummy.

Alone in the vestry, the bishop broodily reflected on the episode. He had just been blessed and kissed by a killer for promising absolution in dark matter. Admittedly, communication hadn't been good, but it was hard to believe he had allowed himself to be led into that one. Directing a fervent apology at the roof, he left the vestry to resume his search for soup, and had just reached into the food bank to grasp a suspicious looking container, when he was interrupted by two sharp cracks from the churchyard. Soon he was being led by a cleaner to the rubbish disposal area, which had already attracted some witnesses to the incident. Propped against a discarded notice board, and seemingly at peace with whatever afterlife he had entered, his latest penitent was ready for the last rights; a call to the police, and collection. One of the witnesses described the victim being chased into the churchyard by two hoody's and being shot. Looking down at the man he said, 'It was just like watching 'Splat' on *Cool view.'* Turning to the bishop he added: 'Missed the music though.'

Later in the diocesan office, the bishop wrote his statement. National media had received photos of him with police at the crime scene, and had reported a witness claiming that the man had run into the church to seek help. Enquires to the diocesan office about events in the church were firmly directed to the police, who declined to say what took place, or whether the incident was linked to the earlier killing of Strummy.

So now, months later, Strummy's killing was back in the headlines fuelling renewed public incredulity that none of the perpetrators had been brought to justice. Suspicions of a big- money cover- up operation were rife, and the Home Office was forced to deny that it had underfunded the investigation in hope that the public would lose interest. But a mystery whistle blower had encouraged the media to seek links between the killing of the man in the churchyard and a big foreign meat importer.

A few days later, the Home Office announced that the decoding of a mobile phone had provided important leads to the police, and some arrests were made. Two Interpol red notices were issued for wanted persons in Argentina, and it was soon confirmed that the victim in the churchyard was indeed Strummy's killer. A columnist in the 'Truth' wrote: '*The whole episode stinks of corporate corruption and Home Office duplicity,'* and the ensuing public outrage boosted the environmental protests.

It was against this background that the Prime Minister was clearing the cabinet table after a meeting to consider government policy towards environmental damage and climate change. She usually went down to the basement kitchen to do the washing up after cabinet meetings. Domestic staff were employed for such duties, but she had always done the washing up at home, and enjoyed returning the cutlery back to shiny order in cupboards and shelves. It was a deeply satisfying process, since it was devoid of emotion, and entirely logical. Logic was her thing, and ministers were made sharply aware of it if they tried an emotional angle to influence policy matters.

As a working farmer's daughter, cause and effect governed all that she did, because farming was logical as were the causes of environmental damage. She had seen the decline of wildlife since she was young, and was aware that she had also contributed to it by helping her parents intensify production with insecticides and artificial fertilizers on their small acreage. For the same reason she had tearfully reached up to smooth the muzzle of Greg, their big plough horse for the last time.

'Does he really have to go?' she had howled at her parents.

Well, yes. he did have to go. Plough horses and Lord Gannon's yellowhammers had been squeezed from balance sheets well before their farm went bankrupt. There was no way Greg, or even the new tractor, could satisfy demands coming from the approaching horizons of red bricks, and she hated how quickly her locality was changing. Yet it was all so logical, and surprise, surprise, now the planet was behaving logically for the same reasons.

She had been satisfied with the outcome of the cabinet meeting. Beforehand, she had insisted that everyone had to consider what could be done to curb environmental damage, regardless of political consequences or social knock- on effects.

'This has to be a ruthlessly logical exercise,' she had emphasised. 'There will be more than enough emotion when Parliament is forced to confront what has to be done.'

At the end of the meeting, the Minister without Portfolio had asked, 'Permission to be emotional, Prime Minister.'

'Be careful Eric.' she had warned.

'I now despair of ever seeing a Tree Creeper in our garden.'

'You must have faith, Eric,' she smiled. 'Creepers are still flourishing in Parliament.'

Stowing the dishcloths into the washing machine, she went upstairs from the basement with a clear head, and began to prepare for her address to Parliament the following morning.

Banners printed with images of Strummy lined the route as she was chauffeured the short distance to Parliament. In the period before her election as PM she had shared the demonstrators' suspicions about the circumstances relating to Strummy's killing, and this had prompted her demand for a thorough enquiry into the home Office handling of it. But the demonstrations were unhelpful. All the shouts and banner waving would lather Strummy flavoured emotion over a programme of environmental debates just when calmness and impartiality were essential. She thought quickly, then screwed up her speech and phoned the Parliamentary Secretary as a matter of urgency.

Just in time for her arrival in the chamber, a large video screen had been erected above the Speaker's chair, and the sound was being adjusted to counteract the chanting outside.

Apologising for any house protocols that may have been contravened, she explained her last-minute decision to show the latest episode of the *Our Earth* documentary in lieu of her introduction, and asked the security staff to allow some campaigners into the public gallery.

The chanting quickly abated during the viewing of the documentary, and at its conclusion, all was quiet and thoughtful, outside and in the chamber.

The Prime Minister summarised.

'Perhaps that was a repeat viewing for some, but it is still a forceful reminder about the changing conditions on the surface of the earth in the years since it has been mapped from space. Make of it what you will. I can add no more, except to say that our planet doesn't respond to opinion or party politics when you are deciding how, or even whether, to take action to prevent further damage.'

The Speaker introduced an MP who was well known for his belief that climate change was largely caused by natural events.

'Prime Minister, I am sure you are aware of many respected experts who have convincing evidence that climate changes are primarily caused by natural events that occur every so often, and that human activity has very little to do with it.'

The Prime Minister allowed time for the conflicting mutterings to settle down.

'I'm aware of differing expert opinions, and they must all be represented in the coming debates. We are, however, considering the totality of environmental damage, including our intensive acquisition of earth's natural resources, all of which contribute to climate change. Rational discussion using all the evidence available is the only way to reach a consensus on the actions required to reverse it.'

She raised a finger for emphasis. 'Implementing those decisions will of course be our most daunting task.' She fixed her eyes firmly on the Speaker. 'If, as a nation, we decide to take the lead in addressing worldwide environmental decline, then we will have taken the first tentative steps towards a decision which could, and I stress could, be the most significant decision taken in the history of this Parliament. It will not be easy.'

And it wasn't easy.

The RH Wendy Watts had been delegated by the Prime Minister to lead a cross party group of MPs who were willing to research and agree on proposals to put before Parliament. She had been chosen because of her management skills, and having a flair for putting complex issues into plain language.

It was agreed to use the Parliamentary Terrace as a venue for the forums, and part of it had been extended and canopied over to accommodate an IT suite and additional seating. Over drinks and snacks, groups were formed to deal with aspects of environmental concern.

The Thames was at high tide by the time everyone had settled down, and the undersides of the shades swirled with patches of reflected light bouncing back from the wake of a passing cruiser.

'I bet we won't be meeting here in a few years' time,' said the MP for Cliff all.

'Because it will be flooded you mean?'

'Exactly, I doubt if the Thames Barrier will cope with it.'

'Don't worry. Once you tell Jack and his brood that they'll have to give up meat, and holiday breaks in Ibiza, most of us won't be here anyway.'

The speaker returned some rude gestures directed towards them from the cruiser.

'Stop being such a couple of miseries,' chided the group leader. 'We have to be positive. Soon you will be laying the foundations for a better world, so drink up and enjoy the sun. Tomorrow we'll be up to our ears in research.'

In the following days, experts were consulted, IT assistants printed out requested information, statistics were compared, learned papers were dozed over, and Wendy Watts went from group to group assessing progress and summarising what had been agreed.

Much of the research was shared between the groups, because it soon became clear that the root causes of environmental damage were usually interlinked. Finding a solution in one area would invariably lead to problems elsewhere.

As one group leader put it:

'It's no good nit-picking. The world is hurting all over. It's got to be the whole caboodle if we're going to stop the damage.'

Questions were raised about the viability of many commonly voiced solutions. The clean energy group doubted the ability of the motor industry to replace or convert about thirty million UK vehicles to battery power by 2050. The environmental group was concerned about the scale of excavations required to extract sufficient rare minerals for the billions of vehicles worldwide, and general concern was voiced about the practicality of battery powered heavy road vehicles and ocean transport.

'Science will find the answers,' stated the optimistic MP for Fumehaven. 'In the meantime we just cut down on car journeys.'

'How?'

'A mileage tax.'

'That's unfair, I live in the country.'

'Then get on your bike, it will be good for you.'

'It might go some way to solving the obesity crisis,' suggested the group leader.

'I've got the answer,' declared the MP from Parched. 'Instead of workers having to go to jobs, we bring jobs to the workers. We could manage with bikes then.'

'Tell me more.'

'Well, my daughter does a forty-mile return drive to work at Woodgone Childrens Nursery, and there's a Woodgone Nursery teacher who has to drive forty miles to work at Parched Nursery. That's eighty miles driving between them. If they swopped jobs they could walk. There must be thousands who could swop jobs and save millions of road miles.'

'They might really enjoy being where they work, and wouldn't want to change.'

'Fair enough. If that's their choice, they pay more mileage tax.'

The Group Leader agreed, 'Very well, let's propose it, and see how it goes down in Parliament.'

The MP for Drymarsh laid both hands pointedly over a sheaf of papers.

'Like most of us, I'm finding it hard to get straight answers. It's taken three evenings of family time working through this load of faff to find out that methane released from shale gas bore holes might create more greenhouse gas than coal. We can't base our proposals on 'might's.

The MP for Floodstream was also confused.

He read from a sheet of foolscap. 'It says here that there are nine million dogs in the UK, and carnivorous pets have a big environmental impact.' He waved the foolscap. 'And listen to this. 'Owning a medium size dog can create more pollution than an SUV.'

'Get lost!' objected the MP for Searising. 'I'm not getting rid of 'Maggots' for anyone!' Imagine the outcry against a dog ban!'

'We're not here to kowtow to public pressure,' cautioned Wendy Watts. 'If pets cause pollution they must be included in our proposals.'

'Then I propose that all dogs go vegetarian,' suggested the MP for Fumehaven.

'Very well,' conceded the MP for Searising. 'You can tell that to Maggots!'

Wendy Watts added the proposal to her tablet.

The leader of the biodiversity group held up a list, but he wasn't happy.

'These are our proposals for increasing biodiversity. To be frank it wasn't too difficult to agree on them. It would mean reducing pesticides, increasing set-aside for wild areas, preserving marshy areas to stop river floods, and growing more trees. Some of it is being done anyway. Trouble is we stopped producing enough food for ourselves ages ago, so we'll end up having to import even more from countries who don't give a worm for biodiversity.'

The leader of the waterways group was also pessimistic.

'We signed up to the Law of the Sea convention to protect fish stocks and stop pollution, but I've stopped going down to Outflow Bay for a family swim now.

He turned to Wendy Watts who had been tapping into her tablet. 'Sorry for sounding so negative, but we're not getting very far are we?'

She looked up briefly. 'On the contrary, we are clarifying the issues.'

The thoughtful MP from Burntmoor had been quietly writing while listening to the discussions, and now looked up from his note pad.

'It all comes down to billions of us damaging the earth by being selfish in millions of different ways, so I propose we put everything in the same basket and go sustainable.' He raised a forefinger and waited for attention before adding cautiously. 'And perhaps this is the moment to stop skirting round the great big elephant in our room.'

All went quiet. Only the swish of the Thames and rustle of papers could be heard until the MP from Drypond tentatively broached the silence. 'You mean the elephant that dare not speak its name in Parliament?'

'The MP from Burntmoor stood up. 'Yes that's elephant I mean, and I think we all know the elephant I am referring to.' He tapped the table for attention, and raised both arms like a conductor. 'So on the count of three let us see if we can sum up enough courage to speak its name. Are you ready?'

He conducted each count: 'One, two, and three…'

'Population.'

It was repeated in hushed voices.

Silence again descended over the Terrace as the awful implications of the word struck home.

'So what do you propose?' asked Wendy Watts.

'Let's just forget it.' suggested the MP from Flood.

'If it's a problem it cannot be ignored, and we must propose a solution,' demanded Wendy Watts.

'OK, so we phase out family allowance,' suggested the MP from Damphouse, 'and if my daughter finds out who proposed it, I'll be one less mouth to feed.'

Wendy Watts glanced around for any last-minute objections, and jotted the proposal into her tablet.

14. One Way or Another.

Brian Bowls, the MP for Surgingsea was nearing the end of his heartfelt objection to the proposed phasing out of child benefit.

'If allowed to reach their full potential, human beings will continue to give life to barren lands and even go on to conquer and populate hostile worlds in space, because there is no limit to our ingenuity. The aberrations of the past, and indeed most of the current hostilities, have to be regarded within the context of history. The human journey has barely started, and the wonders we have already achieved provide only a glimpse of the wonders we can achieve. So, it is surely disturbing that some of us have promoted a belief that we need to curb the growth of future generations in a fruitless attempt to solve the environmental changes that have occurred naturally throughout Earth's history. And how ludicrous to propose limiting the numbers of the very generations who will find the solutions to such events.

Even China has abandoned its abhorrent one child policy, so can you imagine the distress this proposal must be causing to so many new mothers, and mothers-to-be, across this nation? There is more than enough room for human beings on this planet, and it is beholden on us fellow humans to nurture and care for those who are borne. My appeal to this house is to reject this appalling proposal and ensure that our national resources are allocated fairly, so that subsequent generations can continue to flourish and grow.'

Wendy Watts waited until the barrage of approval quietened down before answering.

'And that is why Mr Speaker, if indeed we are to nurture and care for those who are borne, our prime duty should be to protect the Earth. The Earth we call Mother, the Earth that has nurtured and trusted us through the ages to be the custodians of all living things. Yes, all living things, from the microscopic to the forests and oceans. Living things are in our being. Without them we die, and by destroying them, we destroy ourselves.'

She was conscious of becoming emotional, and it was strange. Like the Prime Minister, emotion wasn't her thing. So often it distorted truth, and fostered injustice, yet something inside her was pushing her into the mood of the moment, and it was emotion.

'How can it be otherwise? Yet as I speak, our earth is being rendered sterile by brute force and greed. Yes, human brute force and greed. We have seen it from space. We have seen the scars, the burning forests, the creeping deserts, the bleeding ice-caps and massive urban sprawling. If Mother Earth had a human face it would be screaming in agony. We know about toxic waterways, polluted oceans, melting glaciers, over-fishing and the un-precedented decline of species, from whales to worms. We have known, and been warned of this for years, yet we are so self-centred and arrogant that we refuse to act on the evidence of our eyes.'

She waved an accusing finger round the chamber.

'Yet only a few of us in this house have had the honesty and courage to denounce the evil pretence of squaring ruthless industrialization with environmental care.'

The list of proposals shook in her hand and her eyes blazed with anger.

'Yes, and how I long to experience the joy of motherhood, and being able to share the beauty of the natural world with a child of my own.'

Her voice cracked as she turned to the RH Brian Bowls.

'But not now! Not in a teeming world of conflict, pillaging and trashed natural beauty. I couldn't be so cruel!'

She sat down to a mixture of hesitant grunting, and sounds of approval from a contingent of *'Our World our Business'* campaigners in the public gallery.

On the front bench the Prime Minister gave her verdict to the minister beside her.

'Emotional, but logical.'

It was decided that the proposal to phase out child benefit was so far reaching and potentially disruptive, that more consideration was needed before MPs ventured out to seek views in their constituencies.

As one MP remarked to his opposite number. 'We've been trying to outbid each other on this one for long enough. Now we're forced to confront our responsibilities.'

'Or our nemesis,' said the other. And it was in the informal meeting venues outside Parliament, that desperate, even mind-boggling alternatives to population control were explored.

Greg Binder, the MP for Floodwell, expressed his worries in the 'Damocles Sword' pub, just off Parliament Square.

'We've got more kids than adults in my constituency. I'd never get out alive if I supported a cut in child benefits.' He wryly acknowledged the wail of fire engines speeding over Westminster Bridge. 'I think a lot of us would prefer the world to go up in flames rather than phase out child benefits.'

'What's the alternative?' asked the Bankburst MP.

'How about a cull of the elderly? There's too many of them, and they're not much use. They also cost a lot to keep going. It might even be popular, because most of them are pleading to be helped on their way when life gets impossible, and I'll want the same.'

'It would save millions on pensions,' agreed the MP from Scorch. 'So, let's keep them going until they reach about eighty, with exceptions for those who can run a hundred yards or do twenty press-ups.'

The MP from Builtover disagreed. 'We can't get rid of the elderly. Most of them have money and houses. We need them as cash cows to prop up our health and care services.

The very small MP from Drypond offered a novel solution.

'We should fund research to make us smaller - let's say half size. For a start it would make me feel better, and we wouldn't have to keep building over the countryside, or importing so much, because there'd be enough land for our own farmers to feed us.'

The MP from Builtover was in favour.

'That's a good idea. It would solve the housing crisis, and it would be cheaper for small space rockets to take to us other planets so we could start all over again.'

'We'd need to watch out for dogs and eagles though.' warned the MP from Bankburst.

Lord Mellis summarised.

'Very well, it seems we are heading towards two choices. He raised a finger. 'We include these proposals,' He raised another finger. 'Or we phase out child benefit.' He waved both fingers. 'And that's what we'll get from the electorate.'

But well to the North, veteran MP Lord Averley was attracted to the prospect of living with less. He had read the draft proposals, and settling back with his third pint in the local pub, described the orchard and big barns which had been replaced by the canning factory.

'That's where we used to do our scrumping.' He held his glass towards the ring of security lights beyond the window. 'It earned me a stick across my hind quarters on a couple of occasions, but those days felt real.' He smiled in contemplation of times past. 'Grazed knees, cut hands and nettle stings were part of life. We were always running around doing things…not always what we should've been doing mind. But we weren't sitting in front of some video screen watching porn and garbage. Good or bad, we felt we were living. Not so many fatties then, either.'

'Careful Ron,' warned the constituency party secretary. 'You can't say things like that.'

'Well, it's true. Just look at your old school photographs; you won't see many fatties there. Okay, so I'm a bit podgy at seventy-five with a gammy knee, but nowadays it's all comfort eating.

He again levelled his tankard towards the canning factory. 'Still, can you blame them after grafting in there year after year? Maybe I'm just an old fart, but if all this growth is supposed to be making us happy, I don't see much of it. Living with less would be better all round. My old mate Lord Gannon is spending most of his fortune reviving village life. I think he's come up with the right idea.'

'What's he doing?'

'Getting it back to how it was before everything was taken over by the big money boys like himself. He's starting up sustainable villages. No online buying, just local stuff, and lots of re-cycling. It's all old hat, like church on Sunday; seasonal eating, and sing-songs in the pub.'

'There must be plenty of do's and don'ts.'

'Bound to be, but he's got plenty who want to live there. Wouldn't you like to ease up a bit?'

'I could do without the London commute.'

'There you are then.' He nodded at the pub clock.

'Look, it's nearly closing time and we're sweating like pigs. This is plain bloody stupid. We can't go on like this.' He took up the draft proposal leaflet. 'I'm going with this, if only for the grandkids.'

By late summer, the heat had become relentless, particularly in the South and East.

Wind turbines, both inland and offshore had done very little twirling, so fossil fuels and solar power had to make up the difference. The worst effects were in the cities, where closely packed buildings acted like storage heaters, and old air conditioning outflows pushed out warm air into the streets. Respiratory emergencies were compounded by increased airborne pollution as rail commuters took to their cars because of buckled rail lines, and many inner-city school pupils were required to stay at home.

Whatever the cause, serious global warming had arrived, and whether in the UK or Europe, those in the emergency services were dreading the next bright blue-sky day. Weather forecasters gloomily announced weekly doses of sunshine over red maps. Radio bulletins and posters stressed the urgency of checking fire alarms, and warned against placing glassware in the sun. Later, as water shortages became acute, residents were advised to put bricks in lavatory cisterns to save water on flushes, and where possible to avoid flushing single, or clear pees. Recycled plastic containers with lids and spouts were available at cost price to store wash water which could also be used for loo flushes and watering greenery. Special non-leak plugs for water storage in baths and shower trays were delivered to each household, and drinking water was supplied from street bowsers.

Life had become difficult, but with it had come some positives. Soup sales continued to do well, and were boosted locally by an enterprising restaurant owner. Madge and Ben saw the sign while filming in Spikewell. A large notice read: 'Cool down with our savoury iced soup,' and the owner explained that the idea came to him when someone requested an iced coffee. He put the soup in a freezer and it proved popular. Later he developed a sorbet version which was equally popular, so Jim informed the distribution agency, and the production team added the iced soup option to the labels.

The general spirit of neighbourliness which had been in evidence well before the heat wave, had fostered more voluntary groups, who, with the aid of a smart phone app, were able to pool their skills to help those who were badly affected, and in the climate of growing trust, offers of help were more readily accepted.

'I'm knackered!' announced Beryl on return from her latest shift. She flopped onto the sofa, and boosted upwards, Jim continued towards the sink where he poured her a glass of water.

She kissed him.

'Hope I don't stink, but we've never been so busy. Two of us had to come off the ward to do a stint in A&E. They've got stretchers down the corridor and the paramedics are just about zonked.' She smiled an exhausted smile. 'The atmosphere is great though. It's even better than when I came out of training. Everyone is saying the same.' She sniffed the air and pulled a face. 'But we've got that poo smell back again, and it's dreadful by the hospital roundabout.'

Jim found the air freshener.

'It's the water restrictions. There's probably not enough water to clear the drains.

He thought back to the way they cured a similar problem at one of his overseas army bases. 'We'll have to organise a synchronised flush along the high street, it might work.'

'Clever boy, I'll put it on the new neighbourhood web and suggest an evening flush just as the *Archers* finishes. If the smell goes we could have a street party to celebrate. She thought for a moment. 'I suppose neighbours often got together like that during the last war.'

And a week later on the high street, someone was indeed recalling what it was like for him during the war.

'Takes me back to my wartime days,' reminisced pensioner Dan.

It was only since the arrival of the water bowser that Dan had made the effort to cross the high street, where he was recognised by just one person in the synchronised flush party. A young man took his container and filled it from the bowser.

'This street was full of gaps where the bombs fell,' continued Dan. 'Just like my teeth.' He ran a finger over his remaining teeth and patted the youngster on the shoulder. 'It was tough, but we helped each other like this lad is helping me. Young or old we just did what had to be done.'

'It was the wartime spirit Dan.'

He gave a shaky smile and chose from a plate of cupcakes.

'Yes and you know what?' His hand trembled as he put a cake to his mouth. 'It feels a bit like it's coming back.'

He'd said his piece and hovered uncertainly by the bowser, knowing that age and appearance had impaired his ability for light conversation with a youngish crowd. The sense of isolation had returned by the time Madge and Ben were beside him with their video gear.

'Dan?' Madge smiled and introduced Ben. 'We're making a documentary about the borough, and would like you to take part in it?'

He felt the warmth of acknowledgement.

'I've got a rough old London voice. You wouldn't want to hear that would you?

'That's exactly what we do want to hear, Dan. We want you to tell your story in your rough old London voice.'

Dan's summary of a boys' life in the High Street during the blitz, and graphic description of a doodlebug taking out four houses where the supermarket now stood, engaged his audience for about ten minutes. He finished to a round of applause and a hug from Madge.

After more cupcakes and friendly chats, he joined the lad who was carrying his water container into the kitchen of his small terrace, then pulled out a 1940's dried banana crate from under the sink, and shuffled through his old 'Dinky Toys' and bits of 'Meccano', until he found a jagged piece of shrapnel which he gave to the lad.

'A piece of history for you lad. It was still warm when I picked it up from the Doodlebug Crater. We don't want something like that to happen again, now do we?'

Later, he moved his chair from the window to sit by the photo of Gwen, his wife. She had been buried in the chapel graveyard, and he often apologized to the photo for not paying her a visit, but he was no longer able to manage the grave, and didn't want to see how much it had deteriorated over the years. He kept shopping to a minimum because his gammy hip made walking uncomfortable, and his old drinking mates had stopped going to the pub since it had been taken over by young pissheads.

So he didn't get out much, and he didn't drink much. But now, the unopened half bottle of whisky beckoned to him from the corner cabinet, and taking it out, he shakily unscrewed the cap and closed up to Gwen's photo.

He'd been wanted again; he'd been applauded for being himself again, and he'd been hugged again. That glow would last over his declining years. To hell with the hangover, he'd let the tears and whisky wash away the loneliness… well, at least for a while.

15 Here We Go Again.

Once again Jim was on the celebrity couch facing Brian and Beverley on their breakfast show, and this time he was alone.

It was surprising it had taken so long. Over a month had gone by since the *Sunday Truth* had headlined: *Doped Britain?* and hundreds of gallons of soup would have been spooned into mouths across the borough since then. This wasn't going to be a laugh-a-second show, but a serious grilling. He had a fair idea what questions would be put to him, but didn't want to come across as a pushy sales representative. So, with that in mind, he rehearsed his answers with Beryl the evening before.

Brian picked up a container of 'Sapiens Carduus Original' soup which had been placed next to a copy of the *Sunday Truth* on the coffee table

'So Jim, as the UK representative and distributor, you must be aware of the controversy surrounding this soup.'

'You mean about it being mind-changing?'

'Exactly, and you must have looked into this?'

'Of course, and so have the Food Standards Agency. Sapiens Carduus thistles are traditional fare in the Eastern Regions of South America. They've been a healthy option on family menus for ages.

'To make people nice?'

'Yes, if you must put it that way, and good health should make you nice, or at least nicer. Anyway, they seem to be calming down some serious trouble in Butkre.'

'But if that regime is subsidising thistle eatables to get the population on their side, isn't that devious?'

'You mean their *Building a Better Nation* programme. They're trying to get things back to how they were before the drug gangs took over. What's wrong with that?'

'OK so that's Butkre, but it's not the UK. Don't you worry that you could be profiting by changing thousands; possibly millions of people away from their natural behaviour into being, well... nice?'

'Not really. I have that soup most days. Not feeling quite so bolshie hasn't bothered me.'

Brian put the container back on the coffee table, and Bev took over.

'So do you believe that the overall drop in crime is because of that soup?'

'I'd like to think so, but can't be sure. Maybe it's something to do with science claiming that judgement exists in dark matter.'

She narrowed her eyes.

'Correct me if I'm wrong Jim, but your soup is really part of a broader mission to soften up humanity to make the world a better place isn't it?'

'I'd like to plead guilty to that.'

'So, you disagree with Bishop Pocklington?'

She picked up the *Sunday Truth* from the coffee table.

'In here he says, and I quote: *'Morality is bestowed on us by God from the moment of birth. Distorting, or enhancing it with something dished out to us from containers is an affront to our humanity and our creator.'*

Jim shrugged. 'If that's what the bishop believes, fair enough, but humanity doesn't seem to be taking much notice of it.'

He was becoming irritated. The word 'humanity' hadn't given him a warm feeling for ages. It brought back the unspeakable smart phone video he he'd been bullied into watching at school. It brought back the visual evidence of prolonged executions he'd seen in conflict zones. And locally, it brought back the report of drunken football fans kicking the homeless man to death in the alley by the supermarket.

'How do you mean Jim?'

'If he thinks this world can be made better by doing it his way, I'm not going to argue with him.'

'But you disagree with him?'

'Not really. He's a great talker, and might be proven right for all I know. But teenage knifings are at record levels in this country; people are still being burnt alive in the Middle East, and there's a strong smell of poo, drifting along too many rivers in our once green and pleasant land… So, yes, I'm on a mission!'

He picked up the container from the coffee table. 'And, this seems to be helping whatever the bishop says.'

Bev cringed. That wouldn't go down well with the producer.

'I like Jim's soup,' confessed Brian later.

'Same here,' agreed Bev. 'Jim was right. I know it's made me more considerate, but honestly, I was only trying to be fair to the bishop.'

A few miles away, the Prime Minister completed the washing up, and turned off the radio. She didn't enjoy listening to the 'Brian and Beverley' show, but felt it was her a duty to endure it, if only to keep in tune with the general emotional climate. This time however, she appreciated the candour of the straight talking guest, who had bolstered her determination to ensure that transparency would be the main feature of her government, and with this in mind, she walked into the cabinet room to record her broadcast to the nation.

A wasp had strayed into the room and she trapped it against a window pane by using her drinking glass and a table mat.

'Too valuable to die,' she chided, and instructing the unsuccessful swatter to open the window for her to release the wasp, went on to deliver her broadcast without a trace of emotion.

'Tomorrow, Parliament will consider a range of proposals to decide whether or not the United Kingdom is prepared to lead the world by being the first nation to move towards a sustainable economy. The challenge is too far reaching for Parliament alone to decide. It has to be a truly democratic exercise, devoid of party politics and falsity. So, it is vital that every citizen plays their part in contributing to this decision. Parliamentary debates will be reported and summarized on dedicated radio and TV channels, and there will also be a government website with links to relevant research, and updates about the health of the global ecology.'

She smiled imperceptibly.

'And yes, there will be a national referendum which must be carried with a substantial majority, because this time we cannot risk ambiguity. So, it is vital that all of you are actively involved in the decision making process. I expect open debates and discussions to take place across the nation during the period of consultation, and Constituency MP's will also be seeking your reactions to the draft proposals.

She held up a small booklet. 'Every household will receive one of these bio-degradable draft proposal booklets, containing recommendations from a cross party group of MPs, who have been looking into ways to reverse environmental damage. The proposals will almost certainly cause controversy; even upset, but the choice is simple. We either take the necessary actions, or we do nothing. There is no middle way.' She lowered the booklet. 'If we choose to do nothing, life may be easier in the short term. But regardless of our feelings, it is worthwhile bearing in mind that the earth is entirely indifferent to our well-being, or even our survival.'

A week or so later, the MP for Builtover thoroughly familiarised himself with the referendum proposals, and taking a deep breath, drove into the controversial housing development on the outskirts of town to seek the views of his constituents.

'So let me get this right!'

The man on the doorstep waved a proposals booklet along his road of new-builds.

'I'm listening to the debates, and can't argue with these proposals, but they'll cause big problems for thousands. As a teacher I should still be able to manage if we decide to save the world, but many of my neighbours are employed in the clothing factory just down the road. The same factory imports cloth from the Far East where chemicals discharged from the dyeing process cause river pollution.'

He pointed to a proposal in his booklet. 'If the cloth is banned because of our eco trading policies they'll be out of jobs, and we're all mortgaged up to the eyebrows. There's no way they could cope without some sort of help, and that would be the same all over, surely?'

The MP was annoyed with himself for feeling apologetic. He had only been elected recently, and had been cursing the diffidence of Parliament for years. He didn't have to be sizzling on a doorstep, and had quite enough of trying skip round tricky questions, so he said what he thought.

'It should put pressure on the clothing industry to clean up its act. But you're right, that's just one of the knock-on effects we'll have to face up to if we go for sustainability.'

'I'm not blaming you personally,' said the teacher. 'But climate change should have been the biggest thing in politics well before I was popped into a cradle. Our school has doubled in size since I've moved here, and parking's a nightmare with all the four-by-fours.' He gave a quizzical smile. 'Still, some things have improved recently. I can't yet fathom, why so many first years have stopped turning up in nappies.' He changed tack. 'Okay, so I've got two sons, but they wouldn't be here now if I knew what sort of world they'd be going into. We moved here because teaching was becoming more like social work, and it was getting to be quite unpleasant where we lived.' He laughed ironically. Then I was told that just producing the materials for our house pushed about 2 tons of CO_2 into the atmosphere. 'So, here I am in a new estate built on green land and feeling guilty about it.'

He brushed his hand over a crack in the wall beneath the window.

'There's a bigger one round the back, and our neighbour has the same. These were built in a hurry when the area was saturated. Now that the ground has baked solid we've got settlement cracks. Our house insurance told us not to worry because they'll close up when it rains, and they'll probably say the same next summer.'

He gave a hollow laugh, and extended his hand.

'Anyhow, thanks for coming round. I'll support the proposals because I don't see any other way, but both of us know that we'll still frizzle here if other countries don't follow suit.'

The MP made to go next door, then did an about turn. What was the point of going further when he was too hot to think straight? He'd give the neighbours a miss.

About a hundred miles to the South, Gerry Binder, the MP for Beesless, was dreading knocking on doors in his constituency. The last time, his car had been badly scratched while he was canvassing in Herring Street. This time he'd hired a car, and was accompanied by a burly constituency team member with a box of proposal booklets ready to replace those which had almost certainly been ditched.

Intent on bracing himself for the reception he was about to receive, he failed to notice the small changes which made the street seem less menacing than on his last visit. The tiny front gardens were cleared of litter, and the scorched lawns showed evidence of care. Droopy flowers in painted soup containers dappled the window sills with splashes of colour, and the children weren't shouting quite so loudly as before. The lady even smiled as she opened the door.

'I know who you are! Just a mo…' She went back into the house and returned with the draft proposals booklet. 'You'll want to know what we think of these, won't you?'

Fearful of the likely response, he tensed up. 'Yes, and any ideas or suggestions you might have of course.'

'Well, we've been having street meetings, and there's still plenty of argy-bargy going on.'

He was surprised. 'Argy-bargy about these proposals?'

'Well, yes, they're important. Nowadays we have street meetings whenever anything important crops up. It's got more neighbourly than the last time you came. We think it's the soup that's been in the news recently, and most of us are buying it whatever that bishop says.' She jabbed at the booklet. 'Excuse my French, but you must have a load of plonkers in Parliament for holding this back for so long? We all knew about this at school, and Sir Tim Battersby has been banging on about it since I was doing cartwheels.' She shielded her eyes against the sun. 'And then you wait until were all sweating cobs before telling us what we should be doing to stop it.'

She leaned forward to touch his arm. 'Don't think I'm just getting at you, but it's bloody typical of you lot.'

It wasn't quite the reaction he had expected.

'So do you agree with the proposals?'

'Most of us do. We don't like them, but something's got to be done.'

'Even cutting down child benefit?'

'Well, it's you lot who've been paying us to have kids! My mum never got paid for having me, but the magazines and TV are forever cooing on and on about babies. Girls feel left out if they don't have kids, and I felt really sorry for my mate who got told she was selfish because she didn't want one.' Anyway, a lot of us got pregnant because babies made us feel we'd done something special, and because people were nicer to us. Now you're saying there's too many of us, and that's been bloody obvious for years!'

Hubby joined them.

'You couldn't make it up, and we get all this gump straight after the last referendum when you lot were banging on about producing more and more stuff. Our cat could run the country better!'

It was getting awkward, and Gerry struggled to find an answer.

'Alright, I agree that it's taken a long time, but this could be the biggest decision we're ever likely to take. We've got to avoid the uncertainty caused by the last referendum by making sure that everyone knows exactly what they are voting for.'

'And if we vote yes, the rest of the world will tell us to get stuffed.'

'They could, but that's their decision.'

'But they're causing most of the damage.'

'That shouldn't stop us from taking action.'

'So we're doing this for our kids… right?'

'Yes and our grandchildren.'

The husband waggled his proposals booklet at Gerry. 'And you reckon this will do the trick do you?'

Gerry shrugged… he'd had enough.

'I don't know. I only know that if we don't take action, it's chips, and if the millions of Mustafa's, Ivanov's, and Chucks in the world don't give a blink about the environment, then it's still chips. So you're right, the rest of the world might tell us to get stuffed, but stuffed or not, at least we will have tried.'

'Well, at least you're straight talking, I'll give you that.'

The water bowser arrived, and a clammy hand shake later, he returned to the car and back to the office. There was no need to knock on any more doors in Herring Street.

Roughly 4000 miles away from Herring Street, Dictator Demshi Jibang was also one of those who didn't give a blink about the natural environment, apart from its ability to keep him in power and exotic meat.

Mitataland occupied a large peninsula edged with mountainous highlands that swept down to a tropical plateau supporting a rich variety of fauna and flora. Beneath the wriggling micro life, an abundance of valuable minerals were ready to be grabbed by those willing to pay the best price, and much of the land was scarred by excavation. Mitataland had also been able to acquire some basic nuclear weaponry, in return for some favourable contracts negotiated by Demshi.

What remained of the jungle was simply a resource for wild animals to be shot by Demshi in his golden hunting carriage, and the rest was set aside for the caged breeding of rare creatures to be sold for outrageous prices as exotic meat.

The young Demshi was doted on by his mother. Nothing was too good for him, and his slightest desires were instantly satisfied. By contrast, his father really didn't want to be bothered with an offspring, and had elevated himself to God well before Demshi was old enough to be a nuisance. But too much exotic meat and sugary things had caused him to slither from his throne when he was quite young. Demshi had barely waited for the gasps of self-adoration to cease before having his father trolleyed into the disposal pit. He then arranged for the throne to be raised a few inches higher, and had his image embossed into the walls of the throne room before crowning himself God.

His rule was absolute. Even small infringements of his laws would result in the offender being forced to compete in the Saturday morning games tournament at the Central Stadium. Demshi's version of the Roman games was roundly condemned by humanitarian organisations, but concerns about rare mineral extraction contracts being awarded elsewhere were usually enough to stifle the outcries.

Anyone performing or listening to music could also expect unarmed combat with a hungry crocodile, or something like it, while Demshi waved his golden wand to conduct the crowd according to his mood. Music was unnerving to Demshi. It gave him all sorts of strange moods which didn't go well with screams. It even caused him to question his status as God, so it was banned in every corner of Mitataland, and he tried to avoid it whenever he went on a 'special' trip.

It was during an add-on extra to one of his special trips that he realised he had the means to raise his status way beyond the ability of most mortals, and it wouldn't be hard to do.

The add-on extra was to be an honoured guest at the annual military parade in Moscow's Red Square.

Taking his seat in the VIP enclosure, he inserted his ear plugs to block the sound of the military band and formed his plan of action as the column of nuclear artillery pieces passed before him.

He had similar artillery pieces in his defence force. Surely it wouldn't be too difficult to install the warhead of a nuclear shell under his throne, and fit it with a dedicated lock and golden button exclusively for his own use. If ever his time came, he certainly wasn't just going to slither ingloriously from his throne like his father. He would go out with a bang, and a big one at that.

So, the shell was installed beneath his throne under the cover of paid secrecy, and the skilled technicians who installed it were allowed a celebratory drink of 'Novichok' and carted off to the disposal pit straight afterwards.

What grand finale could be better than gazing adoringly at his own image, knowing that seconds later he would be in the centre of a blinding flash, having secured a place in history with no other gods left to replace him? He would become immortal… well sort of. It seemed an odd aspiration, but for someone who had indulged in the extremes of everything, how else was he to achieve the ultimate satisfaction?

Yet, and unknown to Demshi, the fate of millions, had already been sealed the moment he ordered three Rainbow Coated Marmosets to be uncaged into the wild to improve his chance of shooting just one, to be roasted in sugar for his delectation.

16. Talk Talk Talk.

Beryl had left for the evening shift, and Jim settled down to watch the first UBC National Referendum Debate in the Wikemill Union Bingo Hall near Leeds.

Immediately after the first question, the debate was cut short by loud rumblings and bangs overhead, then the hall blacked out. Robbed of light and amplification, the team sat ghostly and inaudible like a row of cardboard cutouts, while lesser bangs and rumblings continued outside the hall.

'I think we've just been told something.' announced the chairman once power had been restored, 'But for those viewers who have just tuned in, this is the first special edition of 'Talkback' on the subject of global warming, or perhaps I should say: 'global environmental damage.' He turned to Sir Tim Battersby, the well-respected naturalist and conservationist. 'So, before we were so rudely interrupted, our first question was: 'Are we too late to avoid Armageddon?' Are we too late Sir Tim?'

Sir Tim smiled briefly.

'Well, firstly I'm pleased we will be discussing global environmental damage. Global warming is a consequence of it, and probably the most immediate threat to us, but the two are inextricably linked, and the totality of damage we are causing to the living surface of our planet has never been greater. I doubt if anyone can say whether our activities will lead to our demise, but they have already led to the demise of many species, and unless we act quickly it will be a disaster for all us. '

'Will the referendum proposals halt the damage?'

'If they are practised worldwide, they should halt the damage, but repairing the damage could take much longer, perhaps several lifetimes. Environmental degradation is being inflicted over our planet at an alarming rate, and if the UK finds the courage to move towards sustainability, other nations will need to follow our example very quickly. There must be a be an international response.'

'Some hope of that!' exclaimed Brian Bowls, MP for Surgingsea. 'So, we stop having children, and curb economic growth so our competitors can ride roughshod over us. It would be lunacy!'

Cheers and whoops cut through the rumblings.

He continued. 'All this scaremongering about man made climate change is based on sheer presumption started ages ago by a by a few so-called experts. We need growth; we desperately need houses; modern infrastructure and transport. How else will future generations fulfil their aspirations and compete in a modern world? Of course, economic growth needs resources, but all this hype about trashing forests and murdering orang-utans has snowballed into a fashionable topic for tree hugging campaigners who seem intent on taking us back to the dark ages.'

More cheers and whoops followed.

The presenter invited Emma Dowty to reply, while back in the flat, Jim spoke anxiously to the TV screen: 'Don't lose your rag Emma!'

She half-smiled at Brian Bowls, and spoke thoughtfully, almost apologetically.

'I wouldn't be campaigning against the damage being done to our beautiful planet if I honestly believed what you believe.' She leaned forward to face him squarely. 'I don't doubt your sincerity, and have tried to understand your reasoning, but please don't assume that my generation would wish to go for wealth at the cost of trashing our natural heritage. Neither does it stem my anger towards big business, and politicians who claim that they can square massive economic growth with environmental protection.'

Brian Bowls smiled back. 'Then allow me to assuage your anger by a detailed discussion of the facts young lady.'

She felt the heat rising, but this was the patronising way Ben mimed his: 'Well known politician' response to her, and she summoned up enough self-constraint to remain polite.

'And may I suggest that you try to assuage the anger of our few remaining tigers by a detailed discussion of your facts with them.'

Back in the flat Jim gave her clenched fist approval, and the Chairman quickly turned to the economist.

'So could we support the current population if we took the big step into sustainable living?'

The economist was doubtful.

'It would be difficult to achieve. During the period of transition our standard of living would fall dramatically, and it would be hard to satisfy the food and accommodation needs of our rising population without some radical re-thinking. In any case, the change from continuous growth to sustainability would have to be managed very carefully if we are to avoid pockets of deprivation.'

'What's new!' shouted someone in the audience, 'You're already in a pocket of deprivation!'

The economist acknowledged the interruption.

'Yes, and if we decide to live sustainably, any wealth we make will have to be shared more equitably than it is now.'

'Bring it on!' yelled someone else.'

'Wouldn't that be attempting the impossible?' asked the chairman.

'Not if all the proposals were accepted. Indeed, it might herald a new age of innovation, as solutions to less money centred lifestyles are sought.'

'The London City boys wouldn't like that!' came another voice from the audience.

'Probably not,' conceded the economist, 'and I could be out of a job as well, but sustainability is the only ethical alternative to our rush for growth.' He looked warily across to Bishop Pocklington. 'Although I mustn't stray into your territory, Bishop.'

The bishop raised his proposals booklet then slid it disdainfully to one side.

'But this is not an ethical way to go. The spurious contention that we must discourage growth, and particularly population growth to save the planet, is more likely to lead us along the sinister road towards eugenics.'

He started to rise, but remembering he was not in church, settled for a half-way posture with his hands flat down on the conference table.

'Are loving couples really to be denied the greatest gift that God can bestow? And am I as a representative of God expected to endorse such a practice? Children are a blessing, and should be encouraged. There is no evidence that this world cannot support a growing population, and given international goodwill, millions of acres of less fertile land could be cultivated without the need for intensive pest control or de-foresting. Indeed, population growth will encourage communities to seek new ways of increasing food production, which, if managed carefully, would in turn benefit wildlife as well. So enough of all this 'people are a scourge' nonsense. Each generation inherits and builds on the knowledge and ingenuity of previous generations. Therein lays the key to solving the problems that confront humanity.'

'What went wrong then?' enquired a familiar voice.

'Allow me to answer.' The bishop leaned forward.

'Our obsession with global ecology has replaced our concern for moral ecology. Neither of those ecologies will be restored by destroying the potential genius of the yet unborn.'

He sat down to whoops and vigorous nods of approval from Brian Bowls, while back in the flat, Jim swore at the television. The bishop was impressive, but worse than that, his sincerity shone through every word. It was clear that he passionately believed what he said, and this was a forum where passion and emotion ruled OK.'

Sir Tim remained impartial.

'We are considering environmental damage, and the solutions to it will have to be environmentally effective. This can only be achieved by a full understanding of the causes and dealing with them. Overwhelmingly, the evidence points to the causes being the direct result of human activity, and as an environmentalist it is impossible for me to arrive at any other conclusion. Plastic pollution, massive deforestation, and poisoning of waterways by sewage and chemicals are not caused by global weather cycles. If we decide in favour of the referendum proposals, we may have to make changes in the light of experience, but sound reasoning must be the deciding factor.'

He spoke to the bishop:

'Moral ecology may be sensed by some creatures, but it is a concept I am ill equipped to discuss, so I will leave that to you, Bishop.'

He received some applause, but without the whoops.

Felicity Brownley; a popular author, was clearly upset by the proposals.

'I agree that we have to tackle climate change or environmental damage - call it what you wish, but like it or not we all have feelings, and my daughter is expecting her first child. If we accept these proposals, she could be subjected to envy and hateful comments because these proposals are clearly intended to discourage childbirth. Of course, I want to stop climate change for all our sakes, but this is grotesque beyond words!'

Amid more whoops and applause, the chairman again turned to Emma.

'Yet you decided it would be cruel to bring a child of your own into the world?'

'Yes.'

'Because of your concern for the planet?'

'Yes, but it's not just because of the planet. It's also because we never stop finding ways of being horrible to each other.'

'Yet, the Home Office reports a decrease in crime, and the recent: 'Social Society Survey' reports a huge rise in co-operative neighbourhood activities throughout the country. Life seems to be improving here at least.'

Dan Dent; comedian, and sponsor of youth boxing clubs, stepped in before Emma could reply.

'And the answer to that is in my hands!'

He brandished a container of Sapiens Carduus Original before the audience, and flicked his eyebrows up and down like Groucho Marx.

'Allow me to 'souprise' you. This, my friends, will save the world with its 'souperb' qualities.' He shook the container provocatively at the bishop. 'But first it must be presented to the 'Soupreme' Court of judgment.'

Back in the flat, Jim held his head in despair as the container was passed along the table to the bishop, who merely glanced at it before responding.

'I have already stated my position about substances that change, or are purported to change our state of mind. Am I expected to challenge our creator by inferring that his conception of humankind was so flawed, that we need to regularly consume this sort of thing if we are to live together in harmony? We have all been born with an innate sense of right and wrong. The dilemmas and even hostilities we have to confront can only be solved by applying our natural humanity.'

He half stood again with the container centrally placed on the table between his hands.

'When I cradle a newly christened baby, I am cradling hope.'

He stood up, and to rising amusement cradled and rocked the soup container.

'I am now cradling deceit.'

The hall resounded to cheers and whoops while Jim aimed a string of expletives at the floor. If only the bishop wasn't so persuasive. Again, he worried that Emma might blow her top, but she maintained her calm.

'It would make me so happy to give you my very own bundle of joy to cradle and bless, but not in the cruel human world you speak of so fondly.'

She pointed to herself. 'I would be asking you to cradle my selfishness.'

His nod conveyed understanding. 'Perhaps so, but Emma, your baby could be the answer to the cruel world you are so concerned about.' He passed her a gentle smile. 'A baby was the answer once you know.'

The Cheers and whoops took some time to fade, then a single voice broke through.

'Stick to the soup Emma. We can't wait that long!'

She agreed, and again turned to the bishop. 'When you say, 'humanity' I want to get a warm feeling, but now I can't however hard I try. 'I think of crowd thuggery; wars, religious hate, and the face of my grandma after being scammed of her savings. Maybe the soup won't create the humanity that perhaps we both wish for, but our neighbourhood is friendlier now, and if the rest of the world can be made happier by soup, then please give it a chance.'

Dan jumped in again.

'I'm on your side Bishop. They've all gone soupy where I live. I've had to replace the boxing rings with snooker tables because the local lads aren't so keen to punch each other now. If it carries on like this we won't be able to fight wars because no one will want to join the army!'

The presenter again turned to Emma.

'And do you really believe the soup is helping to reduce crime in Britain?'

'Yes I do, but how can I be sure? It could be what the scientists are saying about judgment being in dark matter. My granddad says his church gets quite full now. He says it's more like it was when he was a boy.'

The bishop was not persuaded.

'If the rise in church attendance is due to thistle soup or unlikely destinations in space, I simply have to accept it, but I cannot endorse it. Church attendance has always been subject to change, and usually due to local factors. I suggest that the increased assistance given to poor families by our local authority has had more to do with improving our neighbourhood than far-fetched theories about dark matter, or strange soup.'

'That's a load of old kelter!' rang out another shout from the back of the hall.

'That's right!' echoed another voice. 'There's nothing new about thistle soup stopping trouble.'

'Do you have thistle soup where you live?' enquired the presenter.

'Always have, and thistle muffins. It all came down from the monks.'

'And do you grow the thistles?'

'Of course - have done for ages. There's thousands in the old monastery gardens. It's only outsider's cause trouble in Kindleberry.'

He shouted back to the first voice. 'Where did you get yours?'

'From you in Kindleberry years ago. We grow our own now - they help with the druggies.'

'Bishop?' The presenter sought a response.'

'Interesting.' The bishop examined the label on the container, but remained po-faced.

Dan Dent raised a warning finger. 'Resist the temptation, Bishop. Consume that and you could become Souperfluous.

Above them, the rumblings started increased in volume,, then merged into an airborne coughing fit followed by a percussive double thunderclap and more sustained rumblings. The hall blacked out again, and the unamplified voice of the presenter requested that everyone stayed seated to avoid tripping over in the dark. This time the power took longer to restore, so those wanting toilets moved carefully into the gangways guided by the lights of their mobile phones. The lights bunched together at the bottom of one gangway, and after some uncertainty dispersed upwards and along the front of the stage to the centre aisle.

'Blocked loos,' someone was heard to say.

'Smells like it,' confirmed another.

'We've been flooded,' said another.

Back in the flat, Jim called Madge. 'They've stopped broadcasting the referendum debate because of flooding. I'm wondering if the UBC could be persuaded to transmit your documentary to them. It would be good for the bishop to see it.'

Madge was confident. 'We're ahead of you Jim. We got onto them as soon as the programme was stopped. The hall has the gear to show it, and their tech team can set it up. I'm just hoping they can prune my commentary.'

Uncertainty spread through the audience as word spread that the hall was surrounded by water, and this was soon confirmed when the deputy chief fire officer trudged onto the stage in waterproofs to explain the situation.

'Well, you've chosen the right weather for your debate. I've not experienced a storm like this during twenty years in the fire service and it's still bucketing down. There's no way I can predict when it will be safe to go outside, so I strongly advise you to stay where you are. We've got dinghies available for those urgently needing assistance, and our emergency contact number is in the booking office. But only genuine emergencies please! Sorry to shout it out, but we are up to here with all the idiot calls we get these days.' He levelled a hand above his head to show how far up he was with idiot calls. 'Run off from the hills is causing the flooding, but it's been made worse by some pear-head who parked his caravan on a slope by the river bank. It slid down the slope into the river and dammed up the bridge outside town, so you're in the middle of the lake it's created. We're tackling it, and once we've managed to untangle the caravan from the bridge, the water level should drop quickly, but you could be here for a few hours yet.'

He made to leave, and then raised an arm to draw back attention.

'Oh, and if your car is at the bottom of the park, don't try starting it until the water's well beneath the underside, otherwise you could hydraulic the engine…OK?'

He was quickly replaced by the manageress who pointed to the rear of the hall.

'Sorry about this Duckies, but you can only use the two top toilets. There's hand cream and paper towels just outside the doors, and please only use the flush for number twos. We're brewing up tea, and there's snacks in the foyer, but don't all come at once because it's just me and the caretaker.'

The chairman thanked her and added: 'Well, 'we're all in this together,' as they say, and will just have to amuse ourselves for a while. We do, however, have the option of watching the first episode of a documentary which claims to demonstrate the calming effects of Sapiens Carduus pills during hostilities in a small Latin American state. It's scheduled to be shown on UBC's 'Troubled Earth' series, so this will be a first viewing. I have been asked to warn you that it does contain disturbing scenes and some strong language, but there's a large seating area in the foyer for those who would prefer to leave the auditorium during the showing.'

Some worried car owners made their way into the entrance lobby. Illuminated by the interior lights, a wide assortment of plastic litter bobbed on the ripples of the temporary lake as it lapped around the bottom steps. Beyond, was just watery blackness, and unable to see how deeply their vehicles were immersed, the car owners turned away from the lobby window and made for the seating area in the foyer, or returned to the auditorium.

Brian Bowls had pointedly walked up the centre aisle into the foyer, and was already chatting animatedly with a largish group who had circled their seats round him. Meanwhile, the remainder of the debating team had remained on stage, and were engaged in conversations with the audience until the documentary was ready for screening. Temporary editing had blacked out some of the sequences, but those that remained were sufficiently disturbing to be received in profound silence, and casual conversation seemed inappropriate for some time after the viewing.

'Perhaps,' suggested the presenter, 'we need time for reflection, and I would be grateful for any opinions I can take back to the production team.'

The auditorium seats provided uncomfortable sleeping, and the roving rumblings warned of another almighty bang and power blackout at any time. So, sleep was edgy, and mixed with leg stretching in the aisles and trips to the foyer.

Emma Dowty also had difficulty sleeping, and in the early light of dawn found herself at the lobby window in company with the bishop. It was clear that the fire service had succeeded in removing the caravan from the bridge, because the water had drained away leaving a coating of sludge and plastic litter over the car park. They watched as a car carefully reversed from the bottom parking row and turned onto the high street. Every so often it stopped for the driver to remove an obstruction, and was soon joined by more vehicles arriving from the feeder roads serving the housing developments flanking both sides of the valley.

'And would you say those developments contributed to the flooding?' enquired the bishop.

'Yes I would,' affirmed Emma.

'Hmm.' The bishop was non-committal as they watched the thickening line of traffic snake upwards to the neck of the valley.

'And do you think they shouldn't be there?'

'I wish they didn't have to be there, but many more houses will have to be built, and many more after that.'

'Because of our growing population?'

'Yes.'

The bishop said 'Hmm' again, and without further comment, went on to ask if she knew any in the team who made the documentary?'

'Yes, I met them after they had done their best to save Strummy when he was attacked by those thugs.'

The bishop was still peeved at being led into giving absolution to the killer.

'And you must know that his killer was in turn killed in St Mary's churchyard while I was in attendance.'

Emma replied impassively. 'Yes, I did know about it. I just hope that those who organised the attack are caught.'

'I quite understand.' The bishop replied sympathetically, and was about to say more when Brian Bowls broke away from his group and placed himself between them.

'So, you saw the documentary then bishop?' He added modicum of rebuke.

'I did. It was courageous and thought provoking. You should have seen it.'

The bishop appeared to dismiss Brian Bowls as a minor irritation, and quickly angled his gaze back to Emma.

'Yes, it was certainly thought provoking.' He repeated it quietly, as if to himself.

She was pleased. 'I thought you would think of it as publicity for the soup.'

'Not at all, it was too graphic and straightforward for that.' He smiled. 'Even bishops have the ability to accept reasoned argument you know?'

'Then have you been persuaded?'

'No, I haven't been persuaded.' It was a firm reply. 'Only by dropping my beliefs could I agree to save the world by employing a medium to change our nature.'

Emma broke into a spasm of laughter. 'I'm so sorry bishop; I thought you said 'briefs.''

'Goodness!' The bishop shared her laughter. 'If only it was that easy. And how wonderful if I could save the world by dropping my, er… briefs.'

'It surprised Emma that she had begun to like Bishop Pocklington. His sincerity was beyond question, and he clearly had a sense of humour. It's just that his church didn't seem to be doing a very good job of making us kinder and more caring… well, not many of us anyway.'

They returned to the window, and steeped in their separate musings, watched a large limousine break away from the High Street traffic and draw up outside the entrance. A chauffeur entered the lobby and into the bishop's thoughts.

'Ah, my transport.' A further thought occurred to him. 'Do you have transport arranged, Emma?'

'I'm catching the next train to London.'

'Then why not be chauffeured home with Sir Tim Battersby and Felicity Brownley. We have spare seats.'

He formed his hands into an arch and tapped his chin. 'Perhaps,' he added, ' we could all benefit from further discussion.'

17. Deep Water.

Assigned to washing up duty and shopping while Beryl did the vacuum cleaning, Jim collected the grocery bag from the sink cupboard, and started down to the end door. As he drew level with the inflatable globe, he noticed it had lost its healthy shimmer and was soft when he patted it. Beryl must have tidied up the pump, so he removed the bung and blew into the air tube until he was dizzy. The globe gave a tired old man wheeze as he replaced the bung.

'That's both of us out of condition, globe,' he remarked, 'but don't lose hope, we're holding a referendum, and it's mostly about you.' He slowly spun the globe until his finger hovered over the UK.

By mid-September, unreasonable quantities of rain had once again confirmed the predictions of previously flooded homeowners. This time however, the local authorities escaped blame for inadequate preparation. Most of them did their best with assistance from local volunteers, but it was clear they would lack the resources and manpower to cope with the changing weather patterns and floods to come.

And sea levels wouldn't have to rise much more before sections of the North Norfolk coastline were swallowed. Teetering on the edge of a crumbling cliff, a holiday camp, plus several coastal hamlets would soon be tumbling onto the beach. Given the worst predictions, wide raggedy inlets would soon be roughing up the smooth bum of East Anglia, and a huge chunk of Lincolnshire could be under the waves.

Emotional debates continued to rage across the country as the full implications of the referendum proposals were thrashed out. But despite the shouts and groans, it all came down to logic. The choice was simple: act effectively or do nothing, and opinion had hardened in favour of the proposals.

It was surprising. Undoubtedly, a vote for the proposals would transform the current population into a flock of sacrificial lambs for coming generations, and fury was directed at politicians and previous governments for doing nothing for so long.

But, as one minister had retorted on a recent 'Talkback' debate; 'It's a democracy, so don't push all the blame onto MP's. If you weren't so stupid and self-centred, you wouldn't have elected a bunch of idiots like us to represent you!'

Gradually, a sense of purpose began to flourish across the country, which took on elements of national pride. After all, Britain had once lorded over much of the world. Surely, now was the time to revive national confidence by uniting in a heroic stand against environmental destruction, and the international indifference that went with it. It really seemed as if tiny Britain might recapture some of its past glory by forging the way into a genuinely sustainable world.

He patted the globe, and an indecisive buzz followed him to the end door as the phone rang.

Beryl picked it up, and beckoned him back while talking animatedly to the caller. An alpaca gown was mentioned, and the conversation continued light heartedly for a few minutes, until Beryl said: 'He's here beside me, Adelita. I'll pass you over...Byeeee.'

'Jim, it is so good to talk to your Beryl,' began Adelita. 'We must meet when we heal the world, and everyone is happy…Yes?'

'I can't wait Adelita. Can we meet at your place please?'

'We let Beryl decide. But now I sound you out.' She repeated it: 'Sound you out.' Is that a correct idiom?'

'Yes, you mean, 'obtain my opinion.''

'Good, I keep practising my idioms for better understanding in English you see. So, are things still hunky-dory with you both?'

'It's all Bob's your uncle here Adelita, and are you still, cock-a-hoop with life in Fortunatus?'

'It's going swimmingly Jim.' She even managed a snobby accent. 'But now I get down to brass tacks.'

'I'm all ears.'

'Very well, then pin them back. Sales are soaring and *Conbran* are making inroads into Europe, but some of the corporations are putting fake information on social media and tailoring it to damage our future markets.'

'Like, 'Soup makes you soft,' that sort of thing?'

'Yes, and messages like that can hit the button with macho regimes, which is why we're starting up thistle co-operatives wherever we can.'

'Sounds like a corking plan.'

'But touch wood on that Jim, our trial co-operatives in Nigeria and Kenya are a big success, and although it's early days yet, the Ethiopian Government has agreed to several co-operatives in the highlands.'

'Bingo!' Ethiopia needs to get nicer, but surely we'd create trouble by planting our thistles everywhere?'

'Not at all, our research team discovered they grow in most countries, although their potency can vary.'

He spoke quietly to the globe. 'We don't know the half of it Globe, but setting up co-operatives will be pricey.'

Adelita spoke through the buzz. "I didn't quite hear that Jim; another idiom?"

'I was just questioning my globe. It's telling me that start up programmes will cost an arm and a leg.'

'Your globe is Bob-on. Start-ups won't generate income for us, so maybe not such a big pay rise this year Jim.'

'I doubt if the team will mind. Anyway, if we go towards sustainability, most of this lovely money you are giving us will be taxed to the hilt to pay for essential services.'

'And quite right too, just like here in Fortunatus.'

'But we're not living in beautiful Fortunatus. I suppose you re feeding your blue birds on the patio.'

'No, it's a clear starry sky right now, and my birds are roosting. But did I hear envy?'

'You did. It's raining cats and dogs here.'

'Goodness! I hope not, and clearly an idiom worth remembering, but now I need your opinion about judgment in dark matter.'

'It makes sense to me, but our Bishop says it's all codswallop.'

She said, 'Hmm' followed by a thoughtful silence, then: 'Did I ever mention Lorrenzo Illani our composer and philosopher?'

'You mean the person who wrote the tune that made Respectico change his ways?'

'Yes, so I give you the lowdown on Lorrenzo, okay?'

'Fire away, Adelita.'

'Lorrenzo is how you say, usually down in the dumps, and depressing to be with, but his music is strange and beautiful. He came here to play me a tune, and said it was for my ears only.'

'Was it good?'

There was another silence while she searched for words.

'I can't describe the effect; it was so powerful.' She corrected herself. 'No… it was so wonderful. He only let me hear part of it, but it filled me with love and sadness. Snatches still come, but I only get tiny snatches.'

'Was it on a CD?'

'Yes, which he destroyed by folding it in half. I was shocked, because I so much wanted to hear it again, but he said that it would be heard again only when the time was right. I thought he had composed the piece, but he insisted it had come to him from dark matter, and refused to say how. Afterwards, he went on and on about slugs in his vegetable patch, and left with all my questions unanswered.'

Jim mentioned finding the dead jihadists at the base of the escarpment with their smart phones tuned to music, and Adelita pondered this for a moment.

'Strange, we seem to be getting a theme, and it could mean something. Meanwhile we wait for Lorrenzo's tune, so keep your ears to the ground Jim, and stay hunky-dory.'

Once again he continued to the rear door, and descended the steps onto a wet high street. It was lunchtime and still raining, but the traffic was moving freely and causing very little tyre spray because of the improved drainage. He been abstractedly watching an overweight man lolloping towards him in running shorts, and only took notice when the man slipped and flopped hard down onto the pavement. He ran to the man, and assisted by another helper, slid him across the pavement and propped him against the cake shop wall before hurrying back for Beryl and the first aid box.

The gasps for air had subsided into heavy breathing by the time Beryl had cleaned and bandaged a badly cut knee.

The man chastised himself.

'That was stupid, but I'm a fat slob and I've got to do something about it.'

Beryl spoke plainly. 'Well, even if you are overweight, don't overdo it.'

'But I only ran from the hospital roundabout.'

'Then do a fast walk next time. You won't lose weight by damaging yourself.'

He trembled with effort of pressing himself higher up the wall.

'Thanks for patching me up.'

Jim could see that the man was younger than he first appeared, and caught buzzes of distress.

'It's just that I've got to lose weight. I can't let the others down by not trying. We're supporting each other you see, and I'm the fattest.'

'Well good for you. It sounds as if you're in a weight watchers club.'

'It's more than that.' He avoided eye contact. 'They're helping me to face the world again.'

'Was it comfort eating?' asked Beryl.

'Yes, and more…' He seemed about to elaborate, then changed tack. 'But you've been great. Don't let me hold you up.'

His legs shook as he straightened up into a standing position, then his eyes rolled back, and he went limp. Jim grabbed him, and with Beryl's help dragged him to the street doorway of the flat, and lowered him onto the bottom entrance step.

Beryl hurried up to the top door. 'Just stay with him, while I get some water.'

Jim shut the street door and turned on the light.

'Sorry for being such a bloody a nuisance,' mumbled the man. 'I'm not worth it. You should have left me where I was.'

'Correction,' said Jim. 'You're worth it because you're trying to improve yourself. Just keep trying and you'll make it.' Jim just managed to remain stony-faced while Beryl instructed the man on straightforward ways to safely lose weight.

The man stood up without shaking and, taking a few tentative steps forward, shuffled round awkwardly, and asked: 'Do you live here?' It was spoken as if he was half expecting to be slapped down for asking.

'Just up the steps' confirmed Beryl.

'Well, would you mind…?' His voice shook as if he was about to ask too much. 'Would you mind if called on you when I look better?'

He seemed to panic. 'Sorry, I didn't mean come inside. I meant just see me when I've lost weight. It would give me something to aim for.'

'Of course we wouldn't mind,' grinned Beryl. 'But only after you have run up these steps of course.'

'I will, I will,' and thanks again. You've been awesome.'

Jim opened the door and shook his head as they watched the man limp back towards the hospital roundabout.

'Boy, if that isn't loneliness, I don't know what is.'

Beryl agreed, then turned onto him with an old-fashioned look.

'And what are you waiting for me to say?'

He sensed danger. 'I don't know. What am I waiting for you to say?'

'But for the grace of…?'

He took a risk. 'Well, fancy forgetting that, but don't let me stop you from saying it.'

She thwacked him with the shopping bag. 'And I suggest that you get on with the shopping while you still can.'

He walked down to his old workplace. It was busy, and he nearly tripped over the rear wheel of a mobility scooter as it backed out from behind the paper rack by the window. 'Sorry's' were exchanged with the occupant as she came to an abrupt stop, and in the same instant, she would have seen the shock in his expression. She was ghoulish, and he felt dreadful, because he had conveyed sharp confirmation of her disfigurement. Somehow, he had to make amends - anything to appease her hurt, but what?

He settled for a second apology.

'Apologies again, I just didn't see you.'

'No harm done.' Her reply was distant, as if he wasn't there. Clearly, this was a routine she had shared with strangers many times.

He persisted. 'Is this your usual waiting spot?'

She nodded jerkily and struggled with the muscular control of her mouth, although her diction was quite good.

'It's too crowded in there. I'm keeping out of the way while sister's doing the shopping.'

He had time to adjust to her face. A smile came through; it was lopsided and tentative, and she continued with less formality.

'It's not so bad now.'

Instinctively he knew what she meant.

'I don't get so many comments as I used to.'

'I wondered if that was the reason.'

She opened up.

'I don't know why, but it's nicer here than it used to be.'

'You mean people are friendlier?'

She nodded awkwardly. 'Although I still try to avoid school closing time, they never give up?'

'The children you mean?'

'Yes,' her personality was coming through.

'How do you cope with that?'

'I get angry. What else can I do?'

There was a short hesitation.

'I cry sometimes when I see my ugliness in people's reactions. It came back to me in your reaction. It gave you a shock, didn't it?'

'It did, but I'm getting used to it. You are breaking through your ugly bit now.'

'You mean my crinkles and lip droops are starting to make sense?'

He smiled: 'You could put it that way.'

Using her thumbs, she stretched her mouth into a hideous grin.

'How's that?'

'Much better.'

He stuck a thumb in each ear and trumpeted at her while waggling his fingers. Then she pulled up her nose and blew a raspberry at him. The store security man stood by uncertainly, but a growing crowd of amused shoppers had already circled round, and began pulling faces and making rude noises at each other until the foyer echoed with silliness and laughter. At last, they ran out of faces to pull, and Jim was just able to make himself heard. Bowing first to his fellow performer, he ordered everyone to stick out their tongues, and announced a 'Grand Raspberry Finale!' on the count of three. Dogs barked; the store manager sat bolt upright in his chair, and outside, incoming customers rushed back to their cars.

Later, in the wake of departing shoppers, the ghoulish woman tapped him on the back.

'How do I look now?'

'Dreadful!' He touched her face. 'But underneath this lot, there's something bright and sparkly pushing its way out.'

She gave him a ghastly smile, and her hand shook as she laid it gently over his wrist. Then they both laughed, and trumpeted raspberries at each other, as her confused sister wheeled her out of the store.

Once inside, he'd forgotten what he came in for, but it didn't matter. Beryl was happy; they had done someone a good turn, and laughter and silliness had found a way into the borough.

And congeniality was not just confined to the borough. Beside the bar in their usual meeting place, Madge and Ben were encouraged at what they were able to report in their new documentary about the public mood towards sustainability.

'It's hard to put a finger on it,' said Madge, 'But there seemed to be more energy and cheerfulness around wherever we went, and I didn't get the usual sense of caginess and having to be careful what I said.'

'Neither did I, until you arrived,' said Ben.

'Close,' warned Madge, 'and it's your round, so hurry up before I wop you one.'

She turned to Jim. 'Most of those we spoke to said they'd had enough of money ruling everything, and governments always going for popularity whatever damage it causes. There's a lot of clever things going on as well. Up north, some of the old canals are being put back into to use, and tons of plastic are being washed and ground up before being loaded into horse drawn barges and taken to redundant foundries be melted down and moulded into portable homes. The plan is to make thousands of them if we go for sustainable living, because they can be clamped together into any size and shape, and taken where they're needed.

'The company let us stay in one in one for a few nights while were recording,' added Ben. It's all 'eco mod cons' inside using wind and solar heating, and they're comfortable. I couldn't even hear Brinod snoring.'

Brinod flicked his eyebrows at Ben. 'Separate bedrooms my Ben. Brinod not close enough.'

'Yes…well, it's all in the documentary.'

'Sounds like a modern take on the pre-fabs made at the end of the war,' suggested Jim.

'Well, I'd be happy to live in one, even with those two.' Madge reached into her shoulder bag and gave Jim some miniatures. 'They can be put together any way you want - a bit like *Lego*.'

Jim assembled the miniatures into a bungalow.

'Are they fire-proof?'

'That's what we were told.'

Ben handed round the drinks, and picked up a bar copy of the *Daily Truth.*

'Let's see what's been happening here while we've been away.'

Dominating the front page was a photo of big Mabel with a bunch of tree saplings in one hand, and a spade in the other. Above her the headline announced: *'Greening the borough. Ironside leads the way.'*

Ben read: *'Local campaigner, Big Mabel Kayford has reached her target of two thousand varied tree saplings planted in and around the estates of Ironside and Spikewell. 'Everyone, including our kids and pensioners really put their backs into it.' she told us.*

Advice and assistance, including the planting of four young oak trees, was provided by the Borough Council Parks Department, and funds were also raised by the Spikewell rock group 'Crotch' on their Facebook page. 'Ironside and Spikewell will soon be the places to live round here,' smiled Mabel proudly. 'And it's been great training for the local kids who want green jobs.'

'Good for Mabel,' said Jim. 'She's nearly made up for getting all those houses being put onto the green belt.' He turned over to the back pages. 'And things get better: *'The King and I'* is being shown at the *Regent*. How's that for progress since we last met?'

Brinod pulled a face over his cherry liquor. 'Yule Brynner; baldy head, not for Brinod.'

'Tough!' said Madge, 'Julie Andrews is great by me.'

A period of silence settled round the table while Ben twirled his forefinger in a puddle of slopped beer. At last, he shared his thinking. 'Does anyone here really believe that other countries will follow us if we go for sustainability?'

'My inflatable globe needs convincing as well,' said Jim. 'It's been swearing a lot recently, and only this morning said, 'We'd better ****well hurry up or it's **** chips for all of us and we **** well deserve it!'

'The Secretary of the UN said about same last night.' added Madge, 'and he got less air time than the handball which dropped Liverpool out of the first division.'

A second thoughtful silence followed.

'But let's be positive,' said Jim. 'If it wasn't for our soup, there's no way the UK would be going for sustainability. 'Also…' he waited for continued attention. 'The green campaigners are doing a great job in pushing Europe to follow our lead, and thistle farming trials are doing well in the Sudan and Nigeria.'

He pushed his mug across to Brinod. 'So come on! Just for the moment let's push aside starvation; barrel bombs, paedophilia, domestic abuse, and wild fires. We deserve a mini celebration, and it's Brinod's round!'

The following morning Jim joined Dawn in St Michael's Church to attend the funeral of a cousin who had opted for voluntary euthanasia. The death of a relative in his early forties was hardly a cause for celebration, but to Jim it marked a significant national shift towards compassion, and it was doubly warming to know that they were paying their respects in Bishop Pocklington's diocese.

It was only after he had moved in with Beryl, that Dawn told him about their cousin Malcolm who lived close-by. They had met on a couple occasions during family visits, but Jim was the rough one, and had to be checked at times. From thereon they both went their different ways, because the demands of army life usually ensured that Jim was away during Malcom's later visits. So, they shared little in common. Dawn had mentioned Malcolm's work with the homeless, and Jim regretted not taking the trouble to know him better. But whatever Malcom was like, no one should have been forced to endure the horrible suffering he had to go through, before the law was changed to give him the means for last minute peace.

After the burial they expressed sympathy to his bereaved wife. She had been crying, but spoke with relief. 'I did my grieving while he was alive,' she explained. 'I tried and tried to arrange a peaceful end for him in Switzerland, but the hurdles and expense proved too much. He was like a zombie for so long, and refused visits from his grandchildren because he feared his appearance would overlay any fond memories, they had of him. His death was a blessing, and I'll never forget the wonderful smile he gave me when the pain left his face at the very end.' She pressed her hands together and glanced upwards. 'God, I'm so grateful for that memory. If we did wrong, please be gentle with him.'

The change in the law was managed sensitively. Money grabbing relatives didn't turn out to be such a problem as the: 'slippery slope to abuse' protagonists predicted. Neither was there quite the rush for compassionate dying as expected. Given the right to die, the anticipation of a prolonged and horrible death for those with a horrible condition, had at last been removed, which greatly improved the quality of their remaining years, and often made treatment more effective. The inevitability of death had been with Jim since his narrow squeak, and it was reassuring to know that now he might not be forced to breathe his last looking like a scarecrow.

He was almost cheerful as he left the church, and put it down to the events of the last two days. Perhaps he was being unduly optimistic, but 'niceness' really did seem to be spreading locally and nationally.

18. Turning Points.

The referendum passed with a large majority in favour of the proposals, and in the following weeks Parliament had begun the complex process of preparing for the change. It had to be done carefully, and the Minister of Trade advised caution. 'Bridging the gap between now, and achieving full sustainability will take time and meticulous planning. We may face criticism or even ridicule from other nations, but nothing will be achieved by upsetting our long-term trading partners, even if we disapprove of their environmental practices.

Debates were often heated, but reason usually supplanted blatant politicking in tackling the maze of complexities leading towards a sustainable economy. Likewise, the media became less shouty. Whoops, whistles, and false laughter had calmed down in talk shows, and Brian and Beverley were no longer so keen to probe guests for emotional pressure points.

So, it was against the background of unprecedented wild fires; accelerating glacial break up in polar regions; disappearing ice caps in mountainous regions, and rising oceans, that Britain stood proudly alone in its determination to go for sustainability.

'Thank goodness we've gone back to being grown up.' smiled doddery Lord Greenfield from his chair by the fire.

'I don't get the 'gone back' bit Dad,' queried his son.

The Lord looked over the top of his newspaper, and for the first time in years allowed himself to be corrected by his son. 'No, you're correct Son. I should have said: 'Thank goodness we've moved forward to being grown up.'

And in a brief rallying cry to the Nation, the Prime Minister brushed against emotion by proudly announcing: 'Now at last, we have achieved national maturity.'

Jim turned to Beryl.

'So that's us sorted. Now let's see how long it takes for the others to grow up.'

'You mean the rest of the world?'

'Yes, the rest of the world.'

'And that's most countries.'

'Yes, especially those who can least afford to lose coastlines.'

And many miles away, the dreadful fate of thousands of Pacific islanders dramatically focused world attention on their dwindling coastline.

Horseshoe shaped; the small island of Banda Bukay was lapped on all sides by the Pacific Ocean. Its sloping volcanic rim was once able to maintain a sizeable population, and a small port flourished in the lake formed inside the crater. Daytime tourism and fish farming helped to boost the economy, but over the years, the sea had risen sufficiently to swamp the port and main agricultural area, which prompted a move to cultivate the upper levels of less fertile land towards the top of the crater rim. Repeated applications for migration onto the nearby mainland were deliberately fraught with legal complexities, and acute food shortages were now a fact of life for the population.

Following warnings that a record-breaking hurricane was raging towards the island, many of the inhabitants made for the mainland in their fleet of small boats, and sailed into the very hurricane they were trying to avoid. A few days later, foreign tourists were sharing the sea with hundreds of corpses.

Worldwide outrage followed, but once again the latest UN climate conference closed with commitments, but little action. So, the race to grab and suck whatever goodies were once covered by ice, or anything else, intensified. The sky would get more smoke; more permafrost would turn slushy; more creatures would be stranded on floating icebergs, and the shining towers of the powerful corporates would grow a little higher in company with the sea. It was all so unbelievingly stupid, as bit by bit the inevitable occurred.

By October, Large chunks of the East Coast had crumbled onto the beach, and during one night of ferocious storms, the North Norfolk Broads were overflowing with salt water.

The following morning a council representative and a despondent holiday home builder faced a forest of reinforcing rods poking up from a rippling extension of the North Sea.

'There's a square mile of foundations under that lot,' complained the builder. 'I suppose it's no good asking for my money back.'

'Afraid not. You'll just have to put your houses on stilts.'

'The council should have done something about this years ago.'

'It was discussed, but the ratepayers would have mutinied at the cost. Anyway, whatever we did wouldn't stop the sea from rising... it behaves like that you know.'

And about forty miles across the water from where the builder stood, similar cries of 'Something must be done!' became more and more persistent as Europe wavered between the worst avalanches on record and unseasonable flooding.

The, *Our World our Business* campaign, had at last teamed up with European eco campaigns under the all-embracing banner of *Green Prelude.*

When asked about the title, Emma Dowty described how the words came to her while she was cuddling a sloth during a break in Costa Rica. But many rough edges had to be rounded off between the different campaigns before genuine accord could be reached.

The most divisive issue was population control, which caused so much upset that it was removed. But soon it became evident that without it, most of the other doors to progress were blocked. So, population control was reinstated, causing many campaigners to leave because of deeply held beliefs, and fear of being shunned by their families and friends. Resulting from this, *Green Prelude* campaigned with reduced membership but greater authority, since there was no need to fudge the big issue. As an elderly Swedish campaigner remarked, 'At last I've been able to join an eco-campaign which has come of age.' Meanwhile, the weather became more belligerent.

The Belgian Minister of Development tut-tutted after closing the conservatory windows, and returning to his breakfast of *Conran* rusks. Forest fires were uncommon in Belgium, yet this one was large enough to cloak part of Brussels in smoke, and trigger his asthma. The traffic pollution had grown steadily worse over the years, and recently he'd taken more than enough ear-bashing from his eco mad offsprings about fossil fuels. First it was globalisation, next it was coal-mining and destruction of the Great Barrier Reef, and not long after that they were outside school waving banners about homeless orang-utans and koala bears. Now it was the *Green Prelude* campaign calling for sustainable development and population control. He laughed openly. At least the new campaign should free him from child minding duties while his two were attending college.

Making up his mind to be a hypocrite no longer, he would tender his resignation unless Parliament was prepared to consider moving towards a programme of sustainable development - even if it did mean following in the UK's footsteps.

From October to mid-November the Government had worked non- stop to head off any likely problems that could be delivered by the weather. More prolonged flooding; storm force winds, and unseasonably high temperatures were all possible and a cold winter was also long overdue.

'We can no longer rely on seasonal weather.' warned the Minister of Environment. 'From now onwards, the seasons are likely to throw anything at us at any time.'

Vulnerable areas were asked to anticipate their requirements for dealing with emergencies, and wherever possible to make use of local facilities and skills to produce the equipment needed. Sheep farming was hugely boosted by a demand for stocks of cold weather clothing, and a range of eco-insulation materials using fleece, and soon, a pattern of industry began to emerge which was based on need, rather than market speculation. So, workforces had to be flexible and ready to take on anything within their capabilities before financial assistance was given. At national level, the planned infrastructure and housing projects were cancelled as being woefully inadequate for the imminent demands of the population, and a multi- discipline task force was assembled to consider alternatives more appropriate to sustainable living.

Every so often, the Prime Minister outlined the complex and controversial decisions which would have to be made, and encouraged the provision of a national forum on the government website enabling individuals or groups to contribute ideas relevant to easing the move into sustainability.

'We are an inventive nation,' she had declared, 'and I expect original thinking and approaches which may not have been considered by government.'

In mid-December, she was back to announce that the UK might not be alone, as discussions were underway in Brussels to explore the new political climate which would develop if Europe also opted to make the move towards sustainability.

But the USA was not amused. By going sustainable, the UK and Europe would start being fussy about US imports. After all, America was suffering from freaky weather as well, but going sustainable was barmy. The UK in particular, was having to provide for millions more than it did during the Second World War, and it would be hard-pushed to keep that many well fed and happy under an eco-regime. But the President reasoned it would be better to avoid diplomatic ructions by offering some friendly words of advice, and waiting for history to repeat itself. After all it was a fair bet that the Prime Minister would soon be sailing over in her eco yacht for a trade deal and big loan.

From all the other nations there came a deafening silence.

19. Feels Like Home.

At the last minute, Dawn and family we're invited to spend the Christmas break with Gary's parents in Lincolnshire. They owned a mixed farm in the Wolds, which under the management of Gary's sisters, had wholeheartedly adopted the national move towards sustainability. Shaun had already been kitted out with weather-proof clothing, and as requested, was regularly practicing; 'Helping out with the mucky work.' by tramping over their tiny lawn.

So, Christmas wasn't to be repeated at Dawn's with Gary and his sisters, which was big a let-down, and Beryl voiced her disappointment from the street window.

'Last year was special, Jim. It was so Christmassy, and that's the only way I can put it.'

He wiped condensation from the inside of the street window and thought back to last Christmas. Yes, last Christmas was special. Unblocking the road grids at the church entrance, was special. The twinkling candlelight and low pedal tones of the big organ was very special. And after the service, the neighbourly rapport outside Dawn's semi was special.

'Yes,' he agreed, 'it was special.'

Outside, there was less traffic than last year, but more twinkly lights, and once again Mary was cradling Baby Jesus on the roof of his old workplace.

He tried to sense 'Christmassy.' It usually conveyed glitter and having eaten too much, but last Christmas was different.

'Strange?'

'What's strange Jim?' She closed up to him and the window clouded over, awarding Mary a second halo.

'Last Christmas felt so real. Don't ask me to explain 'real' though.'

'It's because we went to church to celebrate the birth of Jesus; that's what Christmas is all about.'

'Or that's what Christmas should be all about.' insisted Jim. 'So maybe we could try for an old-fashioned Christmas this year?'

'You mean like the ones we sometimes see on our cards?'

She went down to the smattering of cards on the table and returned with one showing a robin perched on a snowman's pipe, against the background of a church and children's choir.

'Yes like that,' agreed Jim. 'We'll just have to imagine the snow.'

'It would be wonderful, even without the snow.'

He looked down the room. The few cards on the table didn't convey much of a festive mood, and no amount of preparation would persuade the flat to do 'old fashioned;' Beryl deserved something much better during her break, and recalling an item he had heard on the news, he did some googling.

It was a long shot, but the 'Old Goose Inn' in Lord Gannon's sustainable village did have vacancies over the Christmas period, and risking a bad weather travel delay, he booked a room and two return tickets from Kings Cross to Greenvale in Yorkshire.

On the day before Christmas Eve, they took the cases down the steps onto a wet street, and Beryl couldn't contain her excitement as they locked the outside entrance to the flat.

'Oh Jim, I'm so excited, and the uncertainty makes it feel as if we're on a risky adventure.'

'You mean like being held up for hours in a stuffy carriage.'

They crossed over to the lay-by for a taxi.

'We could start a sing-song.'

'Have you heard my singing?'

'Yes…well on second thoughts, I'll buy a book at the station.'

Kings Cross Station echoed with announcements of delayed departures and arrivals, but their train pulled out on time, and soon they were escaping from the tentacles of East London and a never-ending suburbia into open country.

Beryl grasped his hand.

'Whatever happens, it's got to be better than spending Christmas in the flat.'

'Don't make it too special. We're coming back remember.'

'Rotter!' She poked him. 'Anyway, my Gran used to say that looking forward to a holiday was the best bit.'

'So, if we get stuck we can pretend the rest, and still enjoy ourselves.'

She closed up to him. 'I'll hold you to that Jim.'

They arrived at York in time to catch a train on the branch line to Greenvale, and at Greenvale Station followed a sign saying 'Greenvale Carriage' which directed them across the road to a wooden shelter and horse driven carriage. This came as a bonus, and they expressed surprise to the couple inside.

'It's horses everywhere in Greenvale,' explained the man. 'They're our transport system.'

'Using horses makes sense here,' added his companion, 'but just watch where you tread.'

'And these two are full of airs and graces,' said the coachman. 'We take on retired racehorses, but they think pulling carriages is way below their status, and snort to let you know it. I've never worked with such snooty horses.'

He tapped them on the rumps, and with four snorts they were trotting through heavy rain and into a dense avenue of trees which led into an 'olde-worlde' main street. A 'Welcome to Greenvale' sign greeted them from the village green, but a recycling yard and quadrangle of repair shops removed any doubts about Greenvale being a spruced-up tourist trap.

The Goose Inn was convincingly olde-worlde, with a close-thatched roof, and warm glow seeping through the curtains of two large bay windows. As they left the carriage and lowered their cases onto the courtyard, the coachman said, 'Nice pub, you should enjoy your stay - I'll be in there later.'

The horses snorted, and they watched the carriage continue along the main street until it turned onto a side road towards a cluster of farm buildings. From there on, the main street narrowed, and dipping down to a stream, crossed over a small bridge into a cluster of modern bungalows, to reappear as a track which rose upwards through a patchwork of fields to the valley ridge and a row of wind turbines.

'Have you been here before?' asked the man.

'It's our first time,' said Jim. We're hoping it will take us back to our old-time Christmases.'

'You mean when you were young, and couldn't sleep because you might find a pencil and notebook in your sock?'

'That's right,' agreed Jim. 'With me it was a penknife.'

'Then you've come to the right place. I'm Cyril, by the way, and this is Sue. We moved here two years ago, so this is our home now.'

Cyril opened the door for them to enter the lobby. 'We're going in for a drink later. You're welcome to join us once you've made yourselves comfortable.'

Once through the lobby, the climate inside was warm and beery, and the décor was just short of scruffy. Roast rabbit, mushrooms, and mashed potatoes, followed by Greenvale Bakery Christmas Pudding was on the bar chalkboard for Christmas Eve, and Colin on piano would be playing for the 'special' sing-song. Their room was basic but comfy, and beside the eco-loo was a request that nappies be placed in the special recycle bin.

They unpacked, and joined Cyril and Sue in a corner table by the window.

'Now that really is old time Christmassy.' Jim pointed to the menu they had seen on the chalkboard.

'Rabbit is standard fare here,' explained Cyril. 'It's the Greenvale equivalent to fish and chips, and just what our grandparents would have looked forward to in the 1940's and '50's. '

'And like my grandma, guess who gets lumbered with all the skinning and gutting?' said Sue.

'Innards go to the pigs,' added Cyril. 'Nothing is wasted here; it becomes second nature after a time.'

Sue placed her hat and gloves on the table. They were leather stitched and functional.

'There are six rabbit skins in these, and I made the same for Cyril because we were told to expect a freezing winter this year.'

'That's nine rabbit's-worth altogether,' said Cyril. 'I'd nearly become a vegan by the time she'd skinned the last one, and we're still waiting for a freezing winter.'

Beryl tried on the hat, and eager to move the conversation away from gory imagery, Jim asked what life was like for them in Greenvale.

'We love it.' enthused Sue. 'It was all traffic and tension where we lived, and for us, it was having to keep up appearances as well.'

'We were both in marketing.' added Cyril. 'Appearances were important.'

'Anyway,' said Sue, 'one day I came home stressed to the eyebrows after getting a bad performance review at work, and bumped into Cyril's vintage Morris Minor.'

'And after the blazing row,' cut in Cyril, 'we agreed to have separate thinks, then took stock about what we really wanted from life.'

Sue frowned. 'It was so difficult. Honestly, we didn't know what we wanted. We lived in up-market suburbia and had complicated lifestyles, quite apart from work. Cyril was in the golf club, and I did ladies' fitness classes. Then there was the entertaining, and our holiday breaks, but it all felt so shallow.'

Cyril raised a cautionary hand. 'Don't get the wrong idea. We were well paid, but once we got down to the nitty-gritty of what our jobs were all about, we concluded that we weren't doing anything very worthwhile.'

'Then we heard that Lord Gannon had started this community,' added Sue. 'So, we applied to join it and it was such a release. Life is so real here.'

They nodded in unison.

Jim was intrigued. The 'real' word had popped up again.

Sue smiled. 'Delivering lambs last week was very real.'

'Sue's on the lambing rota,' said Cyril. 'Our livestock farmer says she's a natural. She usually comes back smelling of afterbirth, but loves it, don't you darling?'

'It's the feeling that I've helped a beautiful little creature into the world.' Sue smiled as she reflected on her last delivery. 'It's messy and they don't always make it, but so satisfying.'

Jim sensed Beryl's growing broodiness, so he gave her a light peck on the cheek and created a diversion by collecting their glasses for another round of drinks and some crisps.

'Nice beer,' he remarked to the barman. 'I like the earthy taste.'

The barman nodded at the Greenvale Brewery sign. 'Our local brewery has to be earthy. We're all earthy round here.'

A cheer went up. Somebody had scored a bull in the nearby game of darts.

'Fair bombing Ken!' exclaimed someone with very red ears.

Jim squeezed back to the table while the score slate was being wiped clean, and the players moved to the bar for replenishments.

'They take darts seriously here,' stated Cyril. 'Our team came second in the 'Wool Cup' competition recently, and that's the cup to win if you are in one of the local dart playing Clubs.'

Someone announced: 'Middle for diddle,' and Red Ears bobbed before the board. His dart arced into the outer bull.

'Arrer!' exclaimed the man who Jim recognised as their carriage driver.

'But there's room for one more,' announced Ken, and taking his place on the mat, daintily paddled his arm at the board and released his dart straight into the bull, bringing forth more cheers, and capturing most of the interest in the room.

The dartboard chatter took Jim back to his illicit teenager visits to the village pub, although there were some regional variations. 'Right line; wrong station,' could have been derived from York's rail heritage. 'Wire trouble,' and 'Cheeky arrers.' he had heard before, and together with the beer; snooty horses, and Sue's rabbit skin creations, he felt he had already taken in more flavours from the past than he could have reasonably expected.

Beryl nudged him. 'Stop dreaming Jim.'

'Let him dream,' advised Cyril. 'We're allowed to dream here.'

'So, what are you dreaming about Jim?' asked Sue.

Jim waved his hand round the room. 'All this is taking me back.'

'It usually does,' said Cyril. 'Greenvale is all about getting back to basics, and thank goodness the country is following suit. I'm still finding it hard to believe that we've gone for sustainability - let alone most of Europe. By now, we should be warring over fish stocks in the North Sea.' He slid the two unopened bags of crisps across the table.

'Sorry, but we'll have to leave these with you.' He put on his parka jacket, and helped Sue into her topcoat. Tomorrow my parents will be spending Christmas with us, so it will be an early start.'

'We love having them,' said Sue, 'and this year Cyril's mum is doing the cooking.'

'They're vegetarians,' added Cyril. 'So, it won't be roast rabbit.' He extended his hand. 'It's been good meeting you both; with luck we'll meet up again before you leave. You should enjoy Greenvale. The sing-song is noisy, but good fun if you enjoy that sort of thing, and the church service is always worth attending.'

They walked into the entrance lobby, where Cyril just managed to hold the front door against the wind, while Sue retrieved her hat. The barman rushed over to help, and bolted the door.

'It's rough out there!' he shouted. 'So, from now on it's the back door please everyone!'

Next morning, after breakfast, they stepped outside the lobby into an older domain where Christmas Eve shopping was in progress. They could have been extras in a period film set. Pedestrians in functional clothes peered into shop windows selling functional goods, and snooty horses, towing shopping carts and trailers, trotted aloofly up and down the main street. The butcher's shop across the street was strung across with pheasants, rabbits and pigeons, and the dismembered body parts on the cold slab had been arranged to produce a ragged jigsaw of an entire pig.

Beryl pointed to something floppy and crimson that Jim wasn't keen to look at.

'We'd never get that in our butchers.'

He pulled a face. 'Can't say I feel deprived - it's just sustainable living. One pig here is worth two pigs elsewhere I suppose. But I'd like to move away now if you don't mind.'

The graveyard wall had obscured their view of the church when they first arrived. Perched on a rise opposite to the recycling yard, it dominated the main street, and they stopped before a notice board giving details of the midnight service.

Beryl said how much she was looking forward to the service, but Jim was concerned that she might be expecting too much after the grand service they had attended with Dawn and Gary's sisters.

'Yes, but don't be disappointed if it isn't quite so good as the last time.'

'Of course I'll be disappointed, but we must go.'

Stone steps were built into the wall which took them up from the street into the graveyard. It was well kept, but extensively littered with bits and pieces blown over from the recycling yard during the overnight winds. A snooty horse and cart were parked by the entrance porch, and two men were pulling down some plastic sheeting from the lower branches of a yew tree in preparation for loading it into the cart. Beryl and Jim wandered between the graves picking up items as they made their way to the porch, and Jim's attention was drawn to the inscriptions and dates etched into the headstones.

In common with most churchyards and burial grounds over the country, many of the inscriptions affirmed a history of Greenvale residents dying in foreign conflicts. He shook his head at the plaque of a young army private. It didn't make sense, and never did make sense. There had barely been a break between stone age skull bashing and spearing, right through to mustard gas, doodlebugs, and nuclear vaporisation. Yet, it was still going on, and he had been part of it.

But should he be quite so despondent? Maybe there had to be continuous human conflict to prevent continuous human boredom? Pushing the question into his 'Much too cynical' box he raised a splintered letter rack from a small headstone and came face to face with a skull and crossbones. 'Well, that's plain enough,' he thought, and looking hard at the skull, spent a few moments trying to receive some wisdom from the past.

One of the recycling yard men rushed over and phewed with relief after checking the headstone. He raised a thumb to his workmate by the cart and said: 'This lady died from the Black Death. Single graves aren't very common, so we're relieved this one hasn't been damaged. She would have been quite important locally, but the inscription is too eroded to tell us more.' He pointed to the other side of the graveyard. 'Plague victims were often buried in mass grave pits, like the one over there.'

'Did she die in the first or second wave?' enquired Beryl.

'She died in 1666 when the plague came up from London. The first wave wiped out the early village.'

They walked with him to the porch, and dumped the letter rack and litter into the cart as he climbed up to join his workmate. The horse snorted, and they trotted towards the open fields which sloped upwards and over the far side of the valley. Framed by the lychgate, the two figures and the cart enacted a scene that the lady in her skull and crossbones grave must have seen many times from the porch.

Beryl recalled what she been taught about the Derbyshire village of Eyam during the plague of 1666.

'Everyone in the village agreed to go into quarantine. They just locked their doors and stayed inside. Most of them died.'

'I heard about that,' said Jim. 'They even gave up having raves and getting legless to stop the plague from spreading.'

'Do you think there would be as much consideration today if we had second wave of yellow stripe?'

'I doubt it, although with luck we might have souped in enough niceness to stop supermarkets being stripped of loo rolls.'

'I didn't expect to hear such optimism from you Jim.'

'Neither did I, so don't bank on it lasting.'

They entered the porch. Angled towards them on the window sill was a cosy nativity scene. A small plaque read: Greenvale Primary School, and the figures were so well crafted they could have been made by skilled adults. Only the cheesy smiles and fearsome grin on the face of the donkey implied smaller hands. Beryl thought it was lovely, and moved across to the flower arrangement by the door, which she also thought was lovely.

The church was constructed from light grey stone. There were no signs of deterioration in the wooden structures, and everything from the floor to the candle holders were highly polished. Kneelers, woven with local scenes had already been placed on the pew shelves for the midnight service, and warm air was rising from grids beneath the bench seats. They walked down the aisle and Beryl chose a front pew for them to sit on. The chancel window threw fuzzy colours over the floor, and just ahead, the eyes of a big brass eagle fronting the lectern stared down to them. It exuded quality, and skilled craftsmanship was evident throughout the interior of the church.

Conceived in an age without mechanical shovels and heavy lifting gear, serious hard graft would have been required to shape and raise so much stone above the countryside, and like so many rural churches, the sound of its construction would have echoed for years across the Greenvale Valley.

He looked up to the vaulted roof and temporarily cast aside much of his cynicism about the role of the church in the exploitation of the peasantry. It was beautiful; there was no other way to describe it, and it had been designed in confidence that it would last for centuries. Surely something more than just money and small beer, must have inspired those who had created it?

A smug Bishop Pocklington came to mind.

'OK, you win,' conceded Jim. 'I agree. It had to be faith or something like it. So can I have some please?'

Beryl squeezed his hand as they rose to leave.

'I think it's the most welcoming church I've visited.'

Jim agreed, and right on queue they were swathed in colour from the beam of sunlight streaming through the chancel window.

'Perhaps this church is trying to tell us something,' he thought.

They put some coins into the collection box, and on the way out, turned onto the path leading to the other side of the church for Beryl to take some photos. Ground source heat units were installed at intervals alongside the wall, and Jim noted with approval that they were topped with flowers planted inside Sapiens Carduus containers. On reaching the end buttress, Beryl took a photo, then they turned the corner straight into a change of mood. A black cloud had extinguished the sun, and they were greeted by the tombstone marking the burial pit. Then Beryl stopped, and her voice dropped to a whisper of foreboding.

'Jim, look at the rider.'

She was pointing to a horse and cart in the field bordering the graveyard.

Straddling the horse and covered by a black drape, was a skeletal something or other, which could have been human. The horse halted outside a storage shed, then two men came out and pulled off the arms before removing whatever it was and uncoupling the cart.

Jim offered an explanation after walking over for a closer look.

'Well, it wasn't bothering the horse. Looks like it could be Greenvale's equine version of the driverless car.'

By the time they had hurried through the graveyard, down the walled steps, and back onto the main street, the cloud had settled like a big black cap over the valley, and a double wallop of thunder introduced a deluge of rain and hailstones which sent pedestrians and snooty horses rushing for shelter.

They made it into the lobby, and went up to their room for a quick tidy up before going to the bar for a snack while waiting for the rain to stop.

'That's all I bloody needed!' exclaimed someone as they came down to the bar. A stronger expletive followed, and a bar towel flew across the lounge as they went in to order snacks. Somewhere a radio was playing, and the landlord had both elbows on the bar top with his head between his hands.

'Sorry, sorry, sorry!' But here we go again. The last thing I needed was this. Come to that it's the last thing anyone needs. Sorry again if you haven't heard.'

Jim guessed. 'Not another pandemic?'

The landlord nodded vigorously. 'You couldn't make it up!'

'A second bout of yellow stripe?'

'Yes, a new strain. They reckon it's the wild animal markets again. They should have dangled those cruel bastards the last time, but they've been allowed to carry on just like before. How bloody stupid can it get!'

He apologised to Beryl. 'Again, sorry for my language.'

'There's no need to be.' She answered softly. Her spirits had already plunged to rock bottom, and her immediate reaction was to finish with nursing. She didn't want a second bout of fear; physical exhaustion, and witnessing the death of colleagues.'

'Beryl's a nurse,' explained Jim. 'It's the last thing she wants as well.'

'Heck, I can imagine that. With me it could be losing a living.' He spoke with concern to Beryl. 'With you it could be your life.'

Jim searched her expression.

'You shouldn't have to go through that again. Not for a second time.'

'I'll have to Jim. What would the team think of me if I chickened out? Anyway, I couldn't live with myself.'

He understood. In Beryl's shoes, he would have come to the same decision.

They found a table and sat in silence; each in their own way coming to terms with the news. The windows rattled with the percussive effect of thunder, and wet pedestrians escaped into the lobby to become customers. The landlord pressed himself through the crowd with their order, and waved away Jim's cheque card.

'You're not paying for this.' He spoke to Beryl. 'I'll never forget what the NHS did for my dad at York Hospital during the last pandemic.'

They thanked him, and Beryl had a weep.

'That was lovely, and whatever happens I'm not going to be a misery - well, not while we're here anyway.' She gripped Jim's knee under the table. 'And you'd better not be a misery either.'

A small crowd pressed round talking about the pandemic, but there was also talk about the immediate need to prepare for flooding. .

'Where's the flooding?' asked Jim.

'Most of its run-off into the stream at the bottom of the road,' said a man with a tattooed neck. We widened it after the flooding last March, but we don't often have rain like this, and the bottom bungalows could get it.'

'Do you have flood gear?'

'We've made barriers. Every bungalow has an emergency set, and there are larger barriers for the stream, but the pensioners will have a job to cope, and half the village is elsewhere visiting relatives over Christmas, so we need more help.'

'You've got me.'

'And me,' added Beryl.

'Well great, and thanks. It's getting bad out there so we'd better do something. I'll do a scout round to see who else we've got.'

A positive hubbub spread through both bars, and Tattooed Neck took centre stage with the landlord.

'Right, it's still pissing down out there, and I reckon the water will rise up to the lower bungalows if we don't get the barriers up at Runny Bottom. Stable number ten has a load of waterproofs and wellies on pegs if you're not too fussed about sizes. Dennis will cart the sandbags and surround barriers to the lower bank for us to get them up as well. Oh, and Dent will have his boat ready in case. I don't need to tell you it's going to be brass-monkey's cold down there, but we'll need to move fast, which should keep us warm. Right now, it's 'Cheers!' to Dave our star landlord, who's given us some fire-water to start us off.'

A cheer went up as the barman poured out large tots of whiskey into glasses which he lined up on the bar for the volunteers.

'And don't get so knackered you can't get back to our sing song with Colin!' shouted the landlord.

Down at Runny Bottom the rain had eased slightly, but the stream was already rippling onto the banks, so it was important to get the barriers in place to protect the lower rows of bungalows. Beryl joined the straggle of helpers fitting the individual flood panels to each bungalow, and Jim helped with offloading the posts and surround barriers from the carts. Everything had been locally made, and was functional but heavy. Trying to align the barrier posts into the post holes without slipping and sliding into the stream caused some hilarity, but after about two hours of solid humping and heaving, all the barriers were in place.

The continuous rain had found leaky areas in most of the waterproofs, and once everyone had trooped back to the stable, any attempts at privacy and formality disappeared as horse towels were used to dry off, and ill-fitting wellies were wrestled from feet with teamwork and laughter.

Beryl and Jim helped to rub down the horses, and as they walked back up the hill with Tattooed Neck, they gathered that he had recently been demobbed.

'Did you like the army?' asked Jim.

'Mostly; but I didn't always like what I had to do.'
He pointed to his tattoos. 'These helped me feel like a
different person after demob, but I stopped pretending
when I came here. This is a real community and
everyone takes you as you are.' He walked off into a
side street. 'See you at the sing-song if you're going.'

Beryl repeated what he said.

'Yes, this does feel like a real community. It's been
cold and wet, but I enjoyed the daftness, and they're
such a great crowd.'

Jim agreed, and the 'real' word had popped up yet
again.

It had stopped raining by the time they were sitting
down to roast rabbit and mashed potato in the saloon
bar. Beryl had never dined on rabbit before, but it
tasted good, and went well with the organic climate
inside the 'Goose'. The misted-up windows added a
cloying humidity, which was further enhanced by
damp clothes and a horsey towel smell from those
who had come straight up from Runny Bottom.

The jokey-together mood still prevailed, and a fair
amount of banter came through from the preamble to
the sing song in the main bar, along with some
thankfully altered ditties that Jim recalled from his
army days.

Colin, the pianist could be seen from where they
were sitting. He looked a little overdressed for a sing-
song, but rolled up his sleeves, and played something
like 'White Christmas.' joined by the crowd singing
something like 'White Christmas.' Clapping and
laughter followed, then someone yelled, 'I want
Temptation!'

'You sing it, and I'll play it, but expect a few mistakes!' replied Colin.

'Your first mistake was opening the lid of that piano!' yelled another voice.

From thereon, normal conversation was difficult, but Beryl was clearly enjoying herself, and made some appreciative noises to the waiter as he replaced their first course with two oversize Christmas puddings, and too much brandy sauce.

She gave Jim a provocative squeeze of the thigh, 'Yellow stripe or whatever. Right now, I don't care, and I don't care if I'm putting on weight, because I'm really enjoying all this.'

He waited for 'Frosty the Snowman' to expire under a welter of raucous laughter.

'OK but don't overdo it. You'll soon have to make it up that hill into the church.'

'I'm looking forward to it.'

Jim was apprehensive. He didn't want the midnight service to come as an anticlimax to Beryl. The small keyboard he noticed in Greenvale Church couldn't possibly match the sound produced by the large pipe organ a year ago, and Beryl deserved a big uplift after the grim news.

'The church doesn't have a pipe organ, so the music might not sound quite so full as last year.'

'Don't worry about it.' she assured him. 'The church is wonderful, so the music will be wonderful as well.'

Tattooed Neck stopped to have a word with them on his way to the bar.

'Thanks for the help. Water is half way up the barrier at Runny Bottom, so the lower bungalows would have got it. There's a clear sky now, so no worries. Are you going to the church tonight?'

'Yes, is it usually full?'

'Always is. You should enjoy it, the music's great, but be careful when you go outside. It's slippy-slidey everywhere now.'

Jim was worried. Tattooed Neck had inclined his head towards Colin when he said: 'The music's great,' and that left plenty of room for doubt.

'Jingle Bell Rock' came to a boisterous finish, and Colin, who had donned a Santa Claus hat and beard, introduced Greta, who enacted the lyrics of 'I saw Momma kissing Santa Claus' by lavishing him with kisses, and singing nothing like the tune, half a beat behind the piano.

'The landlord threw an apologetic grin to the diners over the countertop, and through whistles and whoops for more, Colin announced that Les would taking over on the accordion after the interval.

'And if that isn't enough,' he added, 'we'll probably see some of you on the hill!'

Jim's apprehension increased. 'On the hill' could only mean the church on the hill.

Outside was icy. Christmas greetings wrapped in steamy puffs of breath were exchanged in the courtyard, as the crowd separated into smaller groups. Some went homeward, and they joined the largest group walking carefully uphill to the church. Straight ahead, through the avenue of trees, the night sky was unusually bright and starry, and detaching himself from the seasonal chatter, Jim imagined he was walking into a tunnel leading to the mysteries of outer space, but Beryl firmly re-directed his gaze through the lychgate towards a warmer welcome inside the church.

'Oh Jim, it's so inviting.'

The stained-glass windows shimmered with candlelight as they crunched along the path to the porch. Once inside, coats were removed, and some - still smelling horsey, were handed to the Usher for stowing in the cloakroom. As they walked down the centre aisle they drew level with Cyril and Sue who were seated in the forward lines of pews. Cyril beckoned them to take the empty pew in front, and after introducing his parents asked, 'So, how are you finding Greenvale?'

'We love it.' said Beryl. 'There's such a community feel, and this church is beautiful.'

'And it's well supported,' replied Cyril's father. 'Are you regular churchgoers?'

'We're barely churchgoers,' replied Jim.' But we went to the midnight service at our local church last Christmas, and realised what we had been missing.'

Cyril turned to Sue. 'How would you describe the services here?'

She smiled almost to herself. 'Distinctly Greenvale I would say.'

'Beryl was intrigued. 'That's really interesting. I don't remember much about the church services I attended at home, except for sometimes getting a warm feeling.'

Jim felt protective towards Beryl's warm feeling when Colin arrived, and switched on the small electric keyboard. He felt even more protective towards Beryl's warm feeling when Greta arrived, and placed some hymn sheets purposefully on the eagle lectern.

But it was no ordinary electric keyboard, and when Colin began to play, it was clear to Jim that the sub-base pedal tones which had so affected him during the last Christmas service, could only be coming from a synthesiser. The sound embraced the congregation like an impartial voice of assurance. It was neither celebratory or particularly Christmassy, yet the ultra-low frequency vibrations got right through to his deepest senses. He had no idea if they affected anyone else in the same way, but they were wonderful to him, and in that moment nothing else mattered.

Then came the voice, bringing with it the sensation of an angel calling down to the congregation. But he didn't belief in angels, so he opened his eyes to Greta who, in her flowing white dress, was singing as an angel might sing with her head tilted upwards towards the vaulted roof. The small choir added the middle harmonies, and Greta's voice soared over them as if she was leading everyone towards the Promised Land.

Beryl dabbed her eyes, and closing up to him whispered; 'I feel so at peace Jim.'

During the music, the Vicar had been slowly walking up to the crib, which had been placed in the centre of the aisle, and as the pedal tones faded, he bowed to it and addressed the congregation.

'For many, this crib represents a wondrous event which is the cornerstone of our faith, and the faith of many others across many nations. To some, it may be no more than a moving story based loosely on actual events, while others may see it merely as an opportunity to exchange gifts and have a good time.

How we react will depend on how we regard this event, and increasingly in this modern world, there are those who perceive Christmas as a time for love and hope; not just towards our fellow men, but increasingly to Earth itself. The Earth with its incredible life forms; the Earth which some believe is indeed heaven, and here in Greenvale, the Earth which is of course integral to our community.'

He stooped to look into the crib.

'And here, Baby Jesus is sharing his first home with many life forms, from tiny bacteria to this fierce looking donkey.'

To a ripple of laughter, the Vicar pretended a frightened retreat before continuing.

'And surely that is how we should perceive our own privileged existence? I have heard visitors comment that Greenvale smells strongly of earth.' He sniffed the air to more amusement. 'And my goodness, so it does! Well, I make no apologies for that.' He turned to Colin. 'So, for just a few moments, let us depart from tradition, and celebrate the national move towards a sustainable Earth by first singing: 'All things Bright and Beautiful.'

Under Colin's skilled hands, 'All Things Bright and Beautiful' blossomed into the sounds of springtime, while Greta's voice chased round the church like a rapturous skylark.

In consideration to those nearby, Jim decided not to sing, and throughout the remainder of the service his attention was drawn to the Crib. He had read the story, and understood the roles of the figures grouped around the tiny person in the cradle. It was such a warm friendly gathering, and how wonderful if one of the figures invited him inside. But it would be dishonest to accept, so he chose to remain on the outside while wishing it could be otherwise.

Beryl thanked the Vicar as they queued to put on their coats in the porch.

'Thank you, and how are you enjoying earthy Greenvale?' he asked.

'It's good to be reminded of our natural roots,' said Jim.

'And it feels so real here,' added Beryl.

'I've heard that so many times from visitors,' smiled the Vicar.

Outside, the churchyard was well lit, and reasoning that Beryl could do without seeing an image of death on Christmas Morning, Jim decided against taking the short cut past the skull and crossbones grave, so they joined the small group on the path down to the lychgate.

Behind them, Colin and Greta were giving it welly with 'That Glorious Song of Old' and they glanced back to a scene which could have been an amalgamation of all Beryl's favourite Christmas cards.

Her eyes were streaming.

'Leaving this church is like leaving a loving home, but it's given me so much hope.'

Jim doubted whether Beryl ever had a loving home, but he shared how she felt, even though his hope was sprinkled with reservations.

On Christmas morning they joined a few residents for breakfast in the main bar where the aroma frying bacon mingled with the remaining smells of roast rabbit, beer, and horse towels from the evening before. The piano still occupied the same position, and Beryl drew Jim's attention to a notice taped across the back which invited customers to join in with Colin and Greta's 'Silly Christmas Sing Song'.

'There you are. We both heard how well Colin and Greta performed when we were having dinner. I don't know why you were so worried about the music in church.'

After breakfast they walked down to Runny Bottom. The bungalow flood panels had been removed, but the surround barrier had been left in place because the stream was still lapping over the bank. They arrived as the elderly residents were being helped into carriages by their relatives, before being trotted up the main street to the church for the morning communion service. Already, the synthesiser could be heard waxing and waning a welcome across the valley.

Beryl wanted the Christmas Eve service to remain the top memory of their stay, so they continued upwards along the path to the wind turbines and gazed down at a plan view of Greenvale. By now the carriages were parked alongside the graveyard wall, and the stooped forms of the elderly were moving through the lych-gate into the church. From below, young voices drifted up to them from a game of football on the sports field, and the strings of kites swirling to and fro at about their level, led down to the hands of children standing on a rectangular green patch bordered by shiny green cabins. Jim thought he recognised the cabins from Madge's description after the publicity team had returned with their latest documentary.

'They look like the recycled plastic mobile accommodation units that Ben and Madge used while they were making their documentary.'

'I'd be happy to stay in one,' said Beryl with a tinge of anticipation.

'Let's think about it then. We might be able to hire one for a couple of weeks. It would give us some idea of what it's like to live here.'

'Would you like to live here Jim?'

'Why not? We could stay here at least until the world settles down. Then we could decide whether to ask my exotic woman if we could live in beautiful Torrosus Viridis.?'

'Oh Jim, that would be wonderful!' She gripped his hands and did a girlie jig. 'But we mustn't get too excited. Let's get yellow stripe over with first.'

20. So long.

The afterglow of Greenvale, and the Christmas Eve service had remained with them both, despite an uncomfortable return trip. Flooding and bank collapses had delayed their return to Kings Cross, and extra passengers had to be accommodated because of a breakdown further along the line. Yet Beryl was even humming 'All Things Bright and Beautiful' while unlocking the door to the flat.

'I'm still full of Greenvale Jim!' She threw her arms round him. I hated leaving, but it's really charged up my batteries, and it's not temporary. I dreaded going to work, but now I just want to get it over and done with…whatever.'

He moved to the television. 'Do you want the news?'

'No, I just want to keep the flavour of Greenvale.' She had already put two bowls of soup in the microwave. 'Let's just have soup and a good sleep. We can worry about the world tomorrow.'

Tomorrow, as expected, the news centred on the new strain of yellow stripe which was spreading at an alarming rate into many parts of the world, but this time the World Health Organization was quick to act by announcing an international emergency, and calling for a co-ordinated response to the pandemic. This time, many countries responded positively by sharing research, and contributing to a vast pool of vaccines to ensure fair and rapid distribution across the world. It was an encouraging start, and announcing British support for co-ordinated action, the Prime Minister contrasted it with the disunited approach to the previous pandemic by saying: 'Thank goodness we have at last realized that splitting up into national tribes of self-interest is no way to defeat a common enemy.'

Early in the New Year a worldwide lockdown was in place, and led by Britain, an attempt was made to reach agreement for a synchronised 'unlock- down' to discourage countries taking competitive advantage of the pandemic. This was rejected by some powers, but with a few unavoidable exceptions the do's and don'ts for avoiding infections were the same within the borders of most countries.

An unusual equality prevailed, which did nothing for exciting life styles, but did provide a thread of common purpose, and a general desire to strive for greater consensus on international matters, including action on climate change and environmental damage.

One hopeful sign of this was a planned European led consortium to negotiate and construct a massive solar energy farm and eco city in the central Sahara. A secondary objective would be to provide accommodation and employment for refugees fleeing from troubled regions in Africa and the Middle East. Regardless of belief, race, politics, sexual or any other orientation, employees were required to work in mixed teams and live in mixed single and family accommodation blocks. As the Global Council for Humanity had optimistically declared: 'Diversity would prove the norm as humanity embraces the new world order.'

Jim sought the globe's opinion. 'Well, all this sounds hopeful globe. So, what do you think?'

'You're joking!' came the buzz.

'Well, at least we've got the gear we need this time,' announced an exhausted Beryl, 'and the extra showers they rigged up are going non-stop.'

It was her third week, and patients were arriving at the hospital in accelerating numbers.

Jim turned on the grill. 'Be extra careful. Your old misery here doesn't want you to get it.'

She answered warily, 'We could both get it, so you be extra careful as well.'

'Is it worse than the last strain, then?' He placed the bowls of soup on the table.

'It's a craftier virus this time. It's got a longer incubation period and has more time to spread.'

'So, it takes longer before you know you've got it?'

'Yes and the critical stage develops faster.'

She waited for the outside wail of an emergency vehicle to fade away.

'Jim?' She laid down her soup spoon and placed her hand on his arm.'

'If anything does happen to me, I'd like to be buried at Greenvale Church.'

In that instant Beryl became very valuable to him. They had already arranged the legal practicalities arising from their deaths, and had listed the handful of names and contact details of relatives and friends. But that had been more to do with organisation, not the vacuum of loss.

'How about a double-decker grave?'

'Jim, how wonderful!' She nearly pulled him off his chair. 'But the Vicar wouldn't approve of an unmarried couple in a double-decker surely?'

'Well, I'd like to sort that out if I can.'

The soup bowls wobbled when he caught the table as he knelt down to ask Beryl to be his wife. If it wasn't love, it was very close to it. Not the same feeling that lost him sleep over Heather Freeman, or Maureen Mc Dermount, but a strong Beryl aura, which had grown stronger during their break in Greenvale.

She said: 'Yes,' and two celebratory glasses of wine and a bedroom interlude later, they watched the news, as once again the rules about hand washing, social distancing and wearing of face masks were emphasised. Big virus-coloured areas on world charts displayed the haphazard progress of yellow stripe, and teams of medics and nurses struggling to do their very best. At least there were no jokey fun seekers raving in isolated churches and woodlands, or stripped shelves in supermarkets. Police patrols were barely needed, and the media presented the facts with very little emotional bias, as yellow stripe claimed victims at about the same rate as its predecessor. This time there really did seem to be a genuine world-wide climate of mutual determination to defeat the pandemic.

A month later it was hard to say whether it was the pandemic, or the floods that were causing most concern. Emergency services and thousands of masked and socially-distancing volunteers were doing their best to alleviate the misery of more flooded homes, and once again Jim gave the go ahead for agencies in the affected areas to open up free soup kitchens.

In many ways, life in the flat hadn't been changed by yellow stripe. After all, it had never been a succession of giddy rave-ups. The demands of their work hadn't allowed for much more than meals, television, and sleep. No wonder their trip to Greenvale had been such a joy to Beryl, and it was reassuring to know that a double decker was waiting for them in the churchyard. Cross fingers, they would be able to share more good times together before it was needed.

'I'm knackered,' was Beryl's usual greeting after a shift, and Jim would occasionally be given a summary, and sometimes tears, about the patients who hadn't made it. It was important that she could get work off her chest, regardless of whether it had been satisfying or dreadful, and as she had exclaimed after a particularly stressful shift; 'It's like a good poo Jim; I feel much better afterwards.'

The phone call came after a week of not being molested, and the kiss, which came in place of their usual hug, was waved to him from the door as she went to the hospital for her last shift.

At the time he thought nothing of it. Two extra shifts over the weekend, and the death of a close colleague had knocked the stuffing out of Beryl, so it was hardly surprising that soup and sleep was about all she could manage after returning from work.

On the following afternoon he received a call from the hospital. It was a sympathetic call, informing him that Beryl was in quarantine and receiving treatment.

He went back to the washing machine and pulled out the sheets. They were tangled, and difficult smooth over the ironing board. He had to try overriding his anxiety by doing something physical, and at that moment it was ironing sheets. He had never ironed sheets before, so not surprisingly he was making a mess of it. A sheet started sliding to floor and he trod on it tipping the ironing board, and causing the iron to drop onto his foot, switching him from anxiety to pain.

'That should amuse her,' he thought, but the anxiety doubled to punish him for construing an incident that might never be shared. Going to the bedroom, he puffed up the hollow in the mattress where Beryl slept, and laid the sheets in hope of getting some sleep later. Then he cursed himself for leaving the pillow cases in the washing machine, which meant rigging up the ironing board for a second time and setting the iron back to the right temperature.

There was also work do on the laptop, and he would need to contact the agency to check how sales were being affected by the lockdown. But he wasn't up to talking with cheery Gordon in the agency distribution office. Work would just have to wait, until he'd exhausted himself by having a big flat clean up, and sleep.

Over the weekend he worked solidly while trying to dampen any anticipation of caring for Beryl in a spick and span flat, and knowing that a call bringing relief or wretchedness could come at any time, he ensured that the phone was always within hearing distance.

Just a week after her admission, the same sympathetic voice informed him of Beryl's death. She had died about an hour beforehand, so would still be warm. Along with the numbness, and intense stab of helplessness, came an irrelevant buzz of events taking him right back to the clubby lights in the hospital, and their bedpan liaison after the traffic pile up.

Beryl was dead, and at that moment, was probably being loaded into the hospital freezer.

Wandering aimlessly round the flat, he tried to find solace in anything - however unlikely. He placed his hand over the hollow formed on her side of the couch, knowing that if he turned on the TV as a diversion, he would instinctively seek her opinion and hear no Beryl. He went into the bedroom, and noticing the small silver box of jewellery on the dressing table, took out a necklace and a brooch.

She was wearing the necklace when they spent Christmas with Dawn, and the brooch at Greenvale. He opened the brooch. Inside was a sepia photo of a youngish man with a waxed moustache. He guessed the brooch had probably been passed down from her grandmother to her mother, and he was looking at her grandfather. She rarely talked of family, and had never mentioned brothers or sisters, so she was almost certainly the only one. Closing the jewellery box, he walked alongside the open wardrobe and brushed against the alpaca gown.

It was too much.

Shakily unhooking it, he pressed it hard to his face, and hugging it tightly, fell onto the bed and wept noisily into its softness for a long time. None of the despair he had witnessed in so many others could have inured him to that moment. He would have jumped into the hospital freezer and wrapped Beryl in the gown it if he could. But he couldn't, and in the days ahead, had to wait for the bouts of wretchedness to ease before summoning up enough will power to register her death, and arranging her burial at Greenvale church.

Spooky in their facemasks, the pallbearers lowered Beryl into the grave, and as the straps loosened, Jim could see there was plenty of room for him when the time came. It was a simple burial, and he didn't scatter any earth onto the coffin because he didn't want a lingering image of Beryl in a deep hole. Inside the church, Colin was playing 'Abide with Me' and the bass tones added a soothing vibrancy to the air. No relatives or friends attended the funeral because of the lock down, and phone calls to her relatives revealed that they even had difficulty in recalling who Beryl was. So, nothing was said at the graveside, which suited him because he just wanted to think of her. The Vicar simply bowed and departed as the hymn faded, and Jim was left alone to decide when to turn his back on Beryl, and walk away from her.

A snooty horse-drawn carriage waited by the lychgate to take him back to the station, and on his way to it, he recalled their Christmas Eve visit to the church, and helping the recycling men to clear the windblown debris from the graveyard. Illuminated by the late afternoon sun, the skull and crossbones headstone stood out in sharp relief, and crossing over to it, Jim laid both hands over the skull and appealed to the lady plague victim to make Beryl feel at home.

It was stupid, but it made him feel better, and he managed a snooze on the train back to Kings Cross.

Entering the flat was the worst part. The top door would always be locked; there would be no cleaning up noises or exchange of greetings, and once again he turned the key into a silent chamber of remnants and reminders.

In the days following the burial, he had shuffled through Beryl's box of paperwork to sift out anything important that may have been missed. For some reason he was disappointed that he hadn't come across anything amorous, or even steamy from previous admirers. The only personal messages were those of thanks from ex-patients, and he apologised as he screwed each one up and dropped it into the re-cycle bin. None of the relatives had any interest in her remaining possessions, so he began removing the African carvings from the long shelf with the intention of giving them to the charity shop. But once clear of the shelf, they acquired the mien of living creatures made homeless, and feeling like a heartless landlord, he put them back. Previously, he had removed Beryl's favourite vase from the corner cabinet with the same intentions, but it seemed like a violation of precious space, and as with the carvings, he returned it. So, he became resigned to living in a flat full of Beryl flavours, but no Beryl.

Only Dawn knew of Beryl's death, and he welcomed their chats, because they pushed him into assuming more cheeriness than he felt. Ben and Madge had returned home, and Brinod was in quarantine back at Miser Terrace so he would tell them once they could continue as a team.

His work as a representative had been constrained by the lockdown, so he made himself useful to the distribution agency as a stand in driver by opting to do late deliveries, since they reduced his time alone in the flat. After one late delivery he parked his van in the yard, and leaned on the roof to look at the sky.

It was dusk, with no traffic noise and no wind. Everything was in high definition from the nearby stars to the Milky Way, and he could discern the roughness of the craters on the half-moon. He had never seen such a clear sky, and night was yet to come. This was the unpolluted sky that the Black Death lady would have seen, and like him, she had probably regarded it with awe and bafflement. He wanted to believe that her bafflement had been resolved in dark matter, and that Beryl was with her. It was a comforting possibility, but the immensity of the vista above, conveyed total indifference and his despondency remained until he was back in the flat.

First turning on the electric fire, he prepared to change and shower. It was chilly, but prioritising the tasks that he least wanted to do, was a way of controlling depression. The shower was tepid, and he had to face the alpaca gown whenever he opened the wardrobe, but after changing and stowing his pants in the washing machine, he felt he had earned his soup and television time on the sofa.

He walked over to close the curtains in the end window. The taller buildings beyond the High Street were in sharp silhouette, and higher still, the planets twinkled against the granular backcloth of the cosmos. It was then he noticed his thumb on the curtain and waggled it. If, over time, the cosmos could create something that ingenious, plus all the complex working bits and pieces attached to it, then surely it had the ability to preserve it in some form or another? He would rot away or get turned to ashes of course, but plants reproduced themselves, so maybe the 'real' feeling that kept popping up might be a unique 'Jim' app, which like a plant seed could reproduce another Jim, and maybe even another Beryl in the right conditions. Thinking about it anymore would get him muddled, although he felt slightly more hopeful as he turned on the TV.

News about the international response to the pandemic continued to be encouraging. The mistakes and experience gained previously enabled speedier development of vaccines, and better co-ordination of resources for worldwide production and distribution. Military co-operation between neighbouring countries made it possible for urgent supplies to be dropped by air to isolated regions, and the rapid production and distribution of reliable testing kits provided speedier detection of infections.

Soon it was obvious, even to hostile neighbours that their mutual interest in defeating yellow stripe was best served by co-operation.

As the head of one military junta put it: 'The enemy aren't such a bad lot really. We'd be killing them by the thousands if it wasn't for yellow stripe.'

And with every landslide, wildfire, and species extinction, it was also becoming patently obvious that the health of the global environment could only be restored by ruthlessly applying globally agreed solutions. There could be no national exceptions.

Speaking for *Green Prelude*, Emma Dowty appealed to world leaders.

'This virus is forcing our nations to come together for the first time since we lived in caves. So please, and for the sake of all creatures great and small, lets us apply the same love to Mother Earth.

By April most of the world had been inoculated, and the shift from competition to sustainability had slowly begun to emerge in a variety of ways.

'At last, there are signs that we are moving towards international collaboration,' announced the UN General Secretary, 'and if it can be maintained, future generations may enjoy a harmonious and healthy earth.'

But it wasn't all sweetness and light. Rare minerals were still being excavated at an unprecedented rate, and ever-increasing numbers of refugees, were still seeking safety and solace from starvation and deeply embedded conflicts. Moreover, the weather had gone crazy. Only a week after a second 'Beast from the East' had blasted the UK with snow and freezing temperatures, the borough was steaming with evaporating melt water. It was impossible to stop sweating, and social distancing came naturally. The last time Jim had experienced humidity like that was in the Arabian Gulf, and on return from the supermarket he dumped his clothes in the wash basket, and was heading for the shower just as the phone rang. It was too early for a call from Dawn. So, guessing it could be Adelita, he prepared to sound cheerful.

'Jim? I told you about Lorrenzo, and the wonderful tune he played to me, yes?'

'Yes, the tune he said came from dark matter?'

'That is the one. Now he says that he has received the signal for the world to hear it. It will be sent to *Green Prelude* who have arranged for it to be played on social media and radio stations everywhere. We are also preparing for it to be heard by a horrible dictator who forbids music.'

'That must be Demshi Jibang. I heard he trades in wild animal meat.'

'He does, and the new strain of yellow stripe probably came from one of his wild animal farms.'

'How will he hear the tune?'

'It will be dropped onto his palace by Respectico's helicopter.'

'Do you have a crew trained to do it?'

'We have the pilot'

'What's the tune called?'

'Lorrenzo calls it 'Eco Remorse.' It's so powerful Jim. I still can't find the words to describe it.'

'Let's hope it works.'

She had already caught the downturn in his voice.

'Jim? Something's wrong. I hear it in your voice.'

He said it straight out. 'Beryl died only recently Adelita.'

'Oh! Jim, Jim, I'm so sorry, that's dreadful for you.'

'I'm still working Adelita, but it isn't enough.'

'What would be enough?'

'Helping to get Lorrenzo's tune to that dictator.'

'It would be too dangerous.'

'I've done plenty of air drops, and it would be safer for the pilot.'

'We've lost Father Dududso. It would be terrible to lose you.'

'It would be something to live for, Adelita.'

'It's that bad is it?'

'It won't go away.'

'Please Jim… you give me a few moments to think.'

He heard the phone being laid down, and the sound of footsteps getting fainter. He guessed she had gone to the patio to think. A few minutes later, the footsteps grew louder as she returned to the phone.

'Very well. First you must get tested, then we arrange a yellow stripe business passport form for your flight to Samsikand next Sunday - I send an e-mail for you to complete the details.'

She heard his sigh of relief, and added, 'Please take care Jim, you're so valuable.'

21. Well Well.

The Airbus dropped onto the runway threshold after steadily losing altitude over swathes of jungle pockmarked with huge excavation sites.

Jim guessed that Samsikand Airport was about fifty miles from the border of Mittataland, and inside the small terminal building, cheery beach scene posters informed arriving passengers that Samsikand would once again be gearing up for holiday visitors when the international lockdown was over.

Alereo: Respectico's helicopter pilot, was just recognisable in his facemask as he waited for Jim in the arrival lobby. After coffee in the snack bar, they walked through the aircraft maintenance area and into a small hangar which housed a bright golden helicopter. There was a strong smell of cellulose in the air, and a mechanic was making some finishing touches with a spray gun.

Alereo patted the nose of the helicopter.

'So here Mr Jim is our beautiful, how I say… 'Musicopter?'

'Impressive.' Jim stooped down to the golden loudspeaker cabinet, which had been secured by quick release couplings to the underside of the cabin. 'So, this is lowered down onto the palace roof?'

'Yes, I hold helicopter steady and you lower it onto roof. Then we switch on speaker, and fly away to music.'

'What about Demshi's palace guards?'

'They think this is Demshi's golden helicopter making special delivery.'

They entered the cabin. The winching and release mechanism was straightforward. Providing there was no gusting wind, and Alereo held the helicopter steady there should be no problems.

'We sleep here.' Alereo pointed to three camp beds draped with mosquito nets. 'Tomorrow morning, we receive signal to go.'

Later, they returned to the airport snack bar for a light meal, and Alereo mentioned the growing popularity of sports and the arts in Miser Terrace. 'You not know Miser Terrace if you visit it Mr Jim. Life is good there now.'

It was welcome news, but it came with a stab. Miser Terrace and Fortunatus Viridis had now become places he would never be able to share with Beryl.

He had a solid sleep, and awoke to the sound of the hanger doors being unbolted by Alereo.

It was bizarre. Here he was in bed and feeling chilly in tropical Samsikand, while heatstroke and de-hydration were adding to the misery of yellow stripe across the UK. He changed quickly, and walked with Alereo to the airport snack bar for breakfast. Every so often Alereo checked his phone for messages, and over coffee announced it was time to prepare for take-off. They returned to the hangar and pushed the helicopter onto its launch pad, then Jim took his place on the jump seat by the speaker release mechanism. Giving a broad smile Alereo raised his thumbs, and once again Jim was being pressed upwards.

Very soon Lorrenzo's 'Eco Remorse' would be received by billions of ears across the world, and as they crossed the border into Mittataland Jim thought back to the suicides beneath the escarpment when he was on army patrol. Adelita had mentioned that a common theme seemed to be emerging, and as they approached Demshi's Palace, he received a portent of something momentous to come. Alereo put the helicopter into collective pitch and they hovered over the palace roof while Jim carefully lowered the golden speaker into place and switched it on.

Was this the moment, he wondered, when all the opposing human masses would be inspired to strive in unison for a healthy and peaceful world?

But striving for a healthy and peaceful world, was far from Demshi Jibang's mind, as he savoured a sugared platypus tongue while admiring enhanced images of himself on the walls of the throne room. Down below, the floor of the stadium was being hosed and scrubbed in readiness for the games, and multiple rows of his subjects were being inspected before proclaiming their morning allegiance to him. Above, came the welcome rattle of his helicopter bringing something caged for fresh roasting, and satisfied with the start to his day, he was soon back to caressing the golden nuclear button.

He was about to swivel his throne round to a better viewing position, when the eco tune burst into every nook and cranny of the palace, and saturated the air with a lament so sad and powerful that he broke down into uncontrollable cries of atonement and remorse.

He wanted to scream and hit himself at the same time, but his weight forbade it. He wanted to strip every bit of self-adoration paraphernalia from the throne room, or better still, get rid of the stupid throne room altogether. But most of all, he wanted to purge himself of all the horror, and self-illusory garbage he had indulged in since his moment of conception.

He grasped his head in both hands as the hideous imagery paraded through. The screams; de-capitations, pleadings, and injured creatures trying to flee his burning forest clearance sites. Moments he had relished, now turned into poison which couldn't be poured from his head.

And how could he seriously believe that history would judge his glorious act of self-destruction as any more than the press of a nuclear button by a spoilt brat playing with a dangerous toy.

But there was nothing he could do, and the torment was unbearable.

The clatter from the helicopter was too loud for Jim to hear the tune. He was only aware of a blinding flash and a mixed cacophony of sounds as he accelerated skywards beside an impossibly obese man grasping a golden button. Instinctively he knew what had happened, and spoke his mind.

'That was a bloody stupid thing to do.'

The man grimaced and tried to say something as he zoomed into blackness.

Alereo groaned. 'Respectico will be angry about helicopter. 'He shook hands with Jim and slid into a greyish mist. 'Ah…this about right for me. Bye, Mr Jim.'

The familiar floaty feeling came on strongly as Jim continued upwards. This time it felt natural, as did the warm clubby feeling as he ventured into a tunnel of twinkly lights. It was becoming all very reassuring, but suddenly an algorithm flicked across, and the blond angel was gazing down to him from a circle of lamps.

'No, we don't want that one again,' said a sensation, and another algorithm promptly returned him to the twinkly corridor and a big, 'Welcome Jim!' banner, which hung above the entrance of a grand hall. Once inside, he was plunged into scenes and characters from his past. Space was no problem. Trips to the seaside with Dawn in their twin buggy included his mum and dad against a wide seascape, and catapult warfare took him straight into Silver Woods sandpit with his yobby mates.

Then another algorithm flicked across the hall, and everything accelerated into a rapid synopsis of life events from the moment of his birth to lowering the speaker onto Demshi's palace. Faces, places, and emotional highs and lows flashed before him. It was like being inside a speeded-up video which occasionally halted to give an analysing pop-up time to complete. Utterly confused, he was left staring into a void, then the lights came on and the sensation apologised again.

'Really sorry about all this, Jim. We went digital a year back and still get glitches. There's no way we could carry on manually with the amount of data we have to handle these days, and programming for the fifth dimension is driving us bonkers.'

'I've got plenty of questions.'

'You'll have to wait until you get your password. Once you get that, it'll be a bit like living inside Facebook without the nasties. Life here is very pleasant once you get used to it, but right now feel free to look around and go where you wish.'

He was drawn to the centre of the hall by the sound of the Greenvale Church synthesiser, and was greeted by a companion who was a mixture of Beryl, and someone else he had once known. She led him up the centre aisle into the pew facing the big eagle lectern, and seated in the pew behind was Beryl and someone almost like himself. Soon all four of them were cheerfully chatting together, then Greta placed her song sheet on the lectern and the church was filled with a sadness far deeper than any outpouring of individual hurt. This was the lament of a selfless entity at the cruelty it had received in return for giving so much beauty and love to its children, and augmented by Greta's voice it ascended into a wail of anguish on behalf of all living things.

Colin kept the bass going, and everyone wept quietly as the vicar led them from the church.

Outside, the graveyard had become the venue for a get-together of historical characters who were sharing experiences across generations, and the real Beryl introduced Jim to a lady wearing an important hat and long crinoline gown.

'Jim, meet Abigail, the Black Death lady. You may remember asking her if she could make me feel at home here.' Beryl hugged Abigail. 'She has been wonderful to me.'

Abigail smiled demurely.

'Good morrow, Jim. Firstly, I find my translator.'

She took a smartphone from her gown pocket and switched over to modern English. 'It's so good to meet you, Jim and we're all praying that your earthly mission will succeed.'

'Will it make any difference, now that we're all dead?'

'Be in no doubt, Jim. We are answerable for the behaviour of the generations we nurture on earth, and will suffer or benefit accordingly.'

'So, in a way, we're still linked to earth?'

'Of course, and if your mission returns the earth to health, it will be reflected in the quality of our deaths.' She laid a reassuring hand on his wrist. 'It is entirely logical, Jim.'

The nearly-Beryl held his hand, and the nearly-Jim and real Beryl held hands as Abigail led them to the church porch to gaze at the scene rising beyond the lychgate.

Dotted with patches of wildflowers and flocks of coloured birds, Jim followed a line of snooty horses being led by their owners up the valley towards a forest of blossoming trees.

'Seems a bit over the top,' he concluded, then the scene instantly changed to a traffic jam, the roar of fighter jets overhead, and flashing blue lights speeding up the valley towards a massive industrial estate.

'Jim!' The real Beryl prodded him. 'Will you never stop being such a miserable cynic?'

###

Thank you for reading the Nice Pill. If you enjoyed this story and have a spare moment I would be very grateful if you could leave a review.

ABOUT THE AUTHOR

Peter Scott grew up in post war austerity Britain, and joined the RAF in his late teens. His overseas postings sparked off an interest in mountaineering and the beauty of the natural world. It also acquainted him with the harm we are inflicting on each other and the ecology of the Earth. Later, as an aircraft maintenance engineer in various countries, he could see how poverty and environmental damage frequently went hand in hand with rapid population growth.

Now settled in Suffolk he dismally concludes that his own precious island will struggle to be a green and pleasant land as it attempts to cater for a population heading towards70 million and beyond.

Apart from being a general misery, he enjoys playing jazz and rock; ranting on the BBC, and writing.

Also by Peter Scott: **'Pimple'** *(Trumpeting for a better world)* on Kindle Books.

Printed in Great Britain
by Amazon